## PRAISE FOR MARYJANICE DAVIDSON AND HER UNDEAD NOVELS FEATURING BETSY TAYLOR, VAMPIRE QUEEN

"Delightful, wicked fun!"

—Christine Feehan, #1 *New York Times* bestselling author

"Think *Sex and the City* . . . filled with demons and vampires."

—*Publishers Weekly*

"[Her] adventures are laugh-out-loud entertainment."

—*Fresh Fiction*

"Be prepared to fall in love with the undead all over again!"

—*Romance Reviews Today*

"What can you say about a vampire whose loyalty can be bought by designer shoes? Can we say *outrageous*?" —*The Best Reviews*

"[Her] prose zings from wisecrack to wisecrack."

—*Detroit Free Press*

"[Davidson] has her own brand of wit and shocking surprises."

—*Darque Reviews*

"Sexy, steamy, and laugh-out-loud funny." —*Booklist*

*Titles by MaryJanice Davidson*

DEJA WHO

UNDEAD AND UNWED
UNDEAD AND UNEMPLOYED
UNDEAD AND UNAPPRECIATED
UNDEAD AND UNRETURNABLE
UNDEAD AND UNPOPULAR
UNDEAD AND UNEASY
UNDEAD AND UNWORTHY
UNDEAD AND UNWELCOME
UNDEAD AND UNFINISHED
UNDEAD AND UNDERMINED
UNDEAD AND UNSTABLE
UNDEAD AND UNSURE
UNDEAD AND UNWARY

DERIK'S BANE
WOLF AT THE DOOR

SLEEPING WITH THE FISHES
SWIMMING WITHOUT A NET
FISH OUT OF WATER

*Titles by MaryJanice Davidson and Anthony Alongi*

JENNIFER SCALES AND THE ANCIENT FURNACE
JENNIFER SCALES AND THE MESSENGER OF LIGHT
THE SILVER MOON ELM: A JENNIFER SCALES NOVEL
SERAPH OF SORROW: A JENNIFER SCALES NOVEL
RISE OF THE POISON MOON: A JENNIFER SCALES NOVEL
EVANGELINA: A JENNIFER SCALES NOVEL

## *Anthologies*

CRAVINGS
(with Laurell K. Hamilton, Rebecca York, Eileen Wilks)

BITE
(with Laurell K. Hamilton, Charlaine Harris, Angela Knight, Vickie Taylor)

KICK ASS
(with Maggie Shayne, Angela Knight, Jacey Ford)

MEN AT WORK
(with Janelle Denison, Nina Bangs)

DEAD AND LOVING IT

SURF'S UP
(with Janelle Denison, Nina Bangs)

MYSTERIA
(with P. C. Cast, Gena Showalter, Susan Grant)

OVER THE MOON
(with Angela Knight, Virginia Kantra, Sunny)

DEMON'S DELIGHT
(with Emma Holly, Vickie Taylor, Catherine Spangler)

DEAD OVER HEELS

MYSTERIA LANE
(with P. C. Cast, Gena Showalter, Susan Grant)

MYSTERIA NIGHTS
(includes *Mysteria* and *Mysteria Lane*, with P. C. Cast, Susan Grant, Gena Showalter)

UNDERWATER LOVE
(includes *Sleeping with the Fishes*, *Swimming Without a Net*, and *Fish out of Water*)

DYING FOR YOU

UNDEAD AND UNDERWATER

# DEJA WHO

MARYJANICE DAVIDSON

BERKLEY
NEW YORK

BERKLEY
An imprint of Penguin Random House LLC
375 Hudson Street, New York, New York 10014

Library of Congress Cataloging-in-Publication Data

Names: Davidson, MaryJanice, author.
Title: Deja Who / MaryJanice Davidson.
Description: Berkley Sensation trade paperback edition. | New York, New York : Berkley Sensation, [2016]
Identifiers: LCCN 2015038123 | ISBN 9780425270394
Subjects: LCSH: Reincarnation—Fiction. | Private investigators—Fiction. | Murder—Investigation—Fiction. | GSAFD: Mystery fiction.
Classification: LCC PS3604.A949 D45 2016 | DDC 813/.6—dc23 LC record available at http://lccn.loc.gov/2015038123

First Edition: September 2016

Printed in the United States of America
1 3 5 7 9 10 8 6 4 2

Cover art by Blake Morrow
Cover design by Katie Anderson
Book design by Kelly Lipovich

*For the victims like Mary Jane Kelly and Isabella Mowbray,*
*whose lot it was to suffer undeservedly.*

*And for the watchers of the world like Louise Élisabeth de Croÿ*
*and Mary Moormon, whose lot was to survive,*
*and tell us what they survived.*

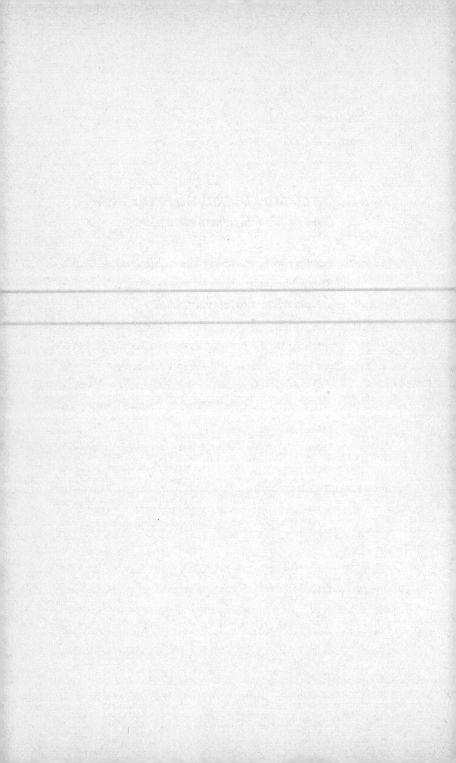

# AUTHOR'S NOTE

Sources for some of the historical figures mentioned in this book are Wikipedia, because nothing says exacting research more than relying on a resource anyone can change at any time. Oh, and Cracked.com. Because they are hilarious. I really need to pitch an article to those bums. To quote another historical figure (Madonna): "I am not ashamed."

All the (fictional) characters' past lives are based on (real) people, sometimes pretty roughly. Not much is known about Jack the Ripper's fifth victim, Mary Jane Kelly; I researched the poor woman as well as I could, then made up a few things, such as how she may have felt about her hometown of Limerick, Ireland.

I took the same liberties with Mary Ann Cotton's poor, doomed daughter, Isabella, whom she poisoned in 1867. Mary Ann killed thirteen people before Isabella, and seven more after, all family members. She explained this away by telling authorities how "weak stomachs" ran in the family. Nobody blinked when her husband(s) and stepchildren succumbed to the hereditary "weak stomach" they did not inherit. Interestingly, reporters caught on before the cops did. And by "interestingly," I mean "how the hell did the cops not catch on to this?"

(I know, I know: I wasn't there, I'm Monday morning quarterbacking, I'm neither a cop nor a doc, etc. And you'd be right; I wasn't there, and I'm not a cop nor a doc. I didn't even go to college. But come on. Hereditary? For victims who were not blood relatives and thus did not inherit jack shit? Come *on*. Gad, this happened over a century ago and I'm still super pissed about it.)

Albert DeSalvo did not, to the best of my knowledge, have a sibling; I made one up for the purposes of storytelling. And recent research, including DNA evidence, has suggested more than one person was responsible for the Boston Strangler murders, which screws up my book, so I'm ignoring the DNA evidence, which is my right as an American.

Leah makes mention of Lavinia Fisher, who is generally acknowledged as the first female mass murderer in the United States. Born in 1793, Lavinia and her husband opened a hotel in South Carolina, as people have a right to do, and started robbing and murdering their guests, which is frowned upon. The number of their victims is unknown, and their method of execution was pretty foolproof, to a point. Lavinia would ply the guest with (poisoned) tea, and then her husband would creep up to the guest's room after the poison had taken effect, stab him to make sure he was super-duper dead, and rob him. The plan broke down when they ran across a guest who hated tea and poured it out when Lavinia wasn't looking. (D'oh!) It all went to hell from there, possibly literally in Lavinia's case.

Interestingly, once she knew she was to be executed, Lavinia informed the authorities that they couldn't hang a married woman. They agreed . . . and hanged her husband the day before. (The gentlemanly thing to do, I suppose. Apparently hanging a widow is a little more chivalrous.) Her last words were along the lines of, "If anyone has a message for the devil, give it to me." So she was also something of a stickler for passing on messages to Satan.

The mayor of Boston is my homage to one of my favorite authors, Carl Hiaasen, who is funnier on his worst day than I am on my best. I fell in love with his characters years ago, in particular Clinton "Skink" Tyree, former governor of Florida, current full-time forest hermit, and my current literary crush. If you haven't checked Hiaasen out, you're missing some of the funniest lectures on how we're ruining the planet.

Hiaasen is not a fan of urban development, and he's cursed with the nutty idea that maybe every single square inch of Florida should not be made of concrete. He lets readers know that he disapproves of the daily raping of his home state, in the best possible way. Run, don't walk. Start with *Double Whammy* or *Striptease*. Then become resigned to getting hooked and plowing through his backlist. Damn you, Hiaasen. Now I *care*.

All that to say the scandals that led the mayor of Boston to live in a Chicago public park are based on real-life "racist but not really" comments featuring David Howard, former head of the Office of Public Advocate, and Kenneth Mayfield, former Texas county commissioner. Both men were forced to make amends for 1) correctly using a scientific term as well as an adjective with Old Norse roots, and 2) *not* being racists. Seriously. Look it up if you don't believe me. It's as hilarious as it is depressing. I love when the media tells us what to think. I hate when we obey.

The college degrees Leah ponders in the first chapters actually exist. Yep. You can get a degree in growing marijuana and auctioneering.

The hospital Leah threatens a patient with, Chicago-Read, has a nasty rep in real life. Established in the mid-1800s, it was a hospital for (as they say in comic books) "the criminally insane" with all the shenanigans that implies. Corpses have gone missing. Patients have committed suicide, succeeding in large part due to the poor supervision. (The attending physician at the time of inpatient Martha Grote's suicide declared he "would rather have lost a month's salary than have this thing happen." Really? A whole month? 1 month's salary = 1 human life? That's terrifying math, doc.) In 1901, nurses starved two patients to death. Unsanitary conditions and broken equipment have been thoroughly documented, and in 1993, it lost its accreditation. (Yeah, *finally*, right?)

All this to say Leah's patient was quite right to be annoyed at the prospect of being admitted there, and Leah was quite wrong to threaten her with admission.

Also: no matter what nastiness I make up, there's always, always something worse out there in the real world. Which is also why I don't watch the news, vastly preferring to reread my Sandman graphic novels instead. Take from that what you will.

*As long as you are not aware of the continual law of Die and Be Again, you are merely a vague guest on a dark Earth.*

—GOETHE

*"I think . . . in another lifetime I was probably Catherine the Great, or Francis of Assisi. I'm not sure which one. What do you think?"*

*"How come in former lifetimes, everybody is someone famous? I mean, how come nobody ever says they were Joe Schmo?"*

*"Because it doesn't work that way, you fool!"*

—ANNIE AND CRASH, *BULL DURHAM*

*There is no death . . . the soul never dies and the body is never really alive.*

—ISAAC SINGER

*Tabula rasa: Latin; translation: "clean slate."*

*Why should we be startled by death? Life is a constant putting off of the mortal coil—coat, cuticle, flesh and bones, all old clothes.*

—HENRY DAVID THOREAU

*"Get out of here! Can't you see we don't want you anymore? Why can't you go back where you came from? Now leave us alone!"*

—GEORGE HENDERSON, *HARRY AND THE HENDERSONS*

# PROLOGUE

"Please. Please don't kill me again."

". . . I have to."

So he did.

# ONE

**Clinic notes:** Alice Delaney, Chart #6116

**Date:** 9/17/2017

**INS:** Leah Nazir, ID# 29682

**Cc:** Dr. Riario, CF; Maura Hickman INS ID# 30199

Patient is a well-nourished Caucasian female who presents with anxiety, loss of appetite, fatigue, and night terrors.

"When are we going to figure out what's wrong? This is our fifth session," #6116 complained.

"It will be fine," Leah assured her. Like Liz Lemon, if she rolled her eyes many more times, she risked her optic nerves cramping. "We're getting close. We're not filling a cavity; it's not a one-trip fix. Now take a long deep breath."

"Okay, but I don't—"

"Less talking. More breathing." She kept a smile on her face, which wasn't easy.

Symptoms began thirteen days ago.

Yes indeed, because putting up with unpleasantness for even two weeks is asking too much. Ugh.

Referred by her GP Gary Riario. DOB 8/1/1993.

Gary, Gary. Not a fan of Insighters, unless he needed to refer. Then he was all Insighters, all the time. *What secrets from sticky past lives are you hiding, Gary?* "Feeling all right? Nod, don't speak."

Chart #6116 nodded, eyes closed.

"Meds bothering you?" The hypnotic analgesic, applied five minutes before the session began, sometimes triggered nausea. And catastrophic brain injury. But that almost never happened with the new protocols in place. Acceptable risk.

Chart #6116 shook her head. Oh, well. There was always the chance she might throw up later. Dare to dream!

*I used to be nice. Didn't I?* It was hard to remember. Once upon a time, she liked her patients. Tried to like them, at least.

She bent forward so she was almost looming over #6116 and adjusted the IV. Chart #6116 was lying snugly on the green padded couch, so plush a patient didn't sink into it but was swallowed by the greedy sofa. A necessary evil, as the couch had built-in sensors that continually monitored blood pressure, heart rate, temperature. It was always good to have advance notice if a patient was about to stroke out. Being devoured by a couch did not go over well with her claustrophobes; she kept a cot for them, and monitored their vitals the old-fashioned way.

The diplomas and certificates on the wall behind her trumpeted her expertise via large font and dark dramatic lettering:

> **anesthesiology (*The American Board of Anesthesiology hereby certifies that Leah Nazir, a licensed graduate of etc., etc.*), library science (*By virtue of the authority vested the trustees have conferred upon Leah Nazir etc., etc.*), competitive reading (*Leah Nazir earned this award for participation and completion of the fifth-grade reading club*), and Insighting (*Leah Nazir: Certified Insider, ID #29682*).**

The last one, she knew, either impressed or horrified people. The first one just impressed them. They were indifferent about her library science and fifth-grade reading awards. Maybe it was time to go back to school, get a doctorate in . . . God, anything that sounded like it could be good for a few laughs. Criminal psych. Cannabis cultivation. Fermentation sciences. Auctioneering. Gunsmithing?

"Who are you?"

"My name is Alice Delaney."

"Why?"

"Why? It's . . . it's my name. Is why." Chart #6116's expression = *pay attention, dumbass.*

Chart #6116 was not yet down deep enough. She could only see herself, which was a large part of her problem. Problems.

*Who are you to talk, sunshine? You see yourself and all your past mistakes and has it made you happy or well-adjusted or pleasant to be around?*

Ah . . . no.

Leah double-checked the feed and hummed. She did this more or less unconsciously; she scarcely heard it anymore, though colleagues occasionally teased her about it. It had a tendency to soothe her patients. And herself, of course. If she didn't hum, she might stab.

"Who are you?"

"Alice . . . hmmmm . . . mmmm . . . my name . . . my name is . . ."

"Who are you?"

"My name is James Clark McReynolds."

Excellent. Leah crimped the tube. Past memories would come easier now; Rain Down (generic name: reindyne, courtesy of the good people at Pfizer, discovered by accident in 1987 when Pfizer was trying to develop a heart medicine/diet aid) was invaluable for that, possibly more invaluable than Leah or any of her colleagues. But if she kept the IV running wide open, Alice/James/etc. would fall so far down the rabbit hole they'd never make it back.

"My name is James Clark McReynolds."

"There you go."

"What?"

"Nothing, Judge McReynolds." Leah flipped through the chart. DOB February 3, 1862. DOD August 24, 1946. Aquarius, a masculine sign. A fixed sign, with keywords like "stubborn," "sarcastic," "rebellious." American lawyer and, later, judge. Possibly the most vile wretch to ever sit on a Supreme Court bench.

Even by the standards of the time, Judge McReynolds was a gold-plated jerkass, foisted on the unwary by President Taft, and what the hell had *el presidente* been thinking? Thanks to history's long memory, and her job, Leah knew exactly: Taft was thinking what he was saying, and what he was saying was McReynolds had been "someone who seems to delight in making others uncomfortable." Wasn't that a terrific quality for any judge to have? Why, it ought to be a mandate! Oh, and lest he hadn't been clear, Taft also described McReynolds as "selfish to the last degree . . . fuller of prejudice than any man I have ever known . . . he has no sense of duty."

So naturally, the politicians of the time were in full agreement: Hire that man! And keep promoting him. Eventually promote him just to get rid of him. Promote him again. And again. Eventually give him a lifetime appointment to the highest court in the land. Because in politics, shit flows uphill.

Leah was not surprised to find she was not surprised. Her research—hours and hours looking up birth and death certificates, hours on the online juggernaut that was the Insighter database—helped her figure out who Alice was, and who Alice had been. Chart #6116 was leaking McReynolds all over the place. And that wasn't even the bad news. She had the same thought about almost every patient: if only they'd come to see me sooner. Before she did things she can never undo.

Well. She

*(they)*

were here now. Leah would help as best she could. Of course, her idea of help and her patient's idea of help were likely different.

". . . the only way you can get on the Supreme Court these days is to be either the son of a criminal or a Jew, or both!" #6116 was ranting in a shrill old man's voice.

*Be glad you didn't live to see the twenty-first century, McReynolds. African-Americans in Congress, the House, the White House, and the*

*Supreme Court. Jews roam freely, secure in the absurd notion that religion doesn't have to dictate career paths. Lesbians brazenly being lesbians. Homosexual couples marrying! And then adopting! Legally!*

She swallowed her snicker. "Further, Judge McReynolds." Leah checked the IV crimp. "Go back further. There's all kinds of stuff in there. You have to dig for it."

Her voice changed at once; no hesitation, Rain Down was working nicely and #6116 was deep in EffRe (Effortless Recall). #6116 went from a self-confident young woman to a shrill old man to . . . "My name is Westley Allan Dodd."

*There you go. I cannot tell you how much meeting a serial killer before lunch brightens my Wednesdays.*

"Mm-hmm. Tell me all about yourself, Mr. Dodd. This is your chance to be heard." The thing they all needed. The thing they would kill to get. If she were nicer, she would be sympathetic.

She wasn't nicer.

Leah skipped past the McReynolds section of the chart. Westley Allan Dodd. DOB July 3, 1961, DOD January 5, 1993. Cancer. An astrological sign of contradictions, as keywords were "loyalty," "oversensitivity," "caring," "self-pitying," "dependable," "self-absorbed." Convicted serial killer and child molester. His execution was the first legal hanging, at his own request, since 1965.

The manner of his death was the least unique thing about him. He also claimed a stress-free, happy childhood of wealth and leisure and his first victims were his cousins, because all ordinary children with happy lives molested their cousins and then went on to rape, torture, and kill other children. "Dear Mom and Dad, happy eighteenth birthday to me. Thanks so much for a carefree childhood and instilling appropriate values in me and protecting me from all trauma, but now I'm going to be a sociopath, for funzies. Thanks again!" wrote no well-adjusted teenager ever.

Dodd's first victims: cousins. All victims: below the age of twelve. Number of victims: over fifty. Attitude toward children in ten words or less: "I'm only nice to the ones I want sex from."

". . . told them, I *said* if I escaped I'd immediately go back to killing and raping kids—"

"They should have taken you at your word, Mr. Dodd. Further now. What is your name?"

"My name is Nathaniel Gordon."

"You bet it is." DOB 1834; historical records do not recount exact DOB. But they sure as hell paid attention to his death: May 8, 1862. Nat Gordon, the last pirate ever hanged, and the only slave trader ever tried, convicted, and executed for stealing one thousand slaves. "Real" piracy was punishable by death, but it was hardly ever enforced when the plunder was merely people with dark skin. The paperwork alone hardly made it worth it.

Of the one thousand slaves Gordon stole, 172 were men and 162 were women. According to John Spears, author of *The Slave Trade in America*, "Gordon was one of those infamous characters who preferred to carry children because they could not rise up to avenge his cruelties." Nice.

Hilariously (to Leah, at least; she knew her job had turned her into a jerk *extraordinaire* and that people were right to avoid her at parties), Gordon tried to kill himself the night before his execution. The local authorities found that annoying, especially since it meant postponing Gordon's execution from noon to 2:30 so the guy could recover enough to be murdered by the state. Leah wondered just how that went down: "He was definitely too sick at noon, but now that it's 2:30 he hasn't barfed in over an hour and can walk under his own power." "Great! Let's go kill him. Good news, Mr. Gordon, you're well enough to execute." Or, as Leah preferred to think of it, the classic "well, sir, we have good news and bad news" scenario.

He left behind a mother, wife, and son, but Judge Shipman (a man who almost a century earlier was a hundred times the "justice" McReynolds was) commented on Gordon's real legacy: "Think of the cruelty and wickedness of seizing nearly a thousand fellow beings, who never did you harm, and thrusting them beneath the decks of a small ship, beneath a burning tropical sun, to die in of disease or suffocation, or be transported to distant lands, and be consigned, they and their posterity, to a fate far more cruel than death."

". . . family to support," Gordon was whining from the plush couch. "How can it be a hanging crime to move property?"

So! A pirate, a serial killer, and the worst bigot the Supreme Court had ever seen. And Leah was trapped in a room with all of them. All right, "trapped" was inaccurate, since she had obtained patient consent, drugged #6116, and called all her shadows forward.

Wednesdays!

# TWO

"So what was it?"

"Wrong question," she told Chart #6116. "'Who was it?' would be more accurate."

Chart #6116 rolled her eyes. "I never bought into that past lives crap. It's just one more thing to blame your problems on. I mean—I *believe* it," she added when Leah raised her eyebrows. "I'm not one of those weirdos who say there's no such thing as past lives, that we're just here for one lifetime and then go to heaven or hell or wherever."

Ah, the afterlife. You don't have to learn anything in your single solitary lifetime, and then you can live in the sky forever after! Unless you live in a lake of fire beneath the earth forever after. Well, there were stranger theories. *Tabula rasa*, for one. The goal of goals, an ideal so unlikely as to be mostly unattainable.

What would it be like, born with a clean slate? Nothing to

make up for? Nothing to relive or regret? It was such an amazing concept Leah couldn't grasp it. Like trying to explain the science of reproduction to a preschooler: "He does what? And then *what* happens?"

"It does seem to defeat the purpose of living," Leah put forth with care, shaking off the daydream. "No point in trying to learn from your mistakes since this is your only chance to get it right . . . it calls a lot into question."

"Exactly. I'm not a Denier. But *I'm* in control of *this* life. Whoever I was before, they had their time. Now it's my turn."

"That mind-set can work," Leah said carefully, "sometimes." It depended on who the person used to be. And what that person used to do. If in her past lives #6116 was, say, a humanitarian who mentored needy children in her spare time, then sure. Except . . . "About seventy percent of the populace can remember some or all of their past lives. But it's fragmented, they get flashes. Or they remember it all but they don't feel it." One of her patients had explained it as being akin to watching a movie. You might care about the characters on the screen, but no matter how the events unfold, it doesn't affect the viewer on a personal level. "Or, in your case—"

#6116 shuddered. "Nightmares. But they never bothered me before."

*You weren't escalating before.* "Sometimes a traumatic event will change how a person perceives their past lives."

"Why are you talking like you're narrating a documentary? I know all this."

Leah ignored the bluster. It was barely possible the woman would hear what she was really trying to say. "I've had patients who didn't have any sense of who they used to be, but then a loved one dies, or they survive a violent trauma—assault, rape—and suddenly they're flooded with images of who they used to be."

Then there were the others, the last group, the smallest percentage. About 5 percent of the population not only remember their past lives perfectly, and feel them on an emotional level, they are able to help others access *their* past selves. And to this day, scientists were still arguing about why.

Once upon a time, Insighters were routinely burned alive, thought to be in league with Satan. These days, nobody burned and Insighters were only in league with whatever HMO covered their patient. The meds helped, too, of course.

"Well, none of that stuff applies to me. I was getting along just fine and then I started having nightmares where I was the judge *and* the defendant. We even had the same terrible hairstyle!"

"Traumatic," Leah replied, and managed to keep a straight face.

"You don't know the half of it. And then I dreamed I was on a cruise. Well, a slave ship. But it was like a cruise, because I was white, so I didn't have to row or anything, y'know? Food sucked, though. I kept waking up hungry. And seasick." #6116 made a shooing motion, waving off nightmare-induced motion sickness. "So the meds worked. Right? I mean, obviously, you've got that 'I've got a secret' expression all you Insighters are terrible at hiding."

"Not all of us," Leah mumbled. She made a mental note to work on hiding her expressions better. Just because she was jaded didn't make it right to be lazy, too.

"I always thought it was kind of a joke. Medication + Insighter = hello, memories! But I could almost feel you digging around in my brain. Peeking. Spying." Leah made no comment, just let the silence stretch out. A pity #6116 was only interesting when she allowed her paranoia to show.

"Peeking and spying," she replied. "Yes, that's about right."

"What's wrong with me?"

*What isn't wrong with you?*

*Don't worry, #6116. You're in good (bad?) company; there's plenty wrong with me*, *too.*

Insighters had come along, evolutionarily speaking, shortly after man took up hobbies like cave painting and wearing the fur of the animals they clubbed to death. They weren't always called Insighters, but at least they weren't alone in that the names of their persecutors changed, too.

From shamans to witches (the Salem witch trials were a particularly bad time to be an Insighter), from pagans to Christians, from water dowsers to spiritual mediums, rhabdomancy to haruspices, and today Insighters. Tomorrow, Leah thought with morbid humor, "those weirdos who knew everyone's past life before we killed 'em all."

Though they were accepted (with reservations) as essential medical personnel, her kind had rarely had it easy. People who knew things they shouldn't have always, always been feared. Leah could remember researching as a teenager, shivering at how in the twelfth and thirteenth centuries, not only was it legal to kill an Insighter, there was a strict protocol to be observed: Pluck out the eyes first. Burn the rest. Bury the ashes. Salt the earth the ashes were in.

*And never speak of this again. Can I get an amen*, *brothers and sisters?*

Today it was about clean offices and HMO plans, receptionists and patient referrals. Once upon a time it had been the ducking stool and hot pincers; the modern version (paperwork!) was almost as bad. It was always unpleasant, but at least Insighting was no longer an automatic death sentence.

Unless, of course, you were the late, somewhat lamented Ginny Devon, formerly of Portland, Maine, now embarked on her fourth life, hopefully. Ginny Devon had been less than two years out of graduate school (doctoral thesis: "A Child Shall Lead Them: Children's Insights from Arthur Flowerdew to Shanti Devi") when she was murdered by a patient's disgruntled husband, a serial cheater who didn't appreciate being told he'd once been Henry VIII.

He had waited for her to leave the office, smashed her car window with a recoilless hammer, used a water gun filled with gasoline to drench her face and hair, then tossed a match and settled down to await arrest. He explained to the arresting officers that yon crispy critter had no right to snoop through his past, and certainly no right no discuss it with his wife, who was in the middle of scoring half of his net worth, thanks to, as he described it, a "fireproof prenup" (he was apparently unaware of the dreadful irony).

He had explained to the grand jury that his wife had been out of line to hire someone to snoop through his past lives, like a PI who didn't have to go through legal channels to dig. They had indicted him by one vote. He then explained his thoughts on snoopy Insighters to another jury, which, to the surprise of no one (but to the resigned alarm of Insighters the world over), came back hung. He had been convicted the second time and the judge had passed a wrist slap: ten years, including time served. Out in six. Extenuating circumstances. Temporary insanity. Only dangerous to snoopy Insighters, not the world at large.

Leah was probably safe from Chart #6116 but it wouldn't do to take that for granted. The lady in question had by now swung her legs over the couch, sat up, and puffed a hank of hay-colored hair out of her eyes.

Leah thought, not for the first time or the twentieth, that evil hid beautifully. Because Chart #6116, Alice Delaney, was gorgeous: tall and shapely, generous in the hip and bust, shoulder-length curls she could not stop touching, freckles, big blue eyes, and skin the envy of an Irish milkmaid. Quite bright, too: IQ 139. The best schools. The best food. The best homes. Chart #6116 was in her prime, and knew it, and took pride in knowing it, and looking it. "Is that why I'm having nightmares all the time? Because of who I used to be? How come not before? I'm not a kid anymore, f'God's sake; isn't this stuff supposed to pop up in your childhood?"

"Usually," Leah admitted. "But as we discussed, major life changes can bring past issues to the surface."

Her patient waved that away with a long-fingered hand that was beautifully manicured. "Nothing like that's happened to me. So why now?"

"Because now you're afraid of going to jail," Leah replied, smiling. "You're wiggling like a beetle on a needle to get out of it, and I'm the ace you preemptively tucked up your sleeve." *And if I had a dime for every time I met a patient this way, I would have three dollars and thirty cents.*

"What?"

"As I said. You're afraid of getting caught."

Leah waited, betting on *I don't know what you're talking about* or a variation on the *how dare you!* theme.

"I don't know what you're talking about."

"Not bad. Not especially imaginative, but not bad."

"What?"

"You despise children. They're too noisy, they refuse to sit still, they never do as they're told. Or they will, but only after they've been cajoled a dozen times. Their parents are lax, you are essentially surrounded by brats."

"None of that's against the law."

"No, it's simply how you justified your crimes. You'd take their toys, their silly treasures. Useless things that the children would miss. You liked knowing they looked everywhere. You loved it when they cried. Somewhere in your house you have a sizeable stash of worthless junk that you gloat over."

"That's not—"

"The stealing escalated to assault." She didn't need the chart, which she closed and set on the low table to her left. "You'd catch them, slap them. Push them, kick them. Never in your own neighborhood, of course. You'd drab yourself down as much as you could bear—unflattering ponytails, I would guess, or wigs. Ugly clothing that hid your figure. Padding to make you look puffier than you are.

"But even that wasn't enough after a while. It wasn't enough to make them sad, to make them hurt. You had to make them *gone*. So you escalated to murder one. You keep a list, don't you? The children you don't like. The ones you have decided have wronged you, or don't like you, or ones you loathe though you've never met—they're all the same under it all, don't you think? Just a bunch of whiny brats."

She was *staring*, which Leah was used to, so she continued. "You keep a list of names along with skim milk and chicken breasts and whatever new dry cleaner you've decided to terrorize this month. And you're pretty confident you didn't leave any crumbs. It isn't difficult to kill a child. It *can* be to hide the crime. But you took care. Even so, you're not *entirely* confident. Are you?"

Still staring. Well, that was all right. Better than screaming, or throwing things, or stabbing.

"So!" Leah gave the chart a brisk pat and straightened in her chair. "If there's ever a trial, your well-paid defense douche can claim that you felt remorse, you knew you were sick, you tried to get help, all those poor children, you tried to stop yourself, society's to blame, yak-yak. When sleep won't come, it is only because you're thinking about how awful ending the games will be. When you have night terrors, they're not about your victims. They're about being locked up. About never getting to have fun again. Never being the center of attention again. In prison, you'd just be another inmate. *That's* what makes you sweat. It's hard to know which is worse some nights," Leah finished. "Isn't it?"

"You're not—" #6116 had frozen in mid-tousle, and now peered up at her through rumpled bangs. "You're supposed to help me."

"No. I'm supposed to find your truth. That's what you paid for; that's what you're getting. And your truth is, you were a bad person then, you are a bad person now, and I imagine you'll be a bad person in the next one, too. That last is just my opinion. *That* you get for free."

"No. None of that's—it's all lies. You're trying to trick me."

"No. *You* tried to trick *me*. That's how people like you get caught. It's not enough to hurt and kill; you need to make a game of it. In all your lives, you considered children to be *things*, property, yours to do with as you liked. You knew it was wrong then, you know it's wrong now. You don't care. Hurting them . . . it's just too entertaining. Yes?"

There was a short silence, and Leah waited expectantly. Maybe #6116 would go the entitled route: *You can't talk to me like that*. Or something victim-y: *I can't believe you're doing this to me.*

"You're just trying to bum me out."

"No, I'm not." Leah was honestly surprised. Chart #6116 sounded grieved, almost forlorn, which probably worked great when she wanted someone to pick up the bar tab. Or drop the charges. "This isn't a trick, or a game. These are your lives. I'm not sure you can grasp that, because in all your lives almost everything *has* been a game, and the more deadly serious the better, right? But you're not a good person now. And you weren't then. So I don't see how you can be in the future. What are you learning from your lives? What is the one lesson you consistently take away? To do what you like, regardless of the cost—especially when you're never the one who has to pay."

"You fucking bitch."

"Sure." She nodded. Did #6116 expect her to gasp, to cry? To insist on an apology? It wasn't even the first time that week she'd been called a fucking bitch. "I'm not a good person anymore. Wait. Maybe not ever, maybe I'm like you that way. Just a moment." She hit the speak/sec button that connected her to the office admin. "Deb, I used to be nice, right?"

"Oh, God no," came the prompt reply. "You've never been nice. Not once."

"Thanks, Deb."

"Remember when I told you my grandma died, and you said me leaving early wouldn't bring her back, and payroll wouldn't calculate itself?"

"Thanks, Deb."

"And when Dr. Turnman quit referring patients to you because he thought you might be one of the Horsewomen of the Apocalypse?"

"All right, Deb."

"And remember when the guy who used to be Genghis Khan and Henry Clay Frick *and* J. Edgar Hoover made that chart detailing just how much of an awful human being you are? And we all got copies of the chart? And we all went to his presentation explaining the chart?"

"That's fine, Deb."

"And when my predecessor said you were a worse boss than the foreman of a South African diamond mine?"

"O-*kay*, Deb!" She smacked the disconnect button and turned back to #6116. "See? You're right, you are entirely right: I am a bitch. But your plan to make me angry by calling me things that are true isn't going to work. You came to me for 'help' and that's what I have for you. I'm not saying these things to be mean. If I were being mean, there would be no doubt in your mind, I promise. What I am doing is pointing out that your insomnia and night terrors are from your fear of getting tracked and trapped for the murders."

"Not that it's even true, not that any of what you're saying is at all true, but how would you even—"

*I can see them in you. All of them.*

Ideas, first, the way you make guesses about a person you've just met. Then ghosts, their past actions impacting the patient like pebbles dropped in a pond, only the rings never fade, never stop. And then you can see those other people, those corpses, behind their eyes.

*When you came to me you showed me everything. Everything. It just took a few sessions for me to understand what I was seeing.* "You're not the only one who has trouble sleeping. And not that you care—why would you?—but my rent is late, my estranged mother keeps trying to slither back into my life, and the man who's killed me half a dozen times is getting close again."

The pique was shifting to pissed. "So . . . what, everybody's got problems?"

"Some more than most. You, now. You have prison in your immediate future. That's a sizeable problem."

She was ready for the swing, and #6116 obliged. Leah caught the taller woman's wrist and applied various principles, and what with one thing and another #6116 flipped over the end table and smacked into the far wall. The plainclothes detectives, who'd been waiting outside trying to look like clients, came right in.

"Would you please arrest #6116 for assault?" she asked politely. Leah was always polite to people who were in the service of the law and routinely carried weapons. Being murdered was no fun at all, and even if it was inevitable in her case, she (usually) had no interest in zooming it along. "Among other things?"

"Alice Delaney, you're under arrest."

"Me! That bitch should be arrested; *she* assaulted *me*! And I want her arrested for libel, too!"

"It's not libel if it's true," Leah replied helpfully. "Also, I think you mean slander. Here's something to think about:

perhaps spend less time on felony assault and murder, and more time with a dictionary?"

". . . you have the right to remain silent . . ."

"Yes, yes, I've heard it all before."

"We're talking to Ms. Delaney," one of the cops said pointedly.

"Oh. How embarrassing."

"Like you know the meaning of the word! You're just a—a psychic Peeping Tom! Fucking *creepy* is what you are!"

"Would this be easier on you if I pretended to be hurt?"

#6116's answer was a furious growl and a lunge, fortunately stymied by the other detective, who was now cuffing her as quickly and carefully as she could. Insighters, Leah knew, gave people the creeps, which was a profoundly logical reaction. She didn't blame them for wanting to vacate.

"Right, sorry. Listen, Anna—"

"Alice, you nasty fucking bitch!"

"Mmm. Listen, while you're slogging through the justice system, you should return for a follow-up."

"Follow-up!" Chart #6116 yowled all the way out of the office and down the hall, promising grisly death, arson, murdered family pets, and, worst of all, a lawsuit.

"See?" the receptionist said. Patients being led away, raving and occasionally handcuffed, was nothing new. "You're the worst. Toldja."

"Not *now*, Deb. Listen, your court-appointed therapist will give you another referral for follow-up—"

"You can follow up with my ass!"

Leah trailed after the cops as they dragged her snarling client to the hoosegow, step one of what would hopefully be a decades-long legal process. "Don't worry about a thing. It'll all be covered by your insurance. Less your co-pay, of course."

> Patient advised to return within sixty days for routine follow-up. Thank you for the opportunity to treat Ms. Delano. *Ms. Dellen.*
>
> *Oh, hell, what was her name again? Delaney.*
>
> Report filed CC. INS ID# 29682.

# THREE

*My name is Mary Jane Kelly.*

Mary Jane misses Limerick, Ireland, and yes, that is where she was born and she's aware it's much like a bad joke. *There was a young lassie from . . . from . . .*

But she misses it. Still a wee one when the family moved to the city, her biggest problem back then was trying not to wet her clouts. She doesn't have the accent, not like her da', but the name alone

*(my name is Mary Jane Kelly)*

gives her away, tells the world she's a mick

*(my name is Mary Jane Kelly)*

an Irish mick, a bog trotter, a coal cracker, a fire bush fumblin' Dublin paddy narrow back potlicker wic sid, seven brothers and one sister because them Irish fuck like minks and none o' them are virgins.

She learned most of those hateful names from her mother, who decided Mary Jane Kelly should be earning on her back. Growing girls ate too much and didn't work as hard as the boys. And there were too many girls in the family as it was. Got to make it up to the family some other way, and Mary Jane Kelly never got the knack of sewing, or cooking, or minding the wee ones. So . . .

So here she was, and it was a bad time to be on the streets, a bad time to be in London's East End, but here she was, and some of her customers called her Fair Emma and none of them would tell her why.

Sometimes they called her Dark Mary and that one she did understand: Mary Jane Kelly was a mean drunk. She said terrible things when she was lit; she hit customers, she broke windows, she hurt, she'd been hurt, she yelled at her mother, dead now for two years. So, yes. A mean drunk.

(She hadn't gone to the funeral. Couldn't. The letter from her oldest brother came too late. She didn't care. And she was arrested twice that day.)

She had plenty to be mean about. The fucking East End and the fucking weather and the fucking johns and fucking live-ins who didn't want her but just the money she earned on her back and fucking Barnett, who smelled like fish no matter how much he washed and sometimes she was sure his fish smell was *in* her and she would never never never be clean.

And the fucking Ripper man, whose sole focus was working girls like herself, soiled doves ladies of the evening sluts whores whores *whores.* Like she had aspired to this. Like she and other little girls and boys the world over told their mamas, oh yes, when I get big I want to be a whore whore *whore*. Like her mother looked at her when she was just born and thought, *I'll make her turn pross when she's a teenager. For the family.*

She was six weeks behind on the rent; she owed twenty-nine shillings and it might as well have been twenty-nine thousand.

A problem.

It was November and fucking cold. Another problem. She'd spent her last pence on beer; it was the only thing keeping her warm. Made her want a piss, but . . . *warm*. Sometimes she thought she could be happy if she could just be reliably, dependably warm, all the time.

The only men she met wanted to borrow money. Still another problem, and by far the most annoying and darkly hilarious. *D'you think I'd be slinging my tits out here if I could loan you sixpence, daft man? Fuck.*

And then: a miracle. He's there and he's neat and clean and when she bitches about losing her handkerchief he gives

*(gives! not lends!)*

her his. He has a kind smile. He asks if she's terribly cold. He has a nice voice, low and kind and a little stuttery with nervousness. He buys her another beer. He asks if she has somewhere warm they can go. He says he likes her eyes, her pretty

*(bog trotter coal cracker fire bush paddy potlicker)*

Irish eyes. He says he knows just by looking at her that her mother was pretty, too.

(He's right.)

Amazed at her good fortune, she leads him to her nasty filthy room, which, at least, offers privacy, and she sings "a violet I plucked from Mother's grave when a boy" for his delighted approval. He doesn't care about the noise. In this part of town, at this time of night, no one cares.

She unbolts the door by putting her hand through the window she broke when she was Dark Mary; everyone knows she does this. In truth the room isn't much warmer with unbroken windows, in truth it's dreadful, but there's a bed and blankets and privacy and she can be warm, for a little while she can be warm with a nice gentleman, a good man who gave her a handkerchief and gave her beer and will give her money. He might not hit. Even if he does, the marks from his hands will keep her warm. For a while.

The light from the lone candle is poor and guttering, but she doesn't mind that, she never minds; what about any part of her life does she want to see clearly? It's better like this, in the shifting shadows he could be anyone: rescuer, prince, lover, husband.

*(Her father, come to save her. "What're y'doing in this hovel, girl? C'mon home with me, now. We've all missed y'so much.")*

He's quick, too, he's in a rush and that's fine, that's always fine, and she tries to help him with his clothes, or at least his trousers, and he's helping with hers, tugging in his eagerness and ah, God, it's been a while since a man wanted her with such urgency and she responds to his desire, his need, his *warmth.*

He's yanking, now, pulling hard and there's a flash of silver and he's—he's cutting her clothes off her, the silver flashes so quickly it's like she's in the center of a pool of little silver fish and yes he wants her she's never in her life had a man want her so badly and she's warm, so warm, and her clothes are off and the fish are everywhere and she's warm, she's *hot*, it's like he's splashing hot chocolate on her it's thick and warm and it smells it smells it smells a little like the farm

*(hog day, they're butchering the hogs today)*

like home, like Limerick, the place she never should have left. It's running from her throat, coating her breasts and dripping on the floor, and now it's turning cold and getting tacky and sticky the way chocolate does when it spills and you don't wipe it up right away it's sticky everywhere she's sticky and the fish are still darting at her and she shivers, cold again, always cold, always always always cold.

# FOUR

Deep in the middle of part-time job number sixteen, he watched Leah walk outside, blink up at the sun like some kind of gorgeous mole

*(gorgeous mole? oh, man, you have it so bad)*

and cross the street, heading into the small park where her only friend—so far as he'd been able to find out in two weeks—was waiting on one of the park's four deep green benches.

He'd been on her for two weeks and she was probably crazy. A sweetly curvy, glum, crazy lady with no friends (except the homeless woman in the park), a job she seemed to hate, and no desire to do anything *but* the job she seemed to hate.

Hobbies? Nope. Parties? Nope. Work parties? More nope. Dates? Ever more nope. Family? *Nada*. Friends, plural? Nope. A life full of nope.

He could see her getting depressed, actually see the physical symptoms of crushing depression every time she approached her office building. In the sixty-or-so feet between her car and the building, her shoulders went lower and lower, her mouth grew tighter, her gaze shifted from straight ahead to the sidewalk. Remarkable and so, so sad.

He knew Insighters were trapped in their own world of weird, but this gal was one of a kind among one of a kind. (Would that be *ones* of a kind?) Normally he hated that phrase, since by definition pretty much everybody was one of a kind, but Leah really *was*. Back in the day, they would have yanked her eyes and burned and salted the remains. Having that prospect dangling overhead would make anyone grumpy, he was sure, even if that kind of atrocity hadn't happened in over a century.

Her professional rep preceded her by miles—Leah had been an expert witness in a baker's dozen of criminal trials. History-making trials; Thomas J. Kinter v. Ann Boleyn brought about legislation preventing reincarnated victims from suing reincarnated people who had wronged them in previous lives. Little old ladies spilling hot coffee on themselves and then suing McDonald's for selling them hot coffee was nothing compared to the legal headache of suing someone who reneged on a twenty-dollar bet in 1814 ("So accumulated interest over two centuries means you owe me just under a quarter of a million dollars. So d'you want to write me a check or should I just garnish your wages for your next four lives?").

So there were all sorts of things about Leah in her pro capacity, but nothing at all about her private life. If she even had one. Right now, he was guessing no. And he had the feeling that it was more than the caution employed by anyone whose job meant they were constantly interacting with the potentially homicidal: district attorneys, crusading journalists, loan collectors, reality show stars.

In person—or as close to that as he could get in fourteen days—she was startling. He'd never met anyone odder or more intriguing. As a different sort of freak, Archer Drake figured he ought to know. And then there was the idea that had taken root in his brain that would not leave, the distinct impression he knew her, recognized her from somewhere. Impossible, since he hadn't officially met her. But there, always there, nipping into his brain and making him nuts, all the more so because he couldn't just march up to her and use the lamest of lame lines: *Don't I know you from somewhere? Oh, and I'm not a creep or anything. So, no friends, huh? Hmm? Oh, I know because I've been following you around for days.*

And that was the thing. He was *dying* to meet her, dying to talk to her, dying to ask a hundred questions, dying see if he could get her to flash the grin that was rare as rubies and lit up her face, turning plain to pretty and, when the grin widened, pretty to extraordinary.

He was supposed to watch her, he was supposed to take the money and keep an eye, and not for the first time he was very, very glad Insighters couldn't see him. Because if Leah could see him, she'd see all the way into him, and how do you defend against that? With the disaster of his father's life as the gateway to a chaotic childhood and his cousin's Insighter entitlement, all that as the background in a world where just about everyone knew they'd lived before, his type was ignored and overlooked and invisible.

Thank God.

# FIVE

"Brought you more of that chicken." Leah held out the bag, and Cat set aside the newspaper and took it with the delicate greed of her namesake.

"Thanks. Tough one?"

Cat had recognized the detectives at once; fortunately, Chart #6116 had been easier to fool. "Not really."

"S'why you take all those judo lessons, right? Sometimes they don't like what you tell 'em."

"Mm-hmm." Judo, no. Aikido and Eskrima, yes. She carried an expandable baton in her purse and a balisong in her bra, which was fine, since on a *good* day she was maybe a thirty-four B. All that in this lifetime's attempt to avoid being murdered again. Eskrima had been the easy one; in one of her former lives she'd been expert. Relearning hadn't been akin to relearning to bike-ride, but still, she'd been able to shave a couple of years off her training.

*Enh. Old habits. No need to burden Cat with any of it.*

"So check this," Cat began, nodding at the newspaper neatly folded beside her on the bench. "They got enough votes to move the graveyard."

"Yeah, I know, and a day before you did."

"Don't start," Cat warned.

"Nobody reads newspapers made from paper anymore. It's so much quicker, more accurate, and better for the environment to just—"

"Oh, Jesus spare me from a grumpy eco-terrorist."

"I am not! Well, yes, I'm grumpy, but the rest of it isn't true. And you know the library lets you have online access whenever you want—"

"Do *not* get me started on libraries!"

Ah. Shit. That was a definite lapse on Leah's part. It was never good to bring up anyone's wildly passionate/destructive love/hate relationship, especially one as tempestuous as Cat's with libraries. "Sorry. Sorry."

"And it isn't about getting news." At Leah's pointed silence, Cat elaborated. "It's not entirely about getting news. Newspaper is good for so much *stuff*! Insulation, windows—"

"Windows?"

"Yeah, it gets your windows wicked clean."

"Do you have windows? Somewhere?"

"You can use it for kitty litter, you can stick a sheet on your windshield and it won't get all iced up . . ."

"You don't have a car."

"And if you do the same thing in summer your car doesn't get so hot."

"You don't have a car."

"Eventually, of course, it's great for compost."

Leah blinked and considered her response. Finally: "You don't have a compost pile."

"Who said it was for *my* compost pile?"

"You're like those people who clip coupons for cat food even though you don't have a cat."

"Yeah, but everyone else *does*. Seems like it, anyway. And when they need a coupon, I'll be ready." She took a long look at Leah's expression and added, "Maybe we should let the newspaper war go for a few more days."

"I'm on board."

"Subject change?"

"Agreed. It's so sad," Leah said, looking into her sack. "I pack my own lunch, but I keep hoping to be surprised. But no. It's exactly what I packed for myself. I don't even *like* carrots."

"Not even a love note," Cat teased.

"No." Leah unfolded the note she'd left for herself: *don't forget to get more milk and keep a sharp eye out for your killer and also your ass looks huge in those shorts.* She looked down at herself. "I'm right. It does."

"Does not."

"No boobs, too much ass."

"Nope." Cat had shamelessly read over her shoulder, and not for the first time. Cat was ten years older, twenty pounds heavier, and almost a foot taller. "You don't *have* an ass to look bad. You've got nothin' going on back there."

"Plaid. What was I thinking? Rodney Dangerfield and circus clowns, they can pull off plaid Bermudas. Sometimes I wish my mystery man would hurry up and kill me again already."

"Yeah. Speaking of." Cat peeked into the lunch bag, smiled at Leah, and pulled out a chocolate pudding cup. Then, horribly, she helped herself to Leah's abandoned carrots and began dipping and eating. "You've had that guy sniffin' around you for a few days now."

"Mmmm." She couldn't look at the other woman. Carrots on their own were dreadful enough. She didn't think it was possible to ruin a Jell-O pudding cup. *Wrong again, dolt.* "He is definitely taking his time this life." The quickest he'd ever killed her was when she was nineteen. The longest was this life—she had just turned twenty-six, and was thus far unperforated.

"Can't believe you just wanna let it happen. Whad'ya take all the classes for? Huh?"

"The confrontation," she corrected her. "That's what I want to have happen. I'm tired of feeling him get close but not knowing if today's the day. And he might not kill me this time. I'm supposed to keep learning, yes? Maybe in this life I have learned enough. Maybe I'll kill *him* this time." Wait. That didn't sound like the lesson karma was trying to teach her . . .

"Mmm, yeah, that'll teach him."

"Well. It might."

"You couldn't kill a tick."

"Could, too." Lie. Leah always set them free, to the fury of whoever observed the behavior. Her mother used to *burn* them in ashtrays. Her mother burned everything but cigarettes in ashtrays. *Ugh. Even a parasite did not deserve to be burned alive.* "They are serving their function. They suck away at the lifeblood of various mammals which is what God made them for. Insert witty commentary on politicians and/or Hollywood agents here."

"Will not. Heard all the 'all politicians are dirty har-har-har' cracks I need. And you! Gettin' too lazy to come up with your own jokes, hell with ya, you're getting wicked lazy in your old age."

"I can't tell you how much I've enjoyed our lunch today, Cat, but duty calls."

"You liar, you've got half an hour left. Listen, call the cops on that guy."

"To tell them that I have never actually caught him doing anything illegal but he might be killing me soon, so could they take a break from actual criminals and please arrest him on no charges?"

"Cops do it all the time for Insighters."

"Cops do it sometimes for Insighters when they have more on the arrestee in question than I do." For example: #6116. The cops had her on attempted assault. They could search her car now, her home, and her person based on what Leah had found out and what had happened in her office, legally taped and documented. Thanks to the Twenty-Eighth Amendment, and the waiver all her clients signed as a matter of course, Leah was not bound by confidentiality issues as a doctor or lawyer was. If anything, she was closer to a mandated reporter like a teacher or social worker: it was her duty to inform the state of potential homicidal shenanigans. Thus, anything they found in #6116's car or home was now considered fruit of the poisoned tree. Beyond that, the police and the DA were on their own.

You couldn't arrest for murder someone who had killed in his last life. You couldn't bring a civil suit against such people, either. They could only be legally penalized for what they did this time around—and what a dark circus the legal system had been before that legislation passed! (It was still a dark circus, but perhaps not *as* dark.) But you could spot them, and watch them. You could set traps for them. Sometimes, with people like #6116, it was easy. Sometimes, as in the case of Leah's many-time murderer, it was impossible.

"If he would just kill me already, they could arrest him. What *can* he be waiting for?"

"There's something wrong with you," Cat said without a trace of judgment, which was one of many reasons Leah ate lunch with her.

"I'm an Insighter who hates Insight," she agreed. She didn't know what to do with that; she'd never known. She didn't know whom to ask, either: every one of her colleagues felt the same. "It's such a silly trope, too: starry-eyed newbie ready to change the world slowly turns into jaded jerk. Boring-boring-boring."

"In plaid, even," Cat added around a mouthful of chicken tender. "You look like Rodney Dangerfield with boobs."

"Yikes." So: disillusioned, *and* trapped in a lame trope. In plaid. *Ugh.*

"Can't you ever just . . . you know . . . turn it off?"

Leah shrugged. There was no use telling Cat that every time they ate lunch together, she saw another sliver of Cat's past lives. Enough lunches and the sliver eventually formed the full stake. Over the weeks and months she saw Cat's father beat her mother until the police came again, and did nothing again. She saw Cat in an earlier life, as a child trying to claw his way past a locked door until his fingers were red to the wrists. Went back further and saw Cat as a grown man crying over two fresh cemetery graves; the vision was so clear she could make out the years:

1867–1875. Twins? Dead sons, daughters? Went back further and saw Cat alone, alone, alone.

*Can I turn off being five-foot-five? With no ass and no chest and (almost) no friends? Can I turn off having brown hair? Wait, bad example . . . Garnier alone has eighty shades.* "No," she said after a while. "I can't just turn it off. I can't turn off being right-handed and deeply distrustful of mothers, either."

"You're a sad kiddo."

"Almost always when I watch you eat," she agreed, but was warmed by Cat's sympathy. She might only have one friend, but Cat was a good one, not least because she looked homeless and wasn't, seemed unbalanced and wasn't, sounded indifferent and wasn't. Leah liked dichotomy; Cat more or less defined the term.

"Speaking of eating," the other woman began, "you don't have to bring me lunch every day. I've got mon—"

"Shut up about giving me money, we've been over this." In every lifetime, Cat died alone. In every lifetime, Leah had a roof over her head and never missed a meal. God was a lunatic who needed to be beaten to death. "Don't talk about money again."

"I'll talk about what I like, this is a public park."

"As long as it's not about money."

Cat just stared at her and masticated carrots and pudding.

"Another change of subject?" Leah suggested. The inviolable law of their friendship: either party could suggest or demand a subject change at any time. *It's like our version of a safe word*, she thought, and had to smile.

"Quit leaving yourself mean notes."

Leah shrugged. "I decline."

"Or I won't eat your carrots tomorrow and you can just worry about them being in your lunch all day."

". . . deal," she finally said. *Outwitted again by a woman who uses last year's swimsuit as underwear.*

"Ha! Sucker."

They finished their meals in the closest thing to a comfortable silence Leah knew. That, too, could be considered weird or problematic if she thought about it.

So she didn't.

# SIX

Archer hurried to intercept Leah. This was dumb, this was crazy, this was not what his client was paying him to do. This was the sort of shit that led to his father being locked up.

Watch and report, he had been told. And he'd been happy to take the money. Then.

"I have to know what she's doing," the client had commanded. "It's the only way to know when the time is right."

"Okey-dokey." Being in a—there was no other word for it—lair made Archer want to check himself for ticks. Stacks of *People* and *Us* and *Entertainment Weekly*. Dust. Packets and packets of Sugarless Bubble Yum and packs of orange Tic Tacs filled clean ashtrays. And everywhere, pictures of Leah. Worse, pictures of his client. Worst of all were the pictures of Leah and his client together, feigning humanity while Leah grimaced at the camera in a variety of humiliating costumes. "What did you *do* to her?"

"That's none of your concern. And she did it to me. Now. The time is almost right."

"Are you trying to sound like a comic book villain on purpose?"

His client hissed at him like an irked housecat. "You will watch, and you will inform."

"A Nazi comic book villain?"

"Then, when I'm ready—"

"—you'll spirit her to your lair and make her your bride?"

"That's disgusting." For a creature who lived in a mansion out of *Great Expectations* and paid strange men to follow cute Insighters, the client was ironically judgmental. "I would never. You have a filthy imagination. Now get to work, but use your imagination on your own time. Everything you need to know is in that folder."

"Not everything," Archer had replied, taking another long look around the mansion of horrors. Who knew such monstrosities lurked in Chicago's Lincoln Park? "Are you dressed as a birthday cake in this picture? Why is Leah dressed as the candle? And what's the dog for? Where is this taking place? I have questions about at least ten other pics, too. I'd like to take pics of your pics and take them home and sort of fret over them. And when I'm done with the questions about the pics, I have questions about your house, starting with the fish. And when I'm done with the questions about your house and your fish, I—"

"Get to work!"

"Please," he begged. "Just one question. Any question. What's with the gum and Tic Tacs? At least tell me that much. You eat them together, don't you? And then spit the Tic Tacs–y wads of gum into the ashtrays? Because I can't help noticing there's no cigarette smoke in here. Or cigarettes. Or things to light cigarettes. So please, in the name of God, tell me, *what are the ashtrays for?*"

"Out! Go work for a living, stupid boy!"

"Don't call me a boy!" Anyway, off he went, and after days of lurking it was time to warn Leah. Which probably broke some sort of Pee Eye rule: don't rat out your client to the person you're following for said client. Yeah, that was probably definitely a rule. Oh, well. He could always get another job. And maybe Leah would be glad. Maybe she'd agree to grab a coffee. She could bring her homeless friend if it made her feel safer. She could bring five homeless friends, a dozen, and guns, too, if that would help her feel safe, and/or knives. He just wanted to see if he could get her to smile.

She hardly ever smiled. Archer thought that was the saddest thing ever, and he'd been surrounded by bubble gum and dusty packets of Tic Tacs and squeaky-clean ashtrays in a cigarette-free house full of fetish photography. Although perhaps that was more creepy than sad.

"Excuse me," he called, hurrying to catch up. She was done eating, she didn't want to go back to work, it was broad daylight, so she maybe wouldn't spook . . . it was as good a time as any, and maybe better than most.

"Finally," she said, which should have scared him but didn't. (He'd have time to ponder all that should have terrified him, and didn't, while being stitched up in the ER with a local that should have dulled the pain, and didn't, while being scolded by Leah who should have been contrite, and wasn't.)

"Yeah, hi. Listen, you don't know me." She'd allowed him to catch up to her, had stepped off the sidewalk and into the little alley between her office building and the CVS. The alley was well-lit and clean and not remotely like the kind Bruce Wayne's parents were killed in. Comics had given alleys such a bad rep.

He had hopes she'd led him off the street because she wanted to talk to him in private, and tried not to pant. She could really move when she wanted; it had been tricky keeping an eye on her while keeping up with her. God, she was so *cute*! Even her scowl was cute. And she was definitely scowling at him. *Probably thinks I want to sell her something. "Pardon me, miss, are you satisfied with your life insurance coverage?" Could not quit part-time job number nineteen fast enough.*

He liked her dark hair, falling like a sleek curtain to her shoulders. He liked her dark eyes, big and wide-set, like a sexy hammerhead shark.

*Sexy hammerhead shark? Dude.*

Yep; he had it bad, and that was fine. His last serious girlfriend was over a year ago, and he hadn't gotten laid in eight months, a boss-with-benefits thing at part-time job number twenty. He hoped Leah would help him break his dry spell. Lately he'd been making excuses to himself to not masturbate.

*Not tonight, right hand, I've got a headache.*

*You've always got a headache! When was the last time you took me out?*

*I take you out all the time! You're a part of me!*

*Don't you try to sweet talk me. You're seeing that whore of a left hand, aren't you? AREN'T YOU?*

*I swear, there's nothing between us. It was that one time! I was drunk, I made a mistake, I'm only human!*

*I'm more than just a palm, four fingers, and a thumb, you know!*

*I know, I know . . . I'd never take you for granted, right hand.*

*You're like my right hand! And oh crap, pay attention, you're about to lose Leah.*

He liked her slender frame and medium height; at just under six feet, he was a comfortable head taller. It made him want to fold her into his arms and protect her. It made him want to fold her into his arms and kiss her until she was panting as hard as he was. *I hope she lets me get the whole story out. Also I should probably work out more, because I should not be this out of breath after jogging after her for thirty seconds.*

"—on with it."

"Right. Listen, this is gonna sound weird—"

"Doubt it."

"—but someone's out to get you, and—"

"I know."

"Oh. Oh! Well." He tried a smile to see if she'd reflexively smile back—lots of women did, like people always shook your hand if you stuck it out there, but Leah was po-faced. "It's easier, then. If you know what's going on."

"You would think." She shifted; he was so busy watching her face he forgot to watch her hands. "But in fact, sometimes that makes it more difficult." Then she stabbed him.

"Hey!" It wasn't even a little bit like the movies. In the movies, half the time the bad guy (not that Archer was the bad guy, though later he understood why she thought so, and also, *dammit*!) didn't even know he'd been stabbed at first. Too busy ranting at the hero to notice. Plus the heroes kept their knives so insanely sharp the villain didn't even feel it going in. But Archer knew instantly that she had taken a knife out of her bra

!!!!!!!!!!!!!!!!!!!!!!!!

and stabbed him in the shoulder.

"Son of a bitch! In your bra? What the hell, Leah? What else is in there? In your bra? I should have seen that coming. But I was distracted because, y'know, bra. Ow-ow-ow."

"I—I—" She looked, if possible, more shocked than he did. Not that he could see his face. But he felt pretty shocked, so he probably looked it and ow-ow-ow. "I can't see you!"

"Well, your aim is pretty impressive."

"I—I was wrong. That was disgraceful." She did look remorseful, which went a little way toward cheering him up as blood dripped down his shoulder and pattered on the sidewalk. "It's just as well I could not ram it home in your heart. All those ribs to get through—ugh. Most of the time the blade just glances off them. In the end it's often too much trouble."

"Wait. What?"

"But they will arrest you on my say-so and then you can sit in a cell and think about what you did."

*"What?"*

"Not that you didn't have it coming," she scolded him. Yeah. *She* was scolding *him*. He tried to pay attention as his blood drip-drip-dripped into his battered sneaker, which had seen worse days, but not many. "You should be ashamed, killing me all the time. What is it with you? Were we married in another life? Are you killing me over and over again because I cheated on you?"

"What? No. What?" Waves of weird kept closing over him. First she was very very close and then she was very very far away. In all cases she was telling him off. Was it a dream? And if it was, was it a nightmare? It was weird that he didn't know. He should know. He should be able to figure that much out at the least.

"Listen. I was hired to follow you but I do *not* like the vibe on this job. I wanted to warn you. I betrayed my solemn oath as an amateur private investigator and you took a knife out from between your boobs and stabbed me. Why'd you drag your boobs into it, Leah? Why? They didn't deserve that. They're innocent!"

A smile! And the smile did that thing to her face where years fell away and she looked mischievous and ready to have fun or make trouble or both.

"Private investigators do not take sacred oaths and I did not drag my boobs into anything, and stop calling me by my first name like you know me. Then . . . I was right. I *can't* see you. I'm afraid I have confused you with my murderer. So what you've babbled at me as you go into shock makes sense."

"I'm not going into shock." He shivered so hard for a second he wondered if he was having a seizure. "All right, I'm going into a little bit of shock. Why were you dressed as a birthday candle in that picture?" he shouted because she was very very very very far away. When did she have time to run away so quickly? And she was smaller, now, too. "Come back!"

"Yes, definitely a mix-up, as normally you would have killed me by now." She was looking at him thoughtfully and blinking her wide-set hammerhead eyes, which was a pleasant change from how dispassionate she'd been earlier. "Why can't I See you? Do you know? Will you tell me?"

*I . . . understand . . . none of this. More important, how can I get her to go out with me?* He shook his head in a vain attempt to clear it. "My client wants you and not in a good way. So I came to . . . what's that sound?"

"You're bleeding."

"Bleeding makes a sound?"

"I've signaled for an ambulance. You're hearing the siren."

He blinked at her like an owl, a stabbed owl, and swayed on his feet. He was unreasonably overjoyed when she reached out and steadied him. "Hey, thanks, if I fall, I'll prob'ly bleed more and also it would hurt probably, I dunno, it doesn't hurt as much as it did earlier. Careful, you don't want to get any on you."

She was looking at him in the oddest way. "Thank you. You're right, I wouldn't want any on me. That was thoughtful."

"Okay, and when you didn't stick the knife in my heart, that was also thoughtful, so thanks for not lethally knifing me."

Another smile! Two in thirty seconds! Or had it been an hour? Who cared? She'd fall in love if he didn't bleed out and they'd make babies who were weird and had gorgeous smiles and hammerhead shark eyes. "Beautiful shark-eyed babies," he told her and, to Leah's credit, she didn't flee, or hoist a knee into his balls. "When'd you do that? Make the ambulance come?"

"While you were whining about how I didn't kill you."

"Whining! No wonder you don't have any friends except that homeless lady in the park."

"That lady used to be the mayor of Boston, is not homeless, and never mind about my friends or lack of same. If you aren't my killer, who are you? I don't know why I can't see you, but *you* must know that at least." She took his elbow and gently shook it. "Concentrate. Tell me."

"I keep saying. The client wants you. *Really* wants you."

She stepped back. She hadn't been afraid of him when she thought he was someone else, someone who would have killed her, but now, *now* she stepped back. And that smile was long gone. What. The. Fuck? "Oh, no," she breathed.

"Yeah."

"Not . . ."

"Yeah. Your mom. She really wants to see you. She says the time has come for you to forgive each other and work on your comeback."

She stabbed him in the other shoulder.

# SEVEN

"You can just back right off, Nazir!"

The strange man who had accosted her on the street was in quite a snit. He kept batting the air like a spitting kitten when she came near, which annoyed the intern trying to stitch him up. And though they were in the least romantic place on earth, save for perhaps a sewage treatment plant or a phosphate mine, she was having trouble not staring at his peculiar, gorgeous eyes. One faded denim blue, one a light green like seawater. Even with his shock-induced tiny pupils, they were extraordinary.

*He* was extraordinary, which explained why she was rapidly overcoming her knee-jerk reaction to someone in her mother's employ. He wasn't . . . handsome, exactly. If you took his qualities and examined them separately, he was downright funny-looking, like Julia Roberts or Gotye.

His nose was too long. His mouth was too wide. His eyes

were striking but odd. His hair was, as Madeleine L'Engle described such things, "hair-colored hair," a sort of light brown with dim lighter brown highlights, and he needed a haircut; the ends curled under just below the nape of his neck. His thick bangs were always falling in his eyes—it was a wonder he had been able to spy on her at all.

So, yes: taken apart, odd-looking. Together, it worked. Together, he was somewhat . . . dazzling.

*How annoying.*

"Hey! Nazir! I'm screaming at you in the middle of an ER. Please pretend to care."

She smiled at him. "No more Leah, eh?"

"I'll never call you Leah again, Leah! That Leah, the Leah that was, the Leah I might have had wonderful children with, is dead to me forever."

"You are," she decided, "overly dramatic. And possibly deranged."

"Because I've been fucking stabbed, you heartless psychotic!"

"I'm not psychotic," she said, stung. *Most likely.*

"Warning her, *warning* her, and she stabs me!"

"It's true."

"Twice!"

"I'm sorry about the first one," she added.

"See? She admits it! Ow-ow-ow!" He jerked on the gurney, and seized the doctor's sleeve. "That stuff you said would numb me? Is not numbing me." Then he snapped his head around to glare at her again. "Wait, just the first one? You're only apologizing for the first stab?"

"I thought you were the killer who keeps killing me."

"I don't even know how to be in a conversation with her," he complained to the harried intern. "Ow! You said the Novocain would kick in right away."

"Usually it does."

"Ow, argghh!"

"Unless I did it wrong again."

"*Again?* Here's some advice, doctor—if that *is* your real name," he snarled, then ruined the fierce effect by puffing his bangs out of his eyes. "That is not something a patient wants to hear *ever*."

"I didn't want to be a doctor," the intern confessed. He was a harassed-looking blond twentysomething who needed a haircut and about thirty hours of sleep. Leah had seen skulls with shallower eye sockets. "My dad insisted."

"Why the hell would you tell me that?"

"Sleep deprivation." Leah cleared her throat. "Your father insists because in two lives your father—and mother, actually, in your last one it was your mother—wants to be a doctor, cannot get it done, and makes you go to med school to fulfill their thwarted dreams," Leah told him.

She looked away from their wide eyes. God, when would she learn not to blurt out Insights to strangers? (At least, strangers who weren't new patients.) The intern had been trying to work and was clearly out of his depth and then . . . then she saw him. All of him. Saw his parents, saw their lives. Saw how it could end for him if he didn't break the cycle. A maddening aspect of her "gift": there were plenty of times she interacted with someone for hours (her receptionist) or saw them many times (the woman who cut her hair every six weeks) and never got so much as a glimpse into their lives, past or otherwise.

She cleared her throat again

(stupid nervous tic; anxiety phlegm!)

and added, "Really, you should be a veterinarian. It's the only way I can see you getting out of this tedious cycle."

The intern pounced. "I would *love* to be a vet. People are just gross."

"Awful," Leah agreed.

"Dogs and cats and, I dunno, birds and lizards, that'd be okay."

"Much more interesting. Also," she added, "they don't talk."

"They *don't* talk," the doctor replied, delighted. "But it's too late now."

"It's not, actually."

"All the money they spent, sending me to school." He looked at his bloody gloves and shook his head. "I can't do it to them. They took out loans. They took on second jobs. They helicoptered the hell out of me."

"So?" She had zero patience with parents living their dreams through their progeny. And not much more for the progeny who wouldn't stand up to said parents. Then again, Leah allowed she had a peculiar bias against parents in general, after being raised by the foul unnatural creature who was her mother. "If you won't stand up to them, get used to this life again and again. It's your fourth pass, you know." It was. She could see it, could see the doctor, all of him: George Stanton, DOB 2/6/1821, DOD 6/2/1865. Harry Bennett, DOB 6/3/1865, DOD 1/2/1905. Carolyn Whitman, DOB 1/2/1905, DOD 12/5/1968. All docs. All hating it. All dying in a state of vicious dissatisfaction. The saddest thing about her gift was when she explained their mistakes to people, only to see them turn around and make more of them.

"I'm so sorry to interrupt this bit of career counseling, Dr. Pay Attention to Your Patient. I myself never planned on becoming a Pee Eye, but none of the local art schools would take me and I hated my part-time job at the morgue. But I am a stabbing victim in mortal agony, so fix me already!"

"You are not," Leah said, annoyed.

"Which part?"

"You're not in agony."

"You don't get to decide about my agony," he snapped back. "You don't get to decide anything about me. In fact, you should be way nicer to me so I don't press charges. Like, fourth-date nice." His gaze dropped to her breasts, which she should have minded, but he had such a stupidly hopeful look on his face she did not. On the other hand, he might have been eyeing her cleavage (such as it was) for weapons. Which, since she had two more knives concealed on her person, was wise.

"That reminds me," the doc said, finishing the last stitch with a satisfied grunt. He straightened and rubbed his back, cursed when he remembered he still had bloody gloves on and had smeared just Archer's blood all over his shirt, and yanked them off. "Did you want to press charges, Ms. Nazir?"

She closed her eyes but the outraged shriek came anyway: "*What?*"

"I did have cause," she reminded him.

Archer was so outraged he could only gape at her for several seconds while the doctor cleared away the mess—they were short of nurses at Northwestern Memorial, and it was making everyone grumpy. Finally, he managed, "Right, I forgot, she's an Insighter, so she gets a pass on felony assault because *bogus.*"

The doc nodded. "She does if you killed her before."

He was wrong, but Leah said nothing. Sometimes it was better to let people keep believing the myths. In fact, she could file a complaint about the stalking, but couldn't have him prosecuted for anything he might have done to her in a former life.

"First of all, I didn't kill her before. I've never killed anybody in any life. Second, our judicial system," Archer announced to the room, "needs work." He thought of his father for a moment, and the uncle his father was in prison for killing, and shivered.

"On that we agree." Insighters were rare, like physics geniuses, and like physics geniuses, they were treated with a combination of awe and impatience, and sometimes bone-deep dread. People needed them and resented needing them. They could do things most could not, and their talents weren't quantifiable or controllable. It made for uneasy symbiosis. The Traynor bill, which had been plodding through Congress for years, did nothing to clarify matters. It had made things murkier, and even Leah didn't think Insighters should get away with some of the things they got away with. "I won't press charges. You have been punished enough."

"Got *that* right."

"But when you get out of here, we are going to see It. Also, you will need a new job because you will not be spying on me any longer. Tell It to hire someone else."

"Got *that* right." He paused. "Are you calling your mom It?"

She ignored him. "Dr. Drange, are you admitting him?"

"It's Derange," the doc, whose ID badge was smeared with blood corrected, and what an unfortunate name for a physician.

He was scribbling in Archer's chart. "Overnight at least, yeah. Couple of stab wounds would normally warrant a longer stay, but they're pretty shallow. Messy, but not dangerous."

"What do you know about my stab wounds? You're a future veterinarian! I happen to think they're messy *and* dangerous."

"I think," Derange added, raising a blond brow at her, "your heart wasn't in it."

"Shows what *you* know." Archer was out of his foaming rage and entering Sulk Mode.

*It did, actually. My heart wasn't in it. Well, the second time.*

"I said I was sorry," she said when they were alone.

"You apologized for one grotesque wound, not both."

"As I am certain," she continued, "you are sorry for spying on me and scaring me."

"*Scaring* you? No way in hell. An IRS audit wouldn't scare you. Goddamned Typhoid Mary wouldn't scare you." Since Leah had met Mary Mallon just last year, he was correct. "You don't scare." A half-second pause, followed by, "Okay, sorryIscaredyoubutyoudidn'thavetostabmetwice."

"You're right." She thought for a few seconds. *Am I really going to do this? Yes. I am.* "Can I get you anything?"

He blinked those dazzling eyes at her. "What?"

"You say 'what' a lot. Magazines? Gum? A cigar? Do you want me to call anyone?"

". . . no."

*He doesn't have anyone. Like me.* The thought brought another unwitting smile to her lips.

"Why are you looking at me like that with your sexy shark eyes?"

"I . . ." *Because I can't see you, and I would like to.* "I apologize."

"I'll tell you what I'd like." He shook his head. "I can't believe I'm saying this. I can't believe I'm even thinking it. But . . ."

And that's how she found herself spending the night curled into a surprisingly comfortable chair beside Archer's hospital bed, the beeps and boops of the monitors around her lulling her into a sleep almost deeper than Archer's drugged one.

# EIGHT

Three days later, they were ready to knock on It's door. Three days of Leah making several trips to the hospital to check on a private investigator who had the perfect name for a private investigator (or perhaps an action star): Archer Drake.

"Really?" she couldn't help asking. "You didn't make it up? Or legally change it?"

A shadow had crossed his face when she wondered aloud if he'd changed it and why, but it was gone so quickly she wondered if his wounds were bothering him and she had misinterpreted his expression.

"Go away, it's my real name, stop coming around and challenging the reality of my name, you awful—Laffy Taffy! Mmm, bring banana-flavored next time."

"I will not. There is no worse taste in the world than artificial banana. Well. Lava, perhaps."

Two days of frustrating sessions with clients while all the

time wondering what nonsense patient Archer Drake, condition satisfactory, was getting up to. Two days of anticipating and dreading the confrontation with her mother. Ha! Confrontation . . . her mother would never stoop to acknowledging any of Leah's righteous fury. What was the word to describe a confrontation of one?

And as if all that wasn't nerve-racking enough, two days of repeatedly staring hard at Archer Drake and verifying that, yes, she could not see him.

Unprecedented.

All that to say, for three days she almost forgot to be resigned to her untimely murder.

Upon discharge, Archer had insisted on taking a taxi to his apartment, and they'd agreed to meet at her office later that day. "Are you sure?" she asked for the third time, walking him through the hospital lobby. He was wearing scrubs, a reluctant gift from the admitting physician (his clothes were, of course, ruined), and walking carefully but energetically. "Perhaps you should take the day to rest."

"Cluck-cluck, Leah. No. I want to get this over with. Also, I have a *thousand* questions for your mom. Your mom! I still can't get over that."

"Ugh."

"Yeah, well, it's happening, honey."

"Do not," she warned, "call me honey."

"Whatever you say, sugar bear."

"Good God."

"Hey. Thanks for taking care of me." His odd eyes were sparkling at her—she was unaware that people's eyes could actually sparkle in real life. He was like a live-action anime cartoon.

"Which you should have anyway since you put me in *the hospital* with *multiple stab wounds* but I'm beginning to see you had your reasons. Maybe. I dunno. You're a weird chick, Nazir."

"Call me a chick again, you will be right back in here."

"I believe you, duckling. See you in a few hours." He dropped a fast kiss to her right cheek and she was so surprised she played statue and watched him hurry out the door and back into the world.

Odd man. A very odd man.

# NINE

Her nine o'clock was disgruntled. He had been waiting in the parking lot until the office opened, and Deb, used to dealing with aggrieved clients, let him in. Not for nothing did they have a metal detector at the entrance, as well as security guards, and once he'd been cleared, she called Leah to warn that her 3:00 p.m. was six hours early.

Leah knew from experience that making them wait not only didn't work, it often backfired. They sat out front and struggled with whatever hidden nastiness Leah had been able to help them unearth. Follow-up care was not yet mandated by law—some compared a post-Insighting session to sub-drop—but patients had to sign waivers indicating their refusal of treatment.

So she knew the best way to handle it was to see Charlie Reynolds at once. He declined beverages and a chair, Leah made sure to keep the desk between them, and he got right to it: "You didn't help me even a little. You just made everything worse."

"How is that possible?" she asked mildly, "when I only spent forty minutes with you months ago and you never came back? You can't even get stitches in forty minutes, and I ought to know. *So* much paperwork."

"You were supposed to help me," he continued doggedly. Reynolds was neatly dressed in a dark gray suit, white dress shirt, black tie, black shoes. He had a fedora and was turning the rim over and over in his hands as he played with it and wouldn't meet her eyes. She remembered during their session that the few times he could look at her, his gaze almost immediately skittered away.

"You came to me because your nightmares were starting to bleed into your waking hours. Your daydreams quickly became as bad. You feared you would lose your job as a corrections officer."

"You have to be alert," he told his hat, "all the time."

"Yes, I imagine."

"They have nothing to do but watch and figure out your patterns. Most of them don't mind hurting you; it's their version of pay-per-view. Not personal, just entertaining." He shivered a little. "Not a good time to get lost inside your head."

There was a long silence and just as Leah decided to break it, he continued. "But after you told me those things—those terrible things—it just got worse. And the pictures in my head—they're always there now." He shivered again. She knew it wasn't the air—the office, with all the windows, no shades, and crap air-conditioning—was usually a brisk seventy-eight degrees in the summer. "Always there."

"Yes, well, I warned you about that. Your subconscious is forcing you to face what you did in the thirteenth century."

"That's not what I wanted!"

"But it's what you paid for," she said gently, "and it's what you got. You expected me to take away your nightmares and I told you that wasn't how it worked. All I can do is pull away the curtain between your last life and this one. Once you see past it, you can do something about it. Or not, as is your choice. But you're the one who has to take the next steps."

"I was sleeping maybe four or five hours a night, and showing up late a couple times a month. Now I'm lucky if I get two hours and I was late five days this week. I figure one way or the other, this time next week I won't have a job. Might not have anything."

She nodded. Here was a perfect example of how the laws of the land and HMOs had yet to catch up to the reality of psychological fallout from past lives. Reynolds's job should have been protected under the Family Medical Leave Act. His past was inflicting psychological damage, he should be able to get penalty-free time off to deal with it. Leah saw it as no different than getting a diagnosis of chronic depression and needing time off to adjust: therapy, meds, related psychological issues.

In a perfect world (or at least a less awful one), yes. As things were now, it wasn't illegal or discriminatory to fire people when their past lives were bleeding over into their jobs.

"Mr. Reynolds, I am sorry. But I explained all this to you at your session." He still wouldn't meet her eyes, so she addressed her comments to his tie. "And I strongly encouraged follow-up. I also sent several letters to your home. We don't advise dealing with this on your own; it's too much for most people. The system is in place to help you deal with resurfaced memories—even if it's not yet in place to allow for job protection."

"You have to make it stop."

"*You* have to make it stop." Leah couldn't see his dreams, but she could imagine. Even now, historians weren't sure how many blond, blue-eyed boys Gilles de Rais tortured, raped, and killed. Conservative estimates put it at sixty; some maintain the number is closer to six hundred. Charlie Reynolds knew, but Leah doubted he was interested in being forthcoming. Even one little boy murdered so horrifically would have been too many and she wasn't without sympathy for his plight. But compassion warred with irritation. She had explained these things. He said he understood. She had warned him. He said it was fine. When he hadn't returned for follow-up, she'd left messages that were never returned, sent letters which were returned unopened, finally sent one by registered mail to be sure he was getting them. He was, and chose to do nothing.

"It's all the time now, don't you understand?"

"I do understand. And as I told you, your 'batten down the hatches and wait for it to go away' plan will not work. You have to face what you did. And then you have to—"

"*It wasn't me!*"

She just looked at him.

"It wasn't." He took a breath and visibly calmed himself. "And now it never stops. Not just when I'm asleep and not when I'm daydreaming. I close my eyes and I see all those little boys, all those blond, blue-eyed . . ."

She nodded, wondering what it said about a man who killed small, helpless versions of himself over and over.

". . . and they're screaming and bleeding and the rooms stink of blood, *reek* of it, and it never never stops." He had stepped up to her desk and was leaning over it and nibbling on his hat rim and his face had flushed to the color of a brick. "You made it worse. Everything's worse."

"Mr. Reynolds, please step back and calm down." She'd pressed the white button (*stand by outside office*) at his "you just made everything worse." If she hit the red button (*swarm!*) security would pile in. "No one here wants to hurt you."

"I don't want to hurt *you*." Deep breath. "But I probably will."

Hmm. That could be interesting. Was this man her destined killer? She knew she should have been tense, scared; instead she felt equal parts pity and irritation for the man who knew what he was but still wouldn't face it.

*No*, she decided, looking him over. *He's not my killer. Though it'd be a rich irony if he were, if I were slashed because in my arrogance I didn't see him as a threat. It'd serve me right, and then some.*

"I don't—" He took another breath, straightened, put his hat on. "I don't understand how you can *do* this to people."

He left without another word—and that happened sometimes, too. There'd be this big blowout scene and Leah would be prepared to defend herself, or unleash the forces of good (or at least the security detail), and then they'd just sort of deflate and wander off.

Regardless, Deb made sure he was off the property, security confirmed, and Leah flagged his chart and updated her clinic notes. It was unfortunate, and not uncommon. Just as car salesmen didn't always advocate a new car for everyone, Leah didn't think Insighting solved everyone's problems every time. It was an unfortunate truth she'd been facing since she was old enough to understand it.

Her ten o'clock was a woman who had been a vestal virgin

in 114 BC and again in 19 AD. Both times she had been wrongfully accused of having sex with a Roman citizen, which was considered treason, both times the accusations were false but she'd been found guilty due to the enormous political turmoil at the time, and both times she was buried alive, which was the traditional reprimand for treason (trumped up or otherwise).

As a result, she was a claustrophobic sex addict.

"Oh, Marcia," she sighed. "Again?"

"Swear to God, Ms. Nazir, the cops just *wait* for me."

"They really don't."

"They do!"

"This is Chicago. The police have better things to do than follow you around and wait for you to indulge in acts of public lewdness."

"Nope! They've got nothing better to do than spy on me and wait for me to—to be attacked by my own disease and do stuff they know I can't help. Buncha pervs. With all the porn out there for anyone on the Internet, they've gotta lie in wait for me?"

"Marcia."

"*I'm* the victim!"

"Marcia."

"And the poor guy I was with. He's probably a victim, too. Mark, I wanna say? He looked like a Mark, right?"

"Marcia, Marcia, Marcia! You were busted having carnal relations in the dugout at Wrigley Field. The police take a dim view of such things. And also the public, presumably."

"It's not like it was the World Series or anything." Her patient sulked. "Not even the playoffs."

"Still." Leah forced herself to soften her tone, though the urge to hit Marcia with her tape dispenser was strong. This was not her first arrest for sex alfresco. "I understand you have a disease—multiple diseases—"

"That's right!"

"—but it is not and should never be a free pass."

"Oh, here we go. You're one to talk, Ms. Nazir."

"Beg pardon?"

"Insighters get away with everything."

"That is not true," she said sharply, though an internal wriggling pricked her conscience. She hadn't had to talk to a cop, post-stabbing. There had been no police report, and likely would not have been even if Archer had been inclined to press charges. Which, for some reason, he had not. "And if you have a problem with what I do for a living—which is strange, since you're here of your own free will—I encourage you to seek help elsewhere."

"No you don't! You can't get rid of me that easily."

"Yes, well." Leah, who had been prowling back and forth, sat behind her desk. "Worth an attempt. I have to write you up for this, Marcia, and I have to decide what to recommend to the DA. My inclination is to lock you up somewhere—"

"Hey!"

"—you can get help, somewhere good like Chicago-Read—"

"Good? Really?" Marcia, who had the hips and butt of an anorexic teenager and the breasts of an artificially augmented porn star, spun so fast her chest took an extra second to catch up. "You're gonna lock me up to be starved to death?"

"That was in 1901." *Do not roll your eyes. And definitely don't hit her with the tape dispenser.*

"Are they even accredited anymore?"

"Your HMO takes them . . ." Not what she would call a

ringing endorsement. "Very well, I'll send you somewhere else. The point is, you've proven you won't take steps to manage your illness. You're like a cancer patient who refuses treatment and then is astonished when the cancer progresses."

"Oh, fuck me."

"Yes, well. Part of the problem. Don't you want to get better?" A rookie question, but she couldn't help it. She honestly couldn't tell. "Don't you want to control your urges instead of the other way around?"

"Why? So I can be a better person in my next life?"

"Well, yes, that *is* the general—"

"I got screwed—hilarious, kind of, since I *didn't* get screwed but was found guilty of treason and executed anyway."

"Yes, but—"

"So in my next life I was super careful, followed all the rules, did everything I was s'posed to—and got screwed again! Without getting screwed! Again!"

"All right, but—"

"The only thing following the rules got me was unjustly executed again. So you, and society, can fuck *right* off. Next you'll tell me if I'm a good girl for the next six or seven lives, I'll come back *rasa*."

"Well—"

"Honk the other one."

After ten minutes of cajoling, threats, pleading, threats, and lectures, Marcia sullenly agreed to an outpatient program and no jail time, provided she could . . .

"Keep my nose clean?" her patient suggested, her good humor restored now that she wasn't going back to jail.

"It's not your nose I'm worried about."

"Ha! Good one, Ms. Nazir."

"I wasn't joking!" she shouted after her, but now she was shouting at a closed door. "Dammit." *It's a cliché, but won't someone think of the children?* Several were traumatized—or at least hopelessly confused—by the sight of Marcia's rake-thin thighs wrapped around her date's head like a bony muffler. On the other hand, prisons all over the country had no room at the inn for serial rapists and pedophiles, never mind a rich exhibitionist, so locking Marcia up seemed wasteful at best, and ineffectual at worst.

She knew her eleven thirty was there before he spoke; she sighed as she gestured for him to come in. "Harry, now really."

"I can't help it." Harry Aguan scratched his thick beard, the bristly hair several shades darker than the hair on his skull. He was a trim brunet of average height immaculately dressed in a spotless sky blue short-sleeved button-down, pressed navy slacks, socks that still had the sale sticker on them, and new black loafers. And it was all a waste of time and money, because Harry smelled like seagull shit on fire. "Every time I get in the shower—gaaaaah!"

"Baby steps."

"Which reminds me, the kiddie pool idea didn't work."

"Then we'll have to come up with something else," she said firmly. "Because you certainly can't go on like this."

"I can't drink coffee on the street anymore," he complained. He stretched, then plopped into the easy chair across from her desk, and the motion stirred enough body odor around to make her eyes water. "People keep dropping money in my cup."

"Well, you do reek to the heavens, Harry," she said kindly.

"You say that like I don't know it."

"I say it like you aren't trying as hard as you could to overcome it." There was that niggle in her brain again, the

*(oh look who's talking—you're just killing time until your murder)*

annoying voice pointing out that she was, at best, a hypocrite, and at worst, a terrible human being. Deb had reminded her of that with her usual cheer ("Yet another dissatisfied customer and if you were a restaurant, critics would give you minus stars.") just that morning. *Am I terrible out of self-defense? Or laziness? Are all Insighters in the wrong line of work, or is it just me?*

"You're actually ahead of the game, Harry."

"That must be why all the ladies want me," he snapped.

"We know the root cause of your ablutophobia. Some people never find out why they're afraid."

*Or they do, and they don't care. Like you, Leah!*

"That's enough."

"Sorry, Ms. Nazir?"

"Nothing, just scolding myself."

"Does it work?"

"Hardly ever. Your paralyzing fear of bathing and washing is perfectly understandable." It certainly was; in 1819, Harry's stepbrother had drowned him in the upstairs bathtub when he was six. *These kids today. And also back then.* "But you can overcome it. You *can*. Look, keep up with the sponge baths in the kitchen, and I want you to get a sitz bath."

"Baths don't work," he corrected her sharply. "I can barely stand to pee in there, remember? It took us over eight months for you to get me to stop pissing in the kitchen sink. It's hard enough just to pee in the bathroom, never mind take a—"

"A sitz bath is small, and you're only in water up to your hips.

It's what pregnant women use after they have a baby and are too sore for much else. Trust me, you cannot drown in one." Probably. Not without considerable sustained effort, for certain. "Baby steps, right? Don't get rid of the kiddie pool; store it in your garage for now and we'll work back up to that. In the meantime: sitz bath. Pick one up or order it online. Today. I'll put a note in your chart and your HMO will reimburse. Meanwhile, step up the sponge baths. The hottest part of summer is coming." Oh, God, it was. If Harry was this ripe now . . . it didn't bear thinking about.

"Okay, I'll try. Thanks for seeing me on such short notice."

"Of course. And we'll have a longer session next week, when you can tell me all about the joys of your sitz bath."

"Can't hardly wait," he said, and gave her a crooked smile on his way out.

If nothing else, she thought, giving her patient a wave as he left a trail of stink behind him before opening every window in the room, *it's nice to put my own problems in perspective. I'm due to be hideously murdered in the next several months, but at least I can enjoy many showers between now and then. I don't smell. I don't have sex with strangers in ball fields. This doesn't make me a better person, just a less complicated one.*

Yes, for some reason she was viewing the cup as half-full today, and she even knew why: it had everything to do with the man about to accompany her to the pit of horror she'd grown up in.

She realized, with equal parts unease and anticipation, that she couldn't wait.

# TEN

"I'm really nervous," Archer confessed as they pulled up to her childhood mansion.

"Why, do you think she's unstable?"

"No! God, no."

"Then you're something of an idiot," Leah said, softening the observation with a smile. "She's incredibly unstable. But she would never hurt *you*."

He waved that away, which given that he'd been stabbed (repeatedly) by another family member, struck her as courageous or stupid. Courageously stupid? And he'd passed over the emphasis on *you*, which she also found interesting. "I'm nervous about the questions. I've got so many! What if I forget one? When am I ever going to be back here? God, I thought my family was screwed up."

Leah sighed, shut off the engine, got out of the car. Archer had been more than happy to let her drive; he was understandably sore. Fine with her; she loved to drive. There was something about hopping in a car and just *going* that appealed to her inner chickenshit. She could never summon the courage to pick up and leave her life, but often indulged a rich fantasy world where she did. Taking the long way on virtually every trip factored into that. *I am not driving to my terrible mother's house; this is the beginning of my road trip to Egypt. I will need a new plan by the time I get to Florida. Perhaps I can trade my car for a one-way cruise ship ticket. That is Monday's problem, today I am going to drive. Drive. Driiiive.*

So when Archer asked her to drive, she'd made sure he was buckled securely in the passenger seat of her gray Ford Fusion (which looked an awful lot like a giant electric shaver, which was an awful lot like why she'd bought it), and taken the scenic route around the lake. But it was a gorgeous day, the kind that lures people to the Midwest: bright blue sky, clouds like marshmallow fluff, the breeze off Superior, the sunshine. Chicago's slogan should be "See? Winter eventually ends."

It was exactly as creepy as she imagined to find herself in the old neighborhood; she had not been home—though her apartment was only a half-hour drive away—since high school. If she'd had her way, she wouldn't have been home since middle school. For the thousandth time, she cursed the thick judge. If Nazir v. Nazir had not been a clear-cut case for legal emancipation, she could not imagine what was.

The place looked, from the outside, as it had when she'd last seen it: a gorgeous pile of Prairie-style brick concealing the utter madness within, with all the rich toy trappings out on the broad lawn, which was, of course, a perfect vivid green. Not the back lawn, either; if it cannot be seen from the street, if someone driving by doesn't crane their neck to take in all the accouterments, it hardly counts: a gazebo, a conspicuous absence of lawn jockeys, and . . .

*A koi pond stuffed with* Gosanke *and* Kohaku. *For God's sake. She hates fish. It could have been her idea of a subtle sly commentary on Hollywood's bottom-feeders, except it's neither subtle nor sly, and she has great respect for bottom-feeders.*

Unmoved by the McMansion's clichéd beauty, she marched up the porch steps and hammered on the glassed-in door with both fists. "I know you're in there, you horrible thing! I might kill you this time, so let me in!"

The door opened at once, startling her, and a moment later she knew why she'd gotten such an instant response: her mother hadn't answered the door.

"Leah, I'd like the record to show I tried to talk her out of it." The man, whom she knew was her mother's age but not holding up nearly as well, blinked nervously at her. His pale blue eyes were unusually large and the glasses made them look watery, as if he was always on the verge of an allergy attack. The few gray-blond wisps of hair he had left seemed so thin and fragile the wind could whisk them away, leaving him bald and blinking. "I truly did."

"And when that failed, you . . . hmmm . . . called to warn me?"

He blinked faster. "Well, your mom's my client, not you. Not since you fired—"

"Shut up, Tom." She brushed past her mother's agent into the front hall, immediately confronted by the clichéd sweeping dark walnut staircase, oriental rugs, hutches full of china they did not inherit, and looming over the entire room the gigantic Scarlett O'Hara–ish painting of her mother when she was Leah's age.

Behind her, Archer was introducing himself to Tom Winn of Winner's Talent™ (ugh). Leah ignored them and marched into the game room, which was dominated by a piano no one could play, reducing it to nothing more than a dusting headache for the housekeeper.

Ah, and there she was: Nellie Nazir, former child star, sperm bank shopper, swindler of fortunes, whack job, former smoker. Leah knew her mother would not have dared receive her in the Room O'Crap, stuffed to bursting with old photos of them in their (ugh) heyday, DVDs and downloads of commercials, newspaper articles, magazines . . . Leah needed no reminders of her exploited childhood. Nellie saved that room for people she needed to impress, and Leah had been off that list since her fifth birthday.

So it was no surprise to see It was posed prettily on the couch opposite the piano no one could play, wearing what Leah called the Birthday Outfit.

"What's the occasion?" she asked shortly, eyeing her mother and wondering if maternity was a gene you either had or hadn't. *If you don't have it, as It clearly does not, is there medication for the syndrome? Besides vodka? Perhaps an operation would be required. Like an appendectomy, only in reverse.*

"My darling daughter is home! The prodigal hon!"

*She might mean Hun. As in Attila.* "You've gone too far this time." She considered her mother's past transgressions. "Again. You've gone too far this time again."

"Wow, Leah, you can really get lost in—whoa." Archer skidded to a halt, taking in her mother's mufti: the long pink satin flowing robe trimmed in pink feathers at the cuffs and neck and hem. The pale skin, masses of rich reddish brown hair, expertly made-up eyes sporting enough eyeliner to choke a bear (but somehow It made it work), the long movie vixen red nails and matching lipstick. "You weren't wearing that when you hired me. That's—um—a different look for you."

"Please." Leah crossed her arms over her chest and considered indulging the urge to stick her tongue out at her mother. "She wore it to every one of my birthday parties."

"Mr. Drake, I underestimated you." Her mother flowed to her feet and, trailing feathers, crossed the room to kiss a startled Archer on the corner of the mouth. "I wanted you to watch over my baby so I could figure out the best time to approach her with my wonderful new idea, and you brought her home to me."

"*I* brought *him*," she got out through gritted teeth. It would be a miracle if she didn't crack a molar. "No more spying, Nellie, and no more wonderful new ideas. You know goddamned well I will never work with you again."

"For me," It corrected sweetly. "Work *for* me. Again."

"What's that weird noise?" Archer asked, trying to look everywhere at once.

"My darling girl has the most atrocious habit of grinding her teeth when she's indulging in one of her tantrums. A dreadful noise." It shook her head and looked mournful, her face momentarily hidden by rich brown curls. "The money I spent on orthos."

"The money *I* spent!" Leah took a breath and tried to force calm. "As I was saying. No more spying. You aren't just wasting your time—not to mention my time—but also your money. Oh, excuse me: *my* money."

"Now, Leah." It had the gall to sound reproachful. "We settled that years ago."

Settled = seducing the judge who could have emancipated

Leah and given her control of her money/life/career/happiness/ health insurance.

Leah controlled an urge to pluck her mother like a large pink chicken. "Listen carefully. I will not embark on a comeback with It. I will do nothing to breathe life into the chamber of horrors It calls a career. It should shrivel up and die and give her spot in the universe to someone else."

"I dislike when you refer to me in the third person, darling."

"*That's* the part of all that you don't like?" Archer asked. Tom, she noticed, had fled. This, too, was the pattern of her childhood. At best, Tom enabled her mother. At worst . . . it didn't bear thinking about.

"She gave herself the nickname," Leah explained. "It goes back to her tiresome rant about—"

"I'm a commodity, we're a commodity!" *Oh, God.* Leah buried her face in her hands as Rant #3 commenced. "Hollywood doesn't see men or women, they see products. It always has. And the only way to fight it—"

*Is not to fight it.*

"—is to get on board. So we're Its to them; not people, not names, fine. Exploit that! Just like in that Wild West movie."

"Uh . . ." Archer shot her a look. He seemed to be in the grip of horrified fascination. And her mother's lipstick was on the corner of his mouth. Leah stepped to him and scrubbed it away with her sleeve, perhaps

"Ow!"

harder than necessary.

"She means *Silence of the Lambs.*" *Oh how I wish that Archer had killed me.*

"But that's horror, or a thriller—not a Western."

"You know, Wild Bill," It interrupted, excited. "The bad guy."

"The bad guy was *Buffalo* Bill, you silly twat," Leah corrected. "Remember? 'It puts the lotion in the basket or It gets the hose again'?"

"*That's* why you refer to yourself as—that's a little weird."

"We know," mother and daughter replied in dulcet unison, then glared at each other.

"Because . . . um . . . it's kind of silly. And maybe even immature."

"That's what she's like," Leah said, irritably gesturing at her mother.

"I meant you."

Leah thought about it. It was wonderful to be in a room with Archer and her mother and have his attention on her and hers on him and It—Nellie—was where she belonged: out of the conversation. "Well, 'Mom' is inappropriate because there's not a drop of maternity anywhere there. And 'Nellie' is just silly."

"But 'It' is a shining beacon of good sense and subtle humor?"

"Point," Leah admitted.

"It makes an impression." Nellie bulled her way back into the conversation by reciting her favorite catechism after "it's worth it to be famous."

"Okay, this explains all the strange pics of you and Leah in all those costumes. Why didn't you tell me you were a child star?"

"Because I've been too busy repressing my entire childhood." She jerked a thumb at him. "Pay attention, Nellie. Archer is off the payroll. And the next time you put a dog on my back trail, they'll find pieces of your wardrobe all over the North Side."

Nellie shrugged. "Fine. I could use some new—"

"*All* of it. The costumes, the gowns you wore to the Oscars, anything that ever touched your skin during your so-called career, not to mention mine: shredded. If your clothing was people, family members would not be able to identify them, you understand? Closed casket, you understand?"

"No!"

"Ah, good, It's catching on." Wow, that was going to be a tough one to break. "Nellie Nazir is catching on."

"At least hear the pitch," her mother coaxed, spreading her arms wide like a preacher about to give a blessing. The effect, with the robe and feathers, made it look like she had big pink wings: a sentient flamingo obsessed with its comeback. "It's a hot new series about a mother and daughter who are both prostitutes."

Leah turned on her heel.

"They'll get into all sorts of wacky situations together."

Leah walked faster.

"It's like a buddy movie, with whores. Think of all the side-splitting situations the mother-daughter hooker team could get into. Hilarity will ensue! I promise you! It will!"

"Yes," she replied, "but not for the reason you think. Good-bye, Nellie. We won't meet again."

Nellie rolled her beautiful brown eyes, naturally luminous and always emphasized with lots of blue and purple shadow and liner. "Even you can't hold a grudge that long. Or are you still determined to be murdered?"

Leah bit her tongue, hard. Some things should never be said, because they could never be unsaid. It was a near thing. Her mother had always been ashamed of her daughter's a) plain looks, b) Insighter ability, and c) indifference to the Oscar race. At age four, Leah had explained to her babysitter that he was afraid of dogs and water because in the last four hundred years he'd died of rabies half a dozen times and ended his life foaming, shrieking, and thirsty. "Just leave strange dogs alone, how many times do you have to get chomped before you internalize that?" the exasperated kindergartener had asked the astonished teenager. And Nellie had been less than pleased: "A near-genius IQ and this is what you use it for? Stop that and help me figure out how to seduce the new VP at MGM!"

Nellie considered her daughter's Insight to be at best embarrassing and at worst something Leah did on purpose for attention. Neither were acceptable. And thus, she had no interest in Leah's predictions of her own murder.

"Being murdered," she managed as the room doubled, then

*don't cry don't cry don't cry don't cry don't cry DON'T YOU DARE CRY*

"—will come as a great relief."

She walked out of her house—not a home, it was never a home—determined never to return.

# ELEVEN

Archer, who had felt out of his depth the moment the weird little crying (or did he have allergies?) guy answered the door, was slow to follow. Shock had held him in place for those few seconds.

*Now* he could see it; now he knew why he had the nagging feeling he'd seen Leah somewhere. Somewhere? Everywhere: when she was little she had hawked everything from diapers to Dentyne, juice to jeans, back-to-school to prom fashions, and everything in between. The Girl Next Door, if the girl next door could take one look at you and tell you all the mistakes you made in the fifteenth century.

Her mother had done plenty of TV work, too, but never made it out of the B-list section of *Entertainment Weekly* . . . which still rankled, clearly. Add that to the average American's five-minute attention span for all things TV, it was no wonder he hadn't recognized Nellie—or Leah—during his last visit.

Being in a room with Leah and her mother was unreal, to put it mildly. Her mother's beauty, her affectations (pink satin robe with feathers? really?), exaggerated mid-Atlantic accent, and utter impatience with anything not related to her career comeback, up against Leah's determination and fury.

It wasn't a contest, and a good thing, because Leah would have won handily. Nellie was pale through conscious affectation and the avoidance of suntan booths; Leah was pale with anger. Her dark eyes were played up and made beautiful with makeup; Leah's were beautiful because of the jaded grumpy soul lurking behind them. Nellie was a marble statue; Leah was the real thing. And speaking of the real thing . . .

"Weird to meet you," he told Nellie, and raced out of the room after her daughter. He found her leaning against her electric shaver car, her forehead pillowed on her arms, crying.

*Whoa.*

The woman who coolly stabbed him (twice) three days ago was weeping in the driveway. Archer almost fell down.

"She never," Leah sobbed as he approached. "She hasn't ever cared. At all."

What to say to that? *There there? Don't be silly, of course she does? Look on the bright side, maybe you'll be murdered by the end of the week? Let's turn that frown upside down, tiny dancer!*

"She's awful," was the only thing he could come up with. "I'm so sorry. I can't imagine what living here was like." Then, verrrry carefully, he reached out and gently pulled her into his arms. "Don't cry, Leah. She's not worth the effort to produce the tears. Plus your face will get puffy."

That made her cry harder. *Argh! Just what I was going for, except NO. Of all the times to make a bad joke.*

"And this is ridiculous," she said, sounding angry as well as devastated. She wriggled a little in his careful grasp, not as if she wanted to escape, but to call attention to their first . . . hug? Breakdown? "I haven't cried in three years. I've only known you for three days, why am I looking to you for comfort? But here it is." She sniffed and swallowed and said again, calmer, "Here it is."

It was strange. It was like Leah was almost relieved to hear someone else say it. (Not the puffy face thing. The she's awful thing.) Archer couldn't imagine the guilt that came with resenting—even hating—the person you were supposed to love the most, the person who was supposed to love *you* the most. How it felt to know that your mother saw you as a thing, a commodity to be used until you had nothing left, not for anyone else, not for you.

"Hey, you know what?" he said into her hair, which he was trying very hard not to kiss—she fit perfectly against him, he could rest his chin on the top of her head and sort of fold her into his arms and ohhhh boy if he didn't break this embrace soon, she was going to realize just how much he wanted her. *Are you carrying around a roll of Life Savers?* Okay, maybe not Life Savers. A really big carrot? But why would he carry around a big carrot? *I should definitely stop thinking about the carrot I don't have in my pants and pay attention.* "Let's go have lunch with the mayor of Boston."

That surprised her so much, she stopped crying. She even managed a smile. Which made the whole crazy side trip worth it—to him, at least. He wouldn't presume to assume that Leah felt the same way.

# TWELVE

The ex-mayor of Boston greeted her with, "You know that skinny guy who's been following you for two weeks? He's right behind you."

"Curses. You have foiled me." Archer held out a hand. "I'm Archer Drake, Your Honor. Nice to meet you."

Cat cut her glance sideways. "Someone's been sneaking you my mail." She and Archer were roughly the same height, and she glared into his eyes as her hand swallowed his in a handshake that could decimate metacarpals. "What's your deal?"

"Her mom hired me to keep an eye on her to figure out the best time to approach her for her mother-daughter hooker sitcom idea."

"That," Cat said, dropping Archer's hand, "is unfortunate."

"Leah fired me and stabbed me, though, so I'm just here as her . . ." Friend? Former stalker? Current stalker? Hopeful would-be snuggle bunny? Hey: bunnies like carrots! *WHY THE*

*HELL CAN I NOT STOP THINKING ABOUT CARROTS?* "I'm just here," he finished. Leah caught him peeking at his white fingers. Cat had a grip like a gorilla, a statuesque showgirl-sized gorilla with keen political instincts and an instinctive distrust of Republicans. He shook his fingers and seemed relieved circulation had resumed.

It was late afternoon, and people were streaming out of office buildings on their way home. The little park was deserted save for the three of them, giving them the illusion of peace and privacy, and Leah felt oddly tranquil.

"I won't deny being relieved," she said as she watched commuters scurrying home. "I knew the permanent break was coming and . . . well. She took it all, and I wouldn't have minded so much if she had ever admitted she had been wrong. Wrong to put me to work, wrong to keep my money, wrong to want more out of me, always moremoremore. But she won't ever. So I can never get past it." Ironic, given her profession. How many patients had she told forgiveness wasn't for the person who had wronged them, it was for *them*? To move on. Advice she could not, would not, take.

"Whoa." From the mayor. "That whole thing kinda came out of nowhere. But good for you for getting it off your chest."

"Sorry, forgot you weren't necessarily up on context. My mother and I are done now, and I should feel worse, right?"

"Not our job, tellin' you how to feel."

"My mom keeps slipping me law school applications because of this thing with my father I'm not going into because we're doing your thing now," said Archer. "Nightmare! She's practically wallpapered my bedroom with them. So I know all about annoying parents. We're partners in pain, Leah."

He winked at her and she snorted. Yes indeed, the man she

couldn't see who walked around in a cloud of fun understood exactly how she felt. She sat on one of the benches and looked at her friend and her former stalker and gave in to the rare impulse to cough up.

*I am all alone now; my mother has never looked out for me and will never look out for me and the only thing that's changed is that I finally made it official. But closing a door doesn't mean I can't open a window. Or the door to the storm cellar. Or something like that. What will it hurt to open up, just once? After all the patients who found the courage to open up to someone they knew wasn't exactly loaded with empathy?*

"I think. I want. To tell you guys something." Hmm. Starting was difficult. "About me. About why I'm the way I am."

"It's not all the drugs you did in college?" Cat asked.

"No! Well, mostly no. When you're an Insighter, one of the things they have you do is research your own past lives. Write up clinic notes on yourself—it's practice for the patients you'll hopefully be able to help one day. So. Once upon a time," she began.

"Excellent," Cat said, making herself comfortable on the opposite bench. "Better with pudding, though."

"It *would* be better with pudding. Or . . . you know what, Your Honor? I wish we had marshmallows to roast. And a fire. And chocolate. Oh, well, continue." Archer plopped on the ground at her feet, shook the hair out of his eyes, and peered up at her with those oddly lovely mismatched eyes. "It's gonna be a good story, right?"

"Oh, no. The heroine is either ineffectual and passive, or dies. A lot.

"Once upon a time . . ."

# THIRTEEN

**Clinic notes:** Leah Nazir, Chart #3262
**Date:** 9/17/1999
**INS:** Chloe Hammen, ID# 14932

*My name is Jean Rombaud.*

Jean Rombaud was the French swordsman ordered by Henry VIII to behead Anne Boleyn. Wasn't that thoughtful of the fat tyrannical son of a bitch? He could have had his queen burned, or tortured, or both. When it came down to it, he could have *not* blamed her for miscarriages likely caused by his fat tyrannical sperm (he was as wide as he was tall when he died, for God's sake).

No and no and no. Instead he decided the woman he had pursued for a decade should be buried in pieces. But no messy crude axe for Anne Boleyn; Henry Tudor wanted only the best.

So Jean Rombaud, expert swordsman, blitzed into town, killed the queen, and blitzed back out. And he was troubled by his duty, which was the reaction of a sane man. He had never been hired to cut off a queen's head before. And because of the King of England's Great Matter, he of course knew not just who she was but where she had started and how she had come to the scaffold.

Here was a woman who literally changed the world, here was a man tripping on autocracy, and Europe could not wait to see how it played out (can you imagine the Internet uproar if it had existed back then? Henry Haterz! Anne Rulz!). But Jean, who had a front-row seat to how it would end, did not feel especially fortunate. The opposite, in fact—though not so unfortunate as the queen.

But he wasn't there to debate the politics of legal murder. He wasn't there to make friends or enemies; he was an independent contractor with a job to do. With misgivings, he did it, and he did it well—Anne Boleyn Tudor likely never felt a thing.

And when it was done, Rombaud was, too. "Thank you for the recommendation, here is your legally murdered wife's head, a pleasure doing business with you, I may use you as a reference, good luck with the Reformation."

Then he got the hell out of England, a place that always afterward gave him the creeps. He watched with the rest of Europe as the morbidly obese sociopath went through four more wives, again indulging in the legal murder of wife number five: Katherine Howard, Anne Boleyn's cousin. Rombaud felt bad for the beheaded teenager, but was glad to be away from it all.

The end. Except not really.

# FOURTEEN

**Clinic notes:** Leah Nazir, Chart #3262
**Date:** 4/1/2002
**INS:** Chloe Hammen, ID# 14932

*My name is Louise Élisabeth de Croÿ.*

Louise Élisabeth de Croÿ was the governess for Marie Antoinette's children. She saw the revolution coming from the nursery where she taught her soon-to-be-exiled-and-then-beheaded students about the divine right of kings. (And probably some math, too. She did not teach How to Survive a Revolution.) She watched it all come down, and when her charges were dead or exiled, she faded into the background to work on her memoirs. She outlived her students by decades.

So: survivor's guilt? Yes. She had always backed the Bourbon family; her favorite ring had *Lord, save the king, the dauphin, and his sister* engraved on it, which is rather awful when you consider the Lord pretty much blew that one off.

She should never have gotten the job. The opening came about when the current governess had to flee following the fall of the Bastille; Élisabeth was delighted with her promotion to such a prestigious position, which would prove to be the ultimate mixed blessing.

In addition to educating the royal children, the queen charged Élisabeth specifically with tackling the dauphin's fear of loud noises. The *fils de france* was especially afraid of the barking from all the Versailles dogs.

(*Not* what he should have been afraid of, by the way. But orders were orders. In fact, Louis XVII of France died in a dark room, "barricaded like the cage of a wild animal," having not spoken a single word for seven months. In other words, the child died a dog's death.)

As Élisabeth worked to teach the three Rs (reading, wRiting, revolution) she was ringside for the destruction of the Ancient Régime, moving with the royal family from the Palace of Versailles (after a torqued-off mob of starving women stormed the place) to the Tuileries Palace. Even though society was literally disintegrating around her, Élisabeth refused to abandon her post, ask for paid sick time, or even negotiate for combat pay. She had cause to regret this after accompanying the royals on a dangerous, disastrous escape attempt to flee Paris and form a counterrevolution.

The king of France was a noted ditherer. He was also in extreme denial, to wit: "Aw, only a few peasants are mad. Most of them love me! I'm pretty much a man of the people." (I am paraphrasing.)

All that to say this complicated Élisabeth's life, which was already pretty hectic, what with not losing her mind from being afraid all the time and teaching a little boy not to fear dogs. But her loyalty never broke; it never even trembled.

The monarchy was abolished in 1792 and everyone—including Élisabeth—was imprisoned. Louis XVI lost his head the following January; Marie Antoinette lost hers nine months later. The dauphin would be dead within two years; a dog's death.

Élisabeth survived it all, which was her curse. Devastated by the royal family's executions, she would live decades longer, and would for the rest of her long life regret she had not done more when she wasn't confronted by men trying to convince her they were the dead dauphin. Although Charles X made her a duchess after the Bourbon restoration, the dead were still dead.

She had held the job for three years.

# FIFTEEN

"I thought you were murdered in your other lives."

Leah braved a peek at Archer, who didn't seem a) horrified, b) revolted, or c) bored. Just interested, and concerned.

"The ones where I'm not an impotent observer, yes."

"What are you talking about, impotent? You—"

"It means—"

"Whoa, whoa." Archer had his hands up. "I know what impotent means. From the dictionary, not from any, uh, personal issues. But how can you say you're just a watcher—you got arrested with the entire French royal family! You tried to help them escape, it's not your fault you all got caught. I mean it wasn't your fault." He squinched his eyes shut and rubbed them, hard. "Argh, hate talking about past lives, all the verb tenses get weird."

Leah hadn't considered that. "Well . . . I cared about them and they all died. I couldn't do anything."

"Except learn from it and bring that knowledge into your next life?"

"Except I'm not. I just end up in the middle of some incredible terrible event in world history and can't change anything or do anything." Cripes, it had been so difficult to share this with them and she wasn't sure they were getting it. Which was fair, because she wasn't sure she was, either. But still: frustrating.

"So, what?" the mayor asked. She and Archer were sharing Leah's carrots. "You were always on the sidelines. Or you think you were, which can be the same thing in some cases. So?"

*Nope. They don't get it. Should have kept my flapping mouth shut. Tight.* "That isn't—"

"You were back then, and way back then, and way way back then, and you are now, because Insighters are always on the sidelines, it's pretty much a job requirement, and if no one's ever told you, you're a bit of a chilly bitch. So?"

"So maybe *that's* the problem." They had been in the park long enough for the sun to begin to set, and deep golden rays slanted across Cat and Archer's faces. Leah couldn't help but be pleased that the only two people in her life she cared about

*(you haven't even known him a week! how is that "in your life"?)*

seemed to be getting along. Sharing carrots, even. (Ugh.)

"What, being a chilly bitch?" At Leah's arched eyebrows, Archer added, "I'm just using the mayor's term! You didn't object, so it's agreed-upon. Unless you never want me to say it again. In which case, the term 'chilly bitch' is dead to me."

"That's not necessary," she said dryly, and hoped he couldn't hear the smile lurking behind her tone.

"Were you an Insighter in any of those lives?"

She shook her head. "No. Or not officially." Though around since man first clubbed his first caveman girlfriend and later felt conflicted about it, Insighters had only been officially a thing (with accepted, industry-wide salary ranges, job protection from the government, and HMO coverage) for the last few decades. "If I ever was one, I don't remember that part. Or I'd get a flash of something from another life and put it down to nerves or superstition or being stressed out by the French Revolution."

"It certainly sounded stressful," Archer agreed, and ate a carrot.

They'd only interrupted her tales of woe twice: Archer to ask what happened to Marie Antoinette's daughter (*Madame Royale* Marie-Thérèse, later dauphine of France, survived the Reign of Terror, was the queen of France for twenty minutes, and lived into her seventies), and Cat to comment that Leah's past lives definitely proved that no matter when you lived or what you lived through, job security was paramount.

"Really?" Archer asked, leaning back to look up at Cat, his eyebrows arching in amusement. "That's what you're taking away from all this? When the peasants come to cut off your head, be glad you at least kept your job?"

"It's tough out there," Cat replied, unruffled by the teasing. "Job hunting sucks. Can't take steady work for granted in this economy. Or any other economy, come to think of it. I mean, jeez, even being a member of the ruling family isn't a guarantee. Education is key, y'know."

"*Anyway*," Leah continued, "I think that's the thread. I think maybe I keep getting murdered because I can't *not* be passive.

Or," she added when Archer and Cat opened their mouths, "when I try to do something, anything, and it not only fails, people die. So I've basically taught myself never to get involved, never to interfere." She shook her head in frustration. "Insighting is the perfect job for me. Like Cat said: part of my nature." Her horrible, prickly, bitchy nature, which, incredibly, neither Cat nor Archer seemed to mind. So far. She turned to Archer. "Speaking of natures, have you ever seen an Insighter? Professionally?"

"Uh . . . no."

That was an odd pause. Almost like he was worried she'd be offended. But Leah, who confronted former serial killers, rapists, child killers, dictators, monarchs, and disgruntled postal workers, and had been insulted by the best (and the worst) was almost impossible to offend. When you knew you were going to be eventually murdered, it was hard to work up a state of pissed-off if someone called you a bitch.

She frowned down at him; he was still sitting cross-legged on the ground in front of the bench. "You've never seen an Insighter? Not even once? Most parents bring their kids in at least once, so they can be on the lookout for . . . well . . . anything, really." Unless, of course, they were too busy hauling their preschooler to cattle calls for juice commercials and catalog shoots for back-to-school clothes and runway tryouts for designer swimwear shows.

The flip side of parents like Nellie, who had no use for Insight and refused to acknowledge anyone's view but her own, were helicopter parents. Choppers were obsessed with their children's past lives, and diagnosed same on their own. "She was born on September 11, two hours after the second tower fell, which totally explains her fear of heights! And possibly her fear of fire, planes, and OSHA regulations."

"But she isn't afraid of heights or fire or planes or OSHA regulations."

"Yes, but she *will* be. It's inevitable; she can't fight her past. It will eventually devour her!"

"I'm not sure that's—"

"So what are you going to do about it? Huh? What? Huh? You take Blue Cross/Blue Shield, right? Right? *Right*?"

*I think in my baby's past life I was there, too, except I was Joan Crawford and that's why my baby is scared of wire coat hangers.*

*My preschooler has the attention span of a four-year-old! Obviously he had ADHD in a past life, so you'd better get him started on Ritalin ASAP.*

*My teenage son is moody and hates me, but when he was little he was nice and he loved me. Something has gone terribly wrong in his past life and we have to fix it because it's not normal for teenagers to fight with their parents like this!*

It was a little like patients studying the Internet to diagnose themselves, then telling the doctor the diagnosis and expecting him to fall in line and whip out the scrip pad.

"Nope," Archer was saying. "I've never needed an Insighter."

"Oh. One of those, hmm?"

"Ah, man," Cat sighed.

"What, 'one of those'?"

"Don't do it, Archer," Cat added.

"You know what 'one of those,'" Leah replied. "Are you?"

"It's nothing personal. *You're* great. It's just, your job sucks." He shifted his position. "I think, in general, people can solve their own problems. Or at least be able to try. I think looking back and having regret after regret, being *reminded* of regret after regret, isn't helpful and . . . and that's all, I guess."

"You might as well finish," Cat said kindly as Leah stared fixedly down at him.

"Well, basically, most Insighters are delusional snoops. 'Only I can fix you! Only by beating you over the head with all the fuck-ups you can do absolutely nothing about can you get your life in order, so let's hop to it. That'll be $149.72, by the way.'" At the look on Leah's face, he added weakly, "No offense?"

"We never tell a client to hop to it." She plopped down on the ground in front of him. "Well. I can't say I've never heard that before. Which explains why I can't see you. You're *rasa*, yes?" Slang for *tabula rasa*, the blank slate. Or, to put it another way . . . "I can't see your past lives because your brain isn't wired to access them. You're . . ." She paused and groped for the appropriate phrasing.

"Pure as newborn snow?"

"You stop mixing metaphors right now," Cat warned. "Hate that shit."

"—life-blind," Leah finished.

"Hey!" Archer was pointing at her. "You can't use that phrase, that's *our* phrase. Also, it's bullshit."

"Mmm." Leah had never met a *rasa*; now there was one right in front of her and there wasn't much she could do for him. If Archer couldn't see his past lives, she could not, either. "Am I the only Insighter you've stalked? Um, spent time with?"

He flashed her a wounded look. "My cousin's one. She explained why she gets kind of edgy around me."

"That's good, but what does that have to do with Insighters?" Cat asked, grinning. "There's gotta be lots of reasons people get edgy around you. I'm thinking of half a dozen without even trying."

"Hilarious, Your Honor. Anyway, she told me that Insighters can't see my past lives and it *really* freaks them out."

"Life-blind, huh?" Cat was looking at him thoughtfully. "Jeez. That's gotta be like . . . I dunno . . . missing a limb or something. Sounds wicked hard."

"It's actually wicked fine. Suits my personal philosophy pretty perfectly."

Leah managed a sour smile. This was awfully close to people who weren't alcoholics being unable to understand why alcoholics can't control their drinking. *Look at me! I just say to myself, Self, don't have a drink tonight. And I don't. See? Easy. Now you try.*

She had another theory about this puzzling, interesting man, and it wasn't that he was life-blind. A most-likely ridiculous theory, but this wasn't the time to bring it up. And she was probably mistaken. But if she wasn't . . . she'd never known someone like him before, in all of her lives (that she knew of, at least) and maybe . . .

Hmm.

"My sister saw an Insighter every month for years, and it sure as shit didn't save her. But I never translated that to 'my sister died anyway, ergo Insighters are useless.' It's like telling a cancer patient that because chemo didn't work for so-and-so, it won't work for them, either."

Leah said nothing. Cat never talked about her family. Ever.

"I'm sorry," Archer said after the awkward pause. "How did she die?"

"Drowned."

Another pause while Leah watched Archer scan the older

woman's face. Cat seemed almost preternaturally calm, but then, she often *was* almost preternaturally calm. "If you don't mind my asking, how'd it happen?"

"She was underwater too long."

*Ohhhhh, boy.*

Archer went from concerned to annoyed back to concerned, shaking his head at the grinning Cat. "I figured *that*. God, my heart. I feel like I'm tiptoeing across land mines here. I assumed she was a little kid at the time—"

"Nope. Seventeen."

"And?"

"Drunk."

"Ah."

"Also high."

"Okay."

"My point is, sometimes something shitty happens and it doesn't have anything to do with what happened before."

"Correct," Leah said, "but sometimes it does."

# SIXTEEN

*My name is Isabella Mowbray.*

Mother is desperate and angry, and hides both behind tight smiles, and so it's time for the nasty treats. Isabella doesn't mind; she has been waiting for such things.

Isabella had eight siblings; they are dead. She had two stepsiblings. They are dead. Her grandmother is dead. Her father is dead. Her stepfather is dead.

They had weak stomachs. All her brothers and sisters and her father and her grandmother, and her stepfather and stepsiblings, who were no blood relation, which made Isabella wonder if weak stomachs were contagious, they were all cursed with weak stomachs and they are dead, and Isabella's stomach has hurt for two weeks and she bleeds when she pees.

She doesn't mind. It's lonesome and nerve-racking with just Mother; her strained smiles are terrifying. So is her belly, which is bigger every month. For a while Isabella thought the family stomach weakness had finally caught her mother, too, but eventually realized what was happening and felt better. *She's growing my replacement. When I die she won't be lonesome.*

So that was all right.

Isabella knew what was happening to her more or less from the first headaches. She was only ten, but she had always been an observant child. "Owl's eyes," her mother teased, "always watching me." Dreadful pounding headaches like someone was sitting on her chest and hitting her on the top of her head with a rock over and over and over. At first, her greatest fear was that the headaches would kill her, kill her and leave Mother alone. Then her greatest fear was that they would not.

Head pain, nasty poopies, and tired, all the time tired. Even thinking was exhausting; it was so much easier to lie there and wait for . . . for whatever. Her hair started to fall out, her lovely long dark hair just like Mother's, and sometimes her body would flail and shake out of her control and that would leave her even more drained, and if she wasn't so tired she might be scared.

It would be more frightening if she hadn't seen it before. This would all be so terribly terribly frightening if she hadn't seen it before. Like Father, like Daddy George, like Grandmother, like Michael and Jenny and David and Laura and John and Leah and the little ones whose names she no longer remembered.

If only it didn't *hurt* so much. That's the only thing, really the only terrible thing. Not the smell or the mess or the weakness: the pain.

She hasn't been able to leave the bed for two days; she messes the sheets again. She sees the blood in her mess; she calls her mother over. "It hurts," she says. Not a complaint. More like an explanation. *Here is my problem. I thought you would like to know.* And it seems Mother *does* know. She nods and she bustles back to the kitchen and returns with another small plate of nasty treats: homemade donuts—the whole house smells like hot frying fat and cake dredged through lots of powdered sugar. Isabella's favorite treat, once upon a time.

"These will make you feel better."

Isabella knows this for a lie, she knows Leah and Jenny and David and Laura and the little ones were told the same lies. But what to do? Not obey? Unthinkable.

Like the rest of her dead family, she eats.

# SEVENTEEN

"Aw, man."

"Breathe. It will be all right." Leah was on her knees beside Archer, who was clutching his head in both hands. Cat, unconcerned, had stretched out on the now-unoccupied park bench, lying on her side like a large pinup model in a yellow and black bumblebee sweater (with black sweatpants) and watching Leah soothe him while she munched the last carrot. "I'm sorry. I shouldn't have just blurted it all out like—"

"Your mom killed you in another life? It fucking *murdered* you in another life?"

"Yes, but it's not so bad." Leah tried for humor, not sure if it would work. "In this life she only killed my stage career. So, improvement. Right?" Nope. No response. A poor time for a joke, as she had suspected. She briefly wished she were better at this sort of thing. "Listen, she's slightly less terrible in each incarnation, does that help?"

"No!"

"Uh, did you hear the one about the mother who killed so many family members reporters actually caught on and tipped off the . . ." Why couldn't she *stop*? She saw uncomfortable patients every day, people who couldn't bear what they were telling her or what she was telling him, and she rarely blinked.

But poor Archer just looked so anguished . . . and nauseated . . . like he would vomit and then burst into tears. Or burst into tears and then vomit. She could appreciate the sentiment while hoping he did neither.

"I'm going to throw up on my stab wounds." Right: vomit, *then* cry.

"Terrible idea," Cat offered from the bench. "You'd be looking at a nasty infection at the least. A pain in the ass."

"And *you*." Archer's head shot up. "You're so relaxed you're almost in a coma. Didn't you hear what Leah said? Did you doze off and miss the horrible horrible ending? She died puking and shitting her own blood, for God's sake, from arsenic-coated donuts! Darsenics! Or arnuts! Fed to her by *her mother*! This makes *Flowers in the Attic* look like *SpongeBob SquarePants*!"

"I don't know what either of those are," Cat replied.

"You read *Flowers in the Attic?*" Leah had, of course. She read everything she could find about terrible mothers, starting with Medea and ending with Kris Jenner's latest biography.

"No, I saw the terrible movie. God, I'm gonna be sick."

Astonished that he should care so much in such a short time about a dead preteen he had never met, Leah drew back. He was so aggravated he didn't notice. And Cat, as was her way, was unmoved. It was why they were friends. "Bad shit happens. What have we been sayin'? There's nothing to be done about it now. You're just a kiddo. You'll get it eventually."

"Ugh, you're awful, I hate you." Archer was hiding his face again and out of nowhere Leah wondered how old he was. He seemed much younger than she was, and she hadn't been paying attention when he was filling out forms in the ER (mostly because of all the shouting). Twenty-three, maybe? Not more than twenty-four, surely. "But it's good you two are friends. You're her only friend, did you know?"

"Yup." Cat raised an eyebrow at Leah. "Better take your boy home. He's had a tough week. Stabbed, exposed to your mom, exposed to *you*, stabbed . . ." The older woman got to her feet with a quick movement that made her seem smaller and younger. "Crazy Betty's saving a bed for me."

"Sister Beatrice's name is not Cr—"

"See you tomorrow. Don't have to bring lunch. You're fun just for the company." She poked a long finger at Archer, still on the ground. "*You* bring lunch."

"It's a date," he replied dryly, but he managed to smile up at Leah as she extended a hand to help him to his feet. He got up much quicker than she would have expected; his wounds were healing quickly.

"Come along, then." It was almost impossible not to smile back at him, but she managed. "I'll take you home."

And she did.

# EIGHTEEN

She walked with Archer up the sidewalk to his three-story brick house, tucked away in the tony Gold Coast area, the neighborhood so crowded with large lush trees you couldn't even see the house until you got close. She must have looked curious because he said, while digging for his keys, "I just rent the tower."

"The tower?"

He leaned back and pointed. The third story jutted into a conical tower, big enough around that it was likely a small bedroom. Or a large bathroom. Or a large closet. *Why would they make the closet into a tower? Why am I thinking about towers? Does Archer go to sleep every night in a tower, like a prince in a fairy tale? What in God's name is happening to my life this week?*

By now he'd unlocked the door and swung it wide. "Come in for a minute?"

She had to smile at his hopeful expression. What a sweet . . .

idiot. "I don't know," she said demurely as she followed him inside. "Did you hide the pointy cutlery?"

"I'll risk it." He shut the door for her and she found herself in a three-story living room, complete with blinding white walls and a floating staircase. The room seemed even larger because the only furnishing was a black sectional couch big enough to sleep a family of six, and a plasma-screen TV larger than her kitchen table. "Besides, you prob'ly wouldn't stab me ag— What?"

Leah was openmouthed. "You live *here*? But you're just a kid!"

He frowned and shook his head, messy bangs tumbling almost into his eyes. "I rent the tower, like I said, but I don't know for how long—my landlady's moving and the house is going up for sale. And I'm twenty-eight."

*I must stop gaping like a moron.* "You are not."

He sighed. "Don't you remember what I yelled in the ER?"

"There was a lot of yelling," she replied, swallowing fresh guilt.

"'I've been stabbed seven times so far and I'm not even thirty, if this is what my twenties were like, I dread my thirties, blah-blah.' Do I have to fish out my driver's license?"

*Seven times? In one life?* She actually thought about it while he groaned and started digging for his wallet. "No, no, I believe you," she finally said, trying and failing to keep the uncertainty out of her voice.

"I'm flattered, I think."

"I thought you were younger than me." *Much younger.*

"I'm flattered, I think."

"You seem so—" Immature. Goofy. Lackadaisical. "—younger than me."

Archer laughed. "You're an old soul, Leah. Literally. Y'know, I hear that phrase all the time but I never really got it. Sounded like one of those things dumb people say when even they don't know what they're talking about. But everything you've been through—even the stuff you don't exactly remember, it's had an effect on the you of *now.*" He spread his hands like she was arresting him. "Of course I seem younger. I'm not trying to walk around with the weight of all my past mistakes smashing me down. As far as my brain's concerned, there's just one of me. God, how many of you are there?" He had moved closer and was looking down at her with a wondering smile. "Can you even see them all? Do you know?"

She shook her head. Five, ten, a dozen, thirty, a hundred, a thousand. Most doomed to die young, doomed to end badly, or begin badly, or get bad in the middle and stupefyingly dull at the end until death was a relief, and why wasn't she more worried about that? No, what she worried about were the ethical considerations of jumping the bones of someone she'd stabbed repeatedly (was twice "repeatedly"?). And beyond the bone-jumping, ethical or otherwise, was she actually entertaining the thought of pursuing a relationship with the fresh-faced boy who was two years older than she was?

*He can't see anything about himself, so you can't, either. You can't quantify him. He's an unknown factor and he is throwing you off because he is not someone who keeps happening and happening and happening to you.*

The thought stirred something inside her.

Not her heart. Lower.

"I don't know how many of me there were," she replied. Her

voice sounded, to her ears, too slow. Slurred, almost. Yes, lower than her heart, much much lower. Ummmm . . . "Come here."

"Are you okay? You look kind of . . . nnnffff."

*I am not considering pursuing a relationship. I merely want to bang him. Repeatedly.*

# NINETEEN

Weird day weird day weird day *weird goddamned day!*

That was about all Archer had time for while Leah was backing him into the empty living room, snogging him

*(mental note: stop watching so much BBC)*

like she was—ha, ha!—gonna get murdered tomorrow. Or something. One of Elaine's lines from *Seinfeld*

*(God, is that why I'm crushing so hard on Leah? she reminds me of a dour Elaine? God, what if she dances as horribly as Elaine does, the whole "full body dry heave set to music" thing? that would be so hot)*

flashed through his brain: "We made out like our plane was going down!" Yep. That's just how Leah was kissing him. Like she wanted to eat him while also pushing him away as she vigorously boned him and then never called him again on her way to get murdered.

Not cool. He would put a stop to this right now.

Right now.

Any minute now. He would. It would allll be stopped.

Thoroughly stopped. Stopped dead. Completely, utterly stopped.

"Ouch!"

"I'm so sorry. Here, I'll kiss the stab wounds I inflicted and make them all better."

"You hear yourself, right?" Right. Although, now that he thought about it, the thought of Leah's lips on his wound . . . and then his other wound . . . and then moving lower

*(oh please, God, let her move lower)*

was disturbingly erotic. He managed to pull back and got a heart-stopping, dick-stiffening look at Leah's lovely face and glittering eyes, her dark hair mussed and flyaway, her mouth a rosy bruise from kissing. "Okay, we have to . . . mmm . . . settle down now. Ah!" She'd pounced on him at "okay." "Why wouldn't you listen to the rest of that sentence?" He extricated himself again—Leah was strong for her size, all the murder-prevention training, no doubt—but it took longer this time because his blood was bypassing his arms and heading for his dick. "And just . . . y'know . . . have a discussion. About something."

"I cannot think of anything I wish to do less," she murmured in his ear, and then bit his earlobe. Which, Archer had just discovered, had a line straight to his dick. Who knew? Someone should do a study. Write a paper. Something. "I'm on the pill, and I saw your labs at the hospital. You're fresh as a daisy, STD-wise."

"Uh . . ." Boundaries? Wait, he could go in bare? Go in Leah *bare*? Their first time and any other time? No, no. Boundaries. Bare boundaries. Wait. What was he worried about again?

"I'd like to love you in your tower, so bring me there."

Huh. That was sort of sweet and romantic. And the tower was pretty great. And he *did* want to be a good host. Not showing her the tower would be rude. Think how shamed his mom would be if she found out about his lack of etiquette.

*(Do not think about Mom right now.)*

"No. Here." He grabbed her wrists and sort of pulled her after him as he backed across the room to the couch. "We need to sit here and—"

"Good idea. I like sectionals." She pounced and once again his hands were full of Leah, only this time she'd knocked him prone which made it sooooo much harder

*(that's what she said)*

*(stop that! idiot!)*

to fend her off. Not that he was one hundred percent on board with fending her off. Her lovely, apple-sized breasts were mashed against his chest, her lips were tracing the line of his jaw, finding the stubble and running her tongue over it, one of her knees was between his thighs, spreading his legs

*(unhand me, you brute!)*

and she was holding one of his wrists and stroking a thumb across his pulse point, which caused said pulse to ramp up at least twenty beats. He could feel something hard pressing against his chest,

*(is that a balisong knife in your bra or are you just—cue punch line)*

no, there were two of them, one in each cup, and he should be alarmed but wasn't, and really, what harm could come from letting her molest the bejeezus out of him? What possible harm other than accidental stab wounds from her bra knives?

"Gah," he managed to say into her mouth. "Nnnff. Of all the nights to forget my rape whistle."

That made her giggle and for a few seconds she just laughed and sort of shook against him. He took the chance and brought his arm up around her waist, raised his head, and kissed her gently on her soft, sweet mouth, and never had a closed-mouth kiss been so glorious.

"Okay," she said, sitting up. On him, but he didn't mind. It did leave him well within pouncing range, though, so he couldn't have escaped those hands and that mouth when she decided to start up again. Which was wonderful. Bad! He meant bad. "What seems to be the problem? Do I have to go on a condom hunt?"

"Please stop distracting me with pictures in my head that are alarming and weird and devastatingly sexy," he groaned. "Condom hunt. Would that be like a scavenger hunt? A sex scavenger hunt? Oh my God, someday can we have a sex scavenger hunt?"

"It's a date," she said in a solemn tone, then spoiled the effect by snickering.

"God, you're gorgeous when you laugh." He looked up at her and smiled, and hoped she wasn't troubled by the enthusiastic presence of Lieutenant Winky, who was currently trying to rip itself free of his jeans, most likely because she was sitting on him.

*(Arrgghh yes that's it escape Lieutenant Winky fly be free you lucky bastard!)*

He sat up and willed himself not to burst into horny tears at what he was slowing down. Lieutenant Winky would be furious with him. "Okay. Okay. Okay." He shook his head to get clear. "Okay. God, you're so—I love your mouth and think we should no no *no*!" He sucked in a steadying breath. "First, you're the sexiest thing in the world and I am breaking my own heart by putting a stop to this. Second, you're the sexiest thing in the world. Third, my penis is not a sleeping pill. Fourth, you've had a really emotional day and I don't want to be That Guy and take advantage when you're obviously vulnerable, and fifth, my status as life-blind might count as slumming for an Insighter, so—"

"Wait. What?"

"My penis is not a sleeping pill? That was the weirdest, so I'm betting that's what you zeroed in on." Might be the life-blind thing, too, but no, he was betting it was the penis pill analogy.

She was scowling at him, which terrified him and also called up the urge to kiss the corner of her scowl. "Yes, that's the one."

"Not that I have anything against comfort sex. I love it. Women are always crying when we . . . let me rephrase."

"By all means, rephrase. Then you can explain what you meant about slumming. Then let's go back to discussing the sleeping pill qualities of your penis."

"You leave Lieutenant Winky out of this." She blinked slowly, like an owl, but (thank God!) said nothing. "And you keep those things in there, thank you very much," he said, pointing at her chest. "No fair stabbing me with them."

"Ah. What?"

"And I'm not saying you'd be into slumming. But you can't tell me the thought never even scraped the edge of your mind."

"What, because I can't see your lives? That actually makes you much more attractive to me. Most people are so . . ." She shivered. "Crowded. In their minds. All those past regrets and deaths piling on top of each other in their brains . . . no wonder some of them go crazy. Poor things, they deserve better than me."

"Jeez, don't say that." He was honestly horrified that she had such a crap opinion of her skills. "And there aren't better than you."

He hoped she'd smile and she did, but it was small and sickly. "That's their bad luck, and mine. But getting back to you, I don't know if blind is the right word. I have a theory . . . never mind, it's boring. But you're not boring, which is wonderful."

He snorted, disbelieving. It wasn't especially pleasant, but he knew many Insighters saw the life-blind as developmentally disabled. *You can't do what billions of people can? What else is wrong with you, you pathetic freak?*

"All that aside, I don't want to be the thing you use to distract yourself from getting murdered. And I won't tolerate a one-night stand with you."

"Won't . . . tolerate?"

He checked the immediate area for knives. All clear. If she went for her bra, he was a dead man. "I'm too greedy," he said simply. "I want to be more than that to you. So we're gonna slow down and we're gonna talk, and then I'm going to walk you to the door like a gentleman, and then I'm going to go upstairs and take a long shower so I can cry and masturbate in peace."

The pissy look on her face vanished and she cracked up. "Really? You are? That's . . . ah, God."

"Yeah. Stop l-laughing." He stuttered the "l" because he was starting to lose it, too. *Did I really just tell that to my future sweetie please God let her be my future sweetie . . .* "Not that I'm ruling out casual encounters in general, I just want more with you. Would you honestly be okay with scenarios where we bang so hard and so well you stumble home after pulling the tattered remnants of your clothes back on and I spend the next three days drinking cans of Ensure? Don't answer that. That was a trick question."

All at once, he wanted to stock a supply of Ensure.

"I've never met anyone like you. You're so . . ." She gestured to the air as if she could pull down the word she wanted. ". . . uncluttered. Is it nice?"

"Being uncluttered? And I'm ignoring the condescension in your tone, missy." He was sitting up, ignoring the sullen throb from his pissed-off balls. They would, he knew, make him pay. They'd done it before. "Next you'll pat me on the head and call me a poor baby."

"But is it?"

"Sorry, my brain is missing a ton of blood right now and it'll be another couple of minutes before it catches up. What was the question?"

"Not being afraid all the time." She had a strange look on her face, part wistful and part "I don't really care I'm just making polite conversation until we can kiss again." "Is it nice?"

*(Boom that's it my heart just blew up oh Leah oh shit oh you oh oh oh)*

"I'm going to help you," he said, and Leah's gaze dropped and she couldn't look at him as he continued. "We'll fix this."

"Nothing to fix." Now she was standing—yikes, she could move like a cat when she wanted. Standing and, yep, moving for the front door. "You were right. This was a terrible idea."

"*Now*," he yelped, scrambling after her. "It's a terrible idea now. Later, it's gonna be the opposite of a terrible idea. I'll get some Ensure and it'll be a wonderful terrific idea. Just not now."

She shrugged, one hand reaching for the doorknob. "Sorry to haul you into my nonsense."

He blinked at the odd word choice. *Nonsense? That's her mother talking.*

"It was very nice meeting you."

*No! Stop! Tilt! Abort!*

"Ow!" He shrieked it so loud she whipped around at once. "My wound! Wounds, I mean! They're burning up and I feel all stabby inside! It's a fever from an infection and ow-ow-owie! You can't leave me in mortal agony argh the agony is overwhelming ow-ow!"

She rolled her eyes but, thank God, let go of the door. "Ye gods, Archer. That's awful. Do not quit the day job." Pause. "What *is* the day job, besides stalking me, which we have agreed you shall no longer do?"

"You don't have the kind of time we'd need for me to explain. Right now, I'm a professional housesitter. It's how I ended up living here. The pain," he groaned. "It's washing everything away, including the ability to let you leave. And also, your breasts are like apples, did you know?"

"I'd like to have just one conversation with you that isn't surreal," she grumped. Then, "Apples? Like . . ." She glanced down at herself. "Crab apples?"

"No, more like Golden Delicious. Or Honeycrisp. You're a hammerhead shark with luscious Honeycrisp boobs, God, you are soooo *hot*."

Leah, meanwhile, had started laughing so hard she had to lean against the door. She'd self-consciously crossed her arms across her chest, which only drew his attention to the Honeycrisp goodies. She saw him looking and laughed harder, finally staggering away from the door. She reached for him, curled a hand around the nape of his neck, and drew him in for a kiss on the corner of his mouth. "Oh, Archer," she managed between snorts. "Never, ever change."

"I want to see you tomorrow," he said, sticking his hands in his pockets so he wouldn't grab her, toss her on the couch, and go bobbing for apples. "And the day after. And the day after-after."

"Fine. I'm too tired and emotionally traumatized and giddy to say no to you. Honeycrisp apples. Christ." She went back to the door, opened it, and headed out into the night. "Yes, all right. I'll see you tomorrow. Assuming, of course, I don't get murdered tonight."

"Don't you *dare*," he said, appalled. "That'll screw up all my plans for you." He heard how that sounded and groaned inwardly, but luckily Leah just found it funnier. Even after the door was closed behind her, he could still hear her giggles. It was a sound he planned on hearing, off and on, for the rest of his life.

"Aw, nuts," he said to the air. "We didn't set up a time or anything."

Details. He'd see her again. She ought to count on it, since he was.

# TWENTY

Another thing Leah liked about Archer: he never looked at her like he was expecting something. With anyone else, if they said or did something even slightly off, they'd look at her with that expectant "go on, Insight me, tell me why I'm like this" expression. It was, she decided long ago, like people who walked up to doctors in social situations and demanded a (free) diagnosis on the spot.

*My arm hurts when I do like this.*

*So don't do that.*

*I'm scared of heights. How come?*

*Because you live in a penthouse you cannot afford? Go away.*

Her rather abrupt thought segue had been brought about by her newest patient, a referral from her colleague.

"I was only clinically dead for three and a half minutes," Chart #2256 was bitching. "And look! I'm back. Everything's fine. I'm fine. You're making way too much fuss here."

"Five minutes," she corrected in an even tone. His chart was on the desk, closed. She knew the contents. "I cannot believe you simply went ahead and discounted all my warnings."

#2256 speared her with a level look. "First off, my past lives are my own business."

*Do not smile. But what a delightful attitude. Do not smile.*

"Second," he continued when she didn't smile, "what? I'm supposed to believe you were sooo motivated by concern for my well-being? It's just CYA for you."

"I was motivated by concern for you." Or at least concern for her license. No, #2256's well-being was also a consideration. The man was the poster child for "my way or the highway," and Leah could not help liking him. "I warned you to leave Insighting to pros." She had. "I warned you there was an excellent chance of brain damage." There was. "I warned you that you might die." He had! For several minutes.

"You said Rain Down has caused a lot of flatlines, which isn't necessarily the same thing." #2256 shrugged. "I wanted to see for myself. I'm not comfortable putting all that control in someone else's hands."

"And yet, here you are."

"Yeah, and we've been over this. The only reason I even came to your clinic is because I lost another job and my wife drew a line in the sand. It's not personal, Ms. Nazir. I don't even trust my own mother."

"We have that in common." Reindyne was a hypnotic used exclusively for one purpose: it was often necessary to bring a patient back to revisit past lives. What made it so effective also provided enormous potential for misuse. Without an Insighter and a controlled setting, users could get lost in their past lives.

"Nothing like all your past orgasms raining down on you," a user once pointed out, except all your past disasters did, too, and your past deaths. Every one of them. At once. People could drown in their minds. People *had* drowned.

For herself, Leah could control seeing past lives, but it had taken years of training and practice. When she was little, other lives would just spill over her. Swamp her. Sometimes that meant a three-day migraine; other times it was a seizure. Her mother figure had not been pleased.

"I wanted to see for myself," #2256 continued, scowling. "Frankly, I wasn't sure how necessary you were to the process."

"How about now?" she asked dryly.

His pale blue eyes met her stare straight on. He was a small man, not much over five-three, but had presence and a gaze it was difficult to look away from. "I'm here, aren't I?"

"Mmmm."

Once upon a time, #2256 was an escaped slave named Henry Brown. In 1849, understandably fed up with the institution of slavery, Henry escaped the Virginia plantation where he was considered property and mailed himself to freedom. A fellow slave who was a fair carpenter made a three-by-two-foot wooden crate for the five-foot-eight Henry, who somehow managed to cram his two hundred pounds in it. Two friends took him to the post office, where Henry had himself marked *Dry Goods* and mailed express. He was in Philadelphia the next day, proving once and for all to the good people at FedEx that there is no excuse for anything not to arrive overnight in the twenty-first century.

Brown later moved to Boston and gave himself the middle name Box. Leah wasn't sure why. It was unlikely he would have needed reminding of the twenty-seven-hour ordeal, some of those hours spent upside down.

"This isn't the first life where your stubborn nature, coupled with the impulse control of a fifth grader, nearly got you killed."

"It seems to keep working for me, though," #2256 said comfortably, and she had to smile.

"I wish more of my patients had your determination."

#2256 yawned. "That's a lie."

"It is. How's the claustrophobia?"

"The wife and I did it in our closet last week." At her smirk, his stony features softened. "Granted, it's a walk-in closet, but still."

"No, that's—well. That's very good progress, actually, uh . . ." She glanced at the chart. "Henry. Hooray for you."

He was already on his feet, the follow-up visit merely something to cross off his calendar on his way back to a (somewhat) better life. "Am I the only patient you've had who had the same first name in every life?"

"No."

"Huh." He seemed disappointed, but shook her hand, shrugged off her de rigueur admonitions to take care of himself and stay away from Rain Down, and walked out. She followed him into the lobby, where to her surprise and delight someone else was waiting with her ten o'clock and ten thirty appointments.

"Hey!" Archer bounded to his feet like a six-foot puppy. "You didn't get murdered last night! Great!"

"It *is* great," she agreed, trying not to giggle at Henry's startled expression as he passed Archer and left the building. She even let Archer kiss her on the cheek and, later, was glad. It was one of the last nice things to happen for a while.

# TWENTY-ONE

"It's probably going to be one of your patients," Archer told Leah, who was looking especially scrumptious with her dark hair piled on top of her head like a sexy brunette donut, a dark green straight skirt

*(pencil skirt? pen skirt? something . . . his cousin would know)*

that fell just past her knees, one of those pretty blouses that looked like a fancy T-shirt in a lighter shade, skin-colored pantyhose

*(nude? that's what they call that color, which seems pretty un-PC but it's nude, right? argh, don't think about nude and Leah don't don't)*

and orange and white running shoes.

"Huh," he said, staring down at them.

"What? Have you tried running around in pumps all day? No? All right, then. Also this is Chicago and there is no way you have never seen a woman wearing tennies with a suit. Besides, in a bit I'm going to the park to have lunch with Cat."

"*I* just had lunch with Cat; she's fine. No, really," he added at her frown. "She didn't mind bag lunches at 10:30 in the morning. Also, she's really carrot crazy." That probably wasn't the only kind of crazy she was. It was just too weird that the former mayor of Boston spent gobs of time loitering in a small Chicago park with an Insighter doomed to be murdered.

He no longer thought she was homeless; he decided Cat had a home that she didn't want to go to. There was definitely more to her story and he was dying to hear all about it. He'd hinted that he'd be interested and had gotten, "You're as subtle as a pimple on a dick," as a retort. Archer had tactfully changed the subject.

"So like I was saying, one of your patients is probably going to kill you."

Leah groaned a little under her breath and crooked a finger, like she was going to lead him to her office to make out.

"Idiot," she breathed.

Or maybe not. But he was saved when one of the patients, a pale young man in his early thirties, impeccably dressed in gray from neck to heels, nodded at once. "Oh, sure," he said, "I can see that."

"What?" Leah rounded on the patient, then turned back to Archer. "This is not the appropriate place."

"Yeah," the other patient added, closing last month's *Vogue*. She was a cheerful-looking brunette about Archer's age, in knee-length denim shorts and a black T-shirt with the slogan "The only thing we have to fear is fear itself. And spiders." "She's awful. Impatient and chilly and sometimes I get the vibe like she's just really, really bored with everything coming out of my mouth."

Leah said nothing, just rubbed her forehead and glared at the carpet.

"During one of my sessions I get a little PO'd," Gray Guy said, clearly ready to bond with Spider Shirt Girl over Leah's awfulness, "and called her a chilly twat—"

"Hey!" Archer yelped.

"—sorry." He held his hands up, placating. "It was a rotten thing to say and I'm not proud of it, but I did and it was out there, and she, Ms. Nazir, she just blinks at me real slow, like an owl, and says 'chilly was unnecessary.' I felt like I wasn't even in the room for her."

"It *is* weird that that's the word she picked up on."

"Did you prefer I jumped up and stabbed you?" Leah cried, aggrieved.

"No," Archer told him. "You definitely don't want her to do that." Thank God, he was a fast healer. The wounds were still sore, but he was off the prescription pain meds.

"It was only because she told me I used to be William Simmons. Imperial wizard of the KKK," Gray Suit went on at the raised eyebrows, indignant. "Which is just bullshit. I *like* black people! African-Americans, I mean."

"Oh," Spider Shirt Girl said.

"I'm sorry?" Archer added, not sure of the etiquette of the situation. Sure, most people knew who they'd been before, but it was considered private business. People didn't generally walk up to a stranger and open with, "Did you know I used to cut Washington's hair?"

"And she was just so cold about it," Gray Suit complained. "Just, ho-hum, you were a real shit in a former life, which is why you're a real shit now, don't worry, we take Blue Cross/Blue Shield, see you next week."

"Again: should I have stabbed you instead?"

"That's not a rhetorical question," Archer added. "So don't be fooled."

"I like you okay, Ms. Nazir, but your bedside manner's pretty, um, shitty," Spider Shirt Girl said, slightly apologetic.

"I've dealt with warmer morticians," Gray Suit added.

"Then why are you here?" Leah snapped.

"Oh. Well." Spider Shirt Girl traded glances with Gray Suit; they shrugged in unison. "You're the best. Most other Insighters have to frig around for months or years before they figure out the problem. Or the past life causing the problem, I guess. You're quicker. So . . ." She spread her hands in a "what are you gonna do?" gesture. It was like picking a dentist based on speed. If you had to have a stranger doing awful things to your mouth with pointy sharp things, it should be a stranger good at her job, and who cares if she loves small talk?

"Hmmm." Leah still had that adorably pissy look on her face, but sounded mollified. And "you're the best" didn't do her justice. Leah was almost infamous in her field. People had written papers about her; he'd read several while in her mother's employ. Funny how none of them picked up on the former child star angle, though.

"But I don't want to kill you, Ms. Nazir," Spider Shirt Girl said, almost as an afterthought. "That's what we're talking about, right? Killing you?"

"Right! You're exactly right, excellent." Archer was grateful Spider Shirt Girl was getting him back on track. "Anyway, I had some ideas about that. Maybe we can talk at lunch?"

"You already had lunch with Cat." Leah, he could tell, was still a little peeved. He figured it wasn't that she hadn't known she could be a little, uh, disconnected from her patients. But that was a lot to take in at once, and in just those couple of minutes. Anyone would feel ganged up on. "And I have patients who loathe me waiting."

"It's not loathing," Gray Suit piped up, no doubt trying to be helpful. "It's more like general dislike."

"With a dash of unconscious scorn."

"Yep, that's it," Gray Suit said with an enthusiastic nod. "That's exactly it." He was eyeing Spider Shirt Girl with not a little admiration. "That's really the exact . . . do you want to grab coffee or something? After?"

"Dunno. I used to be African-American. Is that gonna be a problem?"

"Hell, no. I used to run the KKK. I think we can have coffee together without a hate crime happening."

They beamed at each other.

"This is like a cell phone commercial," Leah snapped. "A bad one."

"Oh, shush," Archer said, catching her hand and giving it a gentle squeeze. "It's romantic as shit. And kind of makes you Cupid."

She muttered something under her breath which sounded a lot like "oh, fuck me," but probably wasn't. But she didn't kick him out, and even found a genuine smile for Gray Suit, who was her next patient.

"True love," Archer said, settling down across from Spider Shirt Girl, who'd picked her *Vogue* back up. "Doncha love it?"

"It's just coffee."

"I wasn't talking about you guys."

# TWENTY-TWO

No question, no question at all, but it was one of the oddest meetings she'd ever endured, and she had helped Karen McNamara (who had been Richard McDonald, founder of McDonald's) get over her coulrophobia (fear of clowns). That had been a strange session; she'd never again be able to hear the *ahh—ooo-gaa!* those old-fashioned bicycle horns made without shuddering. Thank goodness, she had no children; a single visit to Chuck E. Cheese now had the potential to send her screaming into the parking lot.

But this one was stranger. Most likely, she assumed, because it wasn't about a patient she could reduce to a pile of paper in a chart. That was always comforting, and it was wrong to feel that way, she knew. Unfortunately, it was the only way she knew how to do it. Much stranger, of course, to be the subject of discussion.

They were compiling a list of people who wanted to murder her.

Also: the Archer factor. That made it very odd indeed, but wonderful, too.

"Okay, so, top of the list: are you treating any psychos who are really into knives? That's usually how you're killed, right? Stabbed? God, I can't believe I just asked you that."

Leah shook her head and helped herself to another Tootsie Roll. Archer had quite the sweet tooth; his pockets were often bulging with candy. Funny how they had not known each other long and still there were things about him she felt safe enough to take for granted. Sometimes she forgot her plan was to get him to lower his defenses so she could ruthlessly molest him, then run off and get murdered.

Well. Not the last bit, obviously. Probably. Maybe?

"Even if I were, I couldn't discuss it with you, and you know that perfectly well," she said, nibbling on the candy. Archer teased her because she savored Tootsie Rolls as opposed to popping them in her mouth and chomping away.

"Yeah, I get that, but we have to start somewhere. I'm betting remembering who killed you in other lives doesn't much help when it comes to finding the killer in this one. Right?"

"Right." She was a little startled at the obvious question, then reminded herself he was life-blind. He had no frame of reference. At all. Astonishing and . . . was that pity? Might be, yes. She squashed it. She did not want to feel pity for Archer. "And sometimes I never knew his name, or hers. Sometimes I never even saw his face. But I'm not an utter imbecile, Archer. Of course I keep an eye out for any obvious psychotics. But my case load tends to be helping patients through phobias. I'm not treating anyone who has done anything worse than having sex in a public place." Except, she recalled, for Chart #6116, assaulting children, which escalated to murdering them. But she wasn't chart #6116's type. Ah, God, what was her name? Angie something. No, Anne. No, Alice! Yes: Alice Delaney, Chart #6116. "There's an occasional exception, but I do try to be careful."

*And it hasn't helped once, you silly bitch!*

"Oh, man, now I officially hate Insighter client privilege. Because you must have some great stories."

"I do," she assured him, half-finished with her first Tootsie Roll. "Marvelous ones."

He was slouched on the couch in her office, looking effortlessly younger than she was in dark blue jeans, a navy blue button-down, sleeves rolled to the elbows

*(who knew fuzzy forearms could be such a turn-on?)*

and loafers without socks. He looked like a college freshman.

It was the smiling, she decided, finishing Tootsie Roll #1. He had an open face and you could read everything on it and he was just . . . just sunny and uncomplicated. She was beginning to understand why the life-blind were so consistently patronized. *There, there, don't worry your pretty little head about bad things because you can't ever understand your own past and thus won't ever understand your present. Poor baby.*

Ugh. Archer was to be admired. And never, ever pitied. For the tenth time in ten days, she wondered again about her theory. About how the life-blind perhaps weren't blind at all. At least, not all of them. But if she was right, it would be an uphill battle. An up-mountain battle, about as easy as persuading people the tooth fairy was real.

*("Your teeth were gone in the morning, right? And there was money under your pillow?"*

*"I need more proof than that."*

*"I don't have any.")*

"Are you okay?"

"Of course."

He arched dark brows. "Because you're attacking that Tootsie Roll like they're making sugar illegal at midnight."

"I crave fake chocolate that looks not unlike petrified cat feces."

"Aw, Leah!" He tossed a pen at her and she, leaning on her desk with her ankles crossed as she masticated, easily avoided it. "Have a heart. I love those things. I don't want to think about cat poop when I'm contemplating dessert."

"Agreed. I withdraw the comment. Want your pen back?"

He shook his head, looked down at his notepad, then back up at her. His eyes, blue and green, watched her. "Now don't get mad . . ."

"Hmm. I assume you're about to tell me something infuriating."

". . . because on short acquaintance I like her . . ."

"Ah. You think the mayor of Boston might harbor murder in her heart."

"Well . . ."

"And so she does." Leah smiled. "Just not for me. Journalists, however, are not completely safe from her."

"She's not a patient, right?"

Leah shook her head. "I would never insult her by implying there are things wrong with her I could perhaps fix."

"But there *are* things wrong with her and maybe you *could* fix them." He shrugged. "None of my business, which makes my next question kind of awkward: can you tell me her story?"

"Oh yes. And it's a good one."

"Yeah, I figured it must be." He patted the space beside him on the couch. "Stop leaning all sexy-like on your desk and come here and sit all sexy-like on the couch instead."

"Your seductive smoothness has melted my reserve," she said with a straight face, then ruined it by giggling.

"God, you are so gorgeous when you laugh."

"Doubtful." But she went to him anyway, and sat beside him. "Do you know how difficult it is, still is, even in this century, for women to excel at politics?"

"Even if I do, you're gonna tell me anyway. Right?"

"Well . . ."

# TWENTY-THREE

Catherine Carey was the first woman elected mayor of Boston, and when the votes were tallied you could hear the sighs of relief all over the city. The incumbent had to go.

Mayor Carey ran as an independent and soundly kicked ass for several reasons. She was beautiful (yes, what diff, except in politics it helps if you're hot, it helps a *lot*), a local (born in Danvers, Massachusetts, home of the former Danvers State Insane Asylum), intelligent (MBA from Harvard Business School, which proved nothing, but an IQ of 146, which did), charismatic (Miss Danvers, 1993; Miss Teen Massachusetts, 1994), and compassionate (she ran her first blood drive at age fourteen; she mailed her lemonade stand money to starving children in Africa).

Also, her Republican opponent, the incumbent, had just been indicted for taking a bribe to push through the Big Dig II Program ("Now Bigger and Diggier!"), and her Democratic opponent burst into tears during their televised debate ("But I don't *know* how we're going to fix the tax situation! Stop picking on me!").

(It later came to light that the man had stopped taking his antidepressants several weeks earlier, which earned him a compassionate scolding from Mayor-Elect Carey.)

As expected, Mayor Carey wasted no time rolling up her figurative sleeves (and occasionally her literal sleeves) and jumping in with both feet (also literally as well as figuratively). In her first year of office she decreased government spending by eight percent (hey, *you* try it), coaxed two local zillionaires to fund the renovation for several local athletic fields, and wasn't a racist.

The last one proved to be her political ruin. While going over the city's proposed cuts to the Boston Public Library budget, Mayor Carey objected strongly, probably because "cuts" really meant "demolition."

"I don't care about Kindles or Nooks or Wikipedia or downloads. We will always need a library. Boston's citizens will always need a place to find a planet's worth of information for free. Rich, poor, other, they'll always need a place that's warm in winter and cool in summer and full of books and computers and maps and magazines and government forms and reading nooks. It is every citizen's birthright and we are not tearing it down because the Internet exists. Bad enough you want to be so niggardly with the budget."

Of course: uproar. The mayor assumed it was because she was digging in her heels on the budget.

It wasn't.

"But niggardly isn't a racial slur."

**RACIST MAYOR REFUSES TO APOLOGIZE**

"But that isn't what niggardly means."

**MAYOR DENIES BEING DISGUSTING BIGOT**

"It means 'stingy' or 'miserly.' It's from an Old Norse word: '*Nigla*.' It means to make a big deal out of a small thing. Kind of like what's happening right now."

**RACIST MAYOR THINKS BIGOTED REMARKS "NO BIG DEAL"**

"For God's sake."

**RACIST MAYOR TRIES TO COMBINE CHURCH AND STATE**

"Fine. I apologize if my correct use of an adjective that isn't a racial slur offends anyone who can't take five seconds to look it up in Merriam-Webster. Hey, you know where you can do that? *The fucking public library!*"

**MAYOR MAKES AMENDS FOR RACIST REMARKS; PLEDGES TO KEEP LIBRARY OPEN**

"Really? That did the trick? You know, the journalists really got us off track with this one. The *Boston Globe* is basically a black hole from which no scandal, however silly, can escape."

**RACIST MAYOR CITES *BOSTON GLOBE* AS BLACK HOLE; THINKS BIGOTED REMARKS SILLY**

"Oh, come on! I didn't mean that I think the *Globe* is solely staffed by African-Americans! A black hole has nothing to do with race!"

**RACIST MAYOR DENIES BEING A RACIST AGAIN**

"It's a region of space-time that nothing escapes! It's called black because it sucks up everything, even light, and doesn't have one thing to do with race or creed or color. Which you can also find out if you use *the fucking public library*!"

**RACIST MAYOR CLAIMS BLACKS SUCK**

"That's it. I quit."

**RACIST MAYOR RESIGNS**

AND THAT IS how the former mayor of Boston came to live part-time in a small Chicago public park.

# TWENTY-FOUR

"Hmm. Okay. It's probably not gonna be Cat."

"She's not even poor," Leah giggled. Somehow they'd ended up prone on the couch, Archer on his back, Leah on his front. This had stemmed in mid-story from her demand to examine his stab wounds, and had progressed to kissing and, of course, the finale of the Tale of Cat.

"No? Really?"

"Boston, right? Most of her family can trace their roots back to Plymouth Rock and she's got a six-figure trust fund. So she didn't just quit being mayor; she quit all of it. Corporations and business suits and shaking hands while kissing babies and politics of *any* kind and now she sort of pokes around the city and sometimes she sleeps in shelters and sometimes she gets a suite at the Marriott but she always ends up in that park. She must really like the ducks."

"She really likes *you*, dork!" Archer gave her a gentle smack on the forehead with the palm of his hand. "Why does that never *ever* occur to you?"

"Um." She tipped her head to the side and thought. "Past precedent?"

"Ooooh, I love when you're a clueless dumbass and then use big words."

She shifted her weight enough so that an elbow went into his ribs and he groaned. Smiling, she sat up and straightened her skirt. And then her hair. And readjusted her blouse. "Don't pout."

"Awwww."

"That is the exact opposite of 'don't pout.' Besides, I know I was hurting you."

"Nuh-uh."

"I was lying on your chest," she said, exasperated. "So, directly on your stab wounds. You should have prevented that—"

"Fat goddamn chance."

"—or at least told me I was hurting you."

"I get off on it."

"No, you don't."

"No, I don't. But I don't mind."

He sat up, shaking his hair out of his eyes. Leah was having a hard time deciding which she liked best: the blue or the green. "Did not mind. Did not care. Still don't care. You can make me your mattress anytime."

"Thank you. Do you want to call it a day?" They'd been discussing past lives and possible future murders for hours; the clinic had long since closed. "You understand that because of confidentiality issues I couldn't exactly hand you a pile of charts and a copy machine and let you have at it."

"And *you* understand that you should wear green all the time.

It makes you look like a sexy leprechaun." At Leah's snort, he continued. "Besides, we've already been over this. I thought maybe we could figure out the type of person this guy or gal could be, and you could watch for them."

*Adorable.* "It's not always someone in my life," she reminded him. She had a brief flash of someone

*(my name is Mary Jane Kelly)*

and a sensation of dread and drowning

*(the knife like silver fish)*

but the memory was gone before she could chase it down.

"Well, it's something," Archer was saying. "Better than your Plan A, which was 'hang around not engaging in a single thing while waiting to be murdered.'"

*I haven't entirely abandoned that one. I'm just hoping to get laid first.*

"And then there's the people you know."

"There *are* the people I know."

"Oh, God, all your hotness plus you're a sworn officer of the Grammar Police." He pretended to swoon, which was a good trick since he was sitting down. "You are the complete package."

She shook her head. *He approves of everything about me. Ergo, this cannot will not shall not last. As I foresaw. Too bad. It might have been spectacular.*

"So, people you know? I mean really know, not just the charts in your office. Because don't studies show we're most likely to be murdered by someone we know?"

"That's true." *Depressing beyond belief. And completely true.*

"I know you don't have a lot of—uh—the nature of your work

demands you keep a certain—um—distance—which isn't to say you're not—uh—you're—"

*Adorable!* "I'm a chilly bitch," she said, smiling, "and my only friend is the former mayor of Boston, who isn't a racist. Oh, and you, perhaps." She speared him with a look. "Are you a friend?"

"Nope." He shook his head so hard his hair flew. "You can't put me in that zone; don't waste time trying. I'm your future snuggle sweetie and never forget it."

"I will absolutely forget it if required to ever use the term 'snuggle sweetie.'"

"Got it." Now that she'd rearranged her clothing, Archer again patted the space beside him on the sofa and she sat. She hadn't bothered to put her shoes back on, so she curled up and tucked her legs beneath her. Archer, meanwhile, had moved over the small empty space on the sofa so fast and hard that he nearly knocked her through the arm rest. "That's better." He patted her knee. "Argh, even your knees are sexy."

"Archer . . ." She rolled her eyes.

"So, people in your life. We can eliminate me—"

"I certainly hope so."

"Don't start that again," he almost pleaded. "I'm begging, here. What about your boss?"

"I'm the boss. I mean, it's not my clinic," she clarified, "but I'm the head Insighter. My supervisor no longer sees patients. She's in administration and likes it that way, and likes that I'm good at my job. She's the last person who would kill me, if for no other reason than it would make her life difficult short term as well as long term."

"Okaaaay."

She smiled at him. "That's *good* news, Archer."

"Yeah, maybe." He would not look at her, just kept making notes. "What about colleagues? Were you ever killed by someone you worked with?"

"Not that I recall. It's not like I've got a mental file cabinet of all my lives and can effortlessly call up even the smallest detail at any time." But oh, wouldn't that be efficient! And convenient! "And they might not love me, but I don't think they loathe me enough to kill me. One of them could knife me out of envy? Malice? Resentment because I refused to chip in for the birthday cake fund?" She would never, *ever* understand the forced socializing expected at work. She had zero interest in their birthdays, or her own, and they in hers, so why pretend? Also, cake? At 10:00 a.m.?

"Don't joke, babe."

"Ugh. Babe?"

She put her tongue out at him, but he refused to be distracted. "People knife each other for a lot less."

"Oh yes! But in this case, none of them care about me enough to want to kill me. They only want to force pastry on me at all hours of the workday. We're all quite jaded, and nobody wants to take on my case load. So again: good news."

He looked at his notes for a few seconds, then back up at her. "Your idea of good news is different from mine. And you're so calm about it. 'Nobody cares about me enough to kill me' is *not* good news, Leah, okay? It's pretty sad news, in fact. More on that later because I can tell you're already tuning me out, but we're definitely not done discussing this, get it?"

She shrugged. *Tack "tenacious" onto "adorable." Tenorable? Adoracious?*

"Okay, what about that nervous-looking bald guy at Nellie's house? Your mom's agent and I guess yours, too, once. He seems pretty furtive."

"Tom Winn of Winner's Talent™ (ugh). Don't be fooled, though. He's a Hollywood agent, he can't help it," she explained. "Tom's furtive because it's his nature, not because he's murdered me a dozen times."

"And you know this how?"

"That wet-eyed bastard has been in my life for years; he's had several opportunities to kill me. Anytime she decided I needed new head shots, for example. The cattle call for the Tampax commercial, for example. The callback for *Sweets to the Suite*, for example. My entire childhood and a chunk of my adolescence, for example." She took a closer look at Archer and saw he was still puzzled. "It doesn't work like that, anyway. It's not going to be some random stranger who knifes me on the subway. It'll be someone I know, even if just briefly. A patient, or someone who referred a patient. A former teacher."

"Then why stab me? I was a stranger!"

"Instinct?" she suggested. But it was a fair question. "It's one thing to intellectually understand my killer is going to strike again and when he does, he'll be known to me. It's another not to fight against someone who's been following me for weeks and then corners me in an alley."

"Point," he muttered.

"Plus as I said, Tom has had over a decade to kill me. And he's entirely my mother's creature, and was even when I was outearning her five to one."

A look of understanding crossed Archer's face. "Oh, she must have *loved* that."

Leah managed a sour smirk. "You can guess how much. It was petty revenge, but it was *mine*. The irony, of course, is that if I'd had no success, she wouldn't have been so driven to keep me working long after I loathed everything about it. And, in fairness to her, I could be quite smug about it. I would read the trades praising whatever nonsense I'd been up to that week, then 'accidentally' leave them for her to read and eat her heart out over."

"Oh, boo-hoo, your mom deserved it."

"Well, yes. But regardless, you can scratch Tom. He's harmless, which is what I always disliked about him."

"That's what they all say. But it's always the quiet ones."

She couldn't restrain the fond smile. "It's sometimes the quiet ones," she corrected. "History proves it."

"Okay, so he's off the list. Also, our list sucks, because we don't actually have any names on it now. I feel like we should put at least one name down—"

"For the false illusion of progress?" she asked sweetly.

"Yep." Archer remained admirably unmoved by her sarcasm. "So here comes the toughie: your mom."

Leah barked a laugh. "Toughie?"

Undaunted (adorable!), he plowed ahead. "I can't imagine how hard even talking about this must be—"

She laughed again; she couldn't help it. He was just so *earnest*, as though he feared hurting her. Nothing had hurt her in forever. Crying in her mother's driveway those few days ago was the first time she'd cried in years. "As in it will be emotionally difficult for me to discuss the possibility that she will indulge in filicide? Ah . . . no."

"This is the part where I pretend I know what filicide means."

"Killing your son or daughter, also known as prolicide.

There's also nepoticide, when you kill your nephew; maricitide, which is killing your husband; parricide, killing a close relative; fratricide, killing your brother; sororocide, killing your sister; uxoricide, when you kill your wife; avunculicide, killing your uncle; and of course my personal favorite, matricide."

"It's awful that you know all that."

"It *is* awful that I know all that."

"Getting away from fucked-up uncles killing nephews, the thing about your mom is, she's kinda killed you in the past."

"You're so cute when you're striving for tactful."

"Thanks," he said modestly. "But you know I'm right."

"Oh, yes. She has most definitely kinda killed me in the past. And because you're not confused enough, I feel compelled to point out she kinda hasn't, too."

# TWENTY-FIVE

"You have no. Good. Stories." Archer was practically fetal on the couch. "I think I have to get up and go kill myself now."

*Why do I keep telling him these things?* To test him? To test herself? To show him the things she sees and knows, an Insighter reaching for the life-blind? She didn't know. But she leaned forward and smoothed his hair away from his face. "It's not so bad."

"It's your *life*, Leah. And it's very bad. They're all very very very very very very very very—"

"Archer."

"—very very very very very very very—"

"For God's sake."

"—very very very bad."

"But it isn't." When he blinked up at her she elaborated. "Yes, those things happened, but it's like watching a movie. I can tell you what Fred Barker's favorite color was but not how he felt when he bit into a slice of watermelon. I don't feel him. Them. I just know things about them."

"And at least one of them was screwed over by her mother. Your mother, I mean." Anger, now, but not heated. She could almost feel the chill coming off him.

"It's her nature," she said softly. "Nothing to be done about it."

"Oh, bullshit." Abruptly he sat up and wriggled his shoulders in what she assumed was an attempt to physically shake off the anger. "This is my big problem with the whole Insight industry."

*This should be interesting.* She raised her eyebrows, wordlessly encouraging him to continue.

"It's like when someone finds out the reason they're a raging bitch in this life is because they were a raging bitch in the last one, and suddenly that's it. Case closed. 'Nothing to be done about it.' Nobody tries to improve. Nobody asks themselves *why* they feel compelled to be a jackass. It's more about embracing your *old* inner bitch. You know what would be even better? Family therapy."

"Sorry, what?" There was never a need for such a thing. Insighters covered . . . well . . . everything. They were available for children, adults, and the elderly. They worked in hospitals and schools, and were everywhere in the legal system: they advised lawyers, they were in the courtroom when clients got sentenced, in the prisons where clients paid their debt. They were in schools and nursing homes and, sometimes, funeral homes. (Although by then, it was often too late for the Insighter to do much besides, "Yes, well, he died. Again, I mean.")

"You know, a setup where the whole family could go talk to

somebody, a professional, not about their past life garbage but where and why they're making wrong turns in this life. They could, mmmm, talk about their feelings and how they felt when they did whatever it is that's wrecking their life and how they plan to *not* keep doing it. They can make their own lives better."

She tried to swallow the laugh, but it escaped anyway. "I'm sorry, I'm so sorry," she gasped, "it just sounds absurd. Sitting around talking without going back at all. Or, rather, talking but only going back to your life *at that time*. It would never work. Frankly, only someone who . . . uh . . ." Too late, she realized the rest of the sentence: "*was life-blind could come up with such a spectacularly ignorant idea.*" ". . . uh . . ."

"And," he sighed, sounding equal parts annoyed and enthralled, "you also look gorgeous when you blush as you've just realized you're sounding like an entitled jerk who is quick to dismiss any therapy outside of her own profession."

"I'm sorry," she said again. "Sorry to laugh and sorry to immediately discount your idea. I just don't see the need for that service when people like me are here."

"That," he said, quirking an eyebrow at her, "might be part of the problem."

"Maybe family therapy would be a good idea for the life-blind, though." Now that she was giving it some thought, it seemed almost . . . logical? There were next to no resources for the life-blind; if they had a problem, there wasn't much set up in the system to help them. And if they were true *rasa*, the theory went that they didn't *need* anything in the system to help them. But the therapy thing sounded interesting. "Although now that I think about it . . ." Then she heard it, and forgot everything.

"Oh my God, is that your ringtone?"

She had frozen at the sound. Her phone, across the room on top of her desk, was shrieking in Faye Dunaway's voice, "I told you! No wire hangers, ever!"

"Is that *Mommie Dearest*?"

"Big fan of cult camp classics, hmm?"

"Not me. My dad. Interesting choice for your ringtone."

Leah shrugged, uncomfortable but unable to squash the small smile, then crossed the room to pick up her phone. "I know, it's childish and petty."

"Yeah, well, so's your mom. Why would she call you? Is that a thing?" Archer's eyes went wide as he considered the possibilities. "Does she call you? Especially after you've sworn you're done with her forever? She blows off your murder and you march out and then a day later she calls and doesn't apologize?"

"No." Leah stared down at her phone, which was still trembling and shrilling, "No wire hangers, ever!" "That is not a thing. She does not do that."

She debated another few seconds, which Archer misread, and he turned toward the door. "Oh. Sorry. I'll let you take—"

She shook her head. "That's not why I'm hesitating." Adorable. He'd been in her house for the Scene. The Final Blowoff Scene. Why would Leah care if he overheard a phone call? She picked up the phone, viper-quick, as if she was afraid she would lose her nerve if she *didn't* pick it up in a hurry. "What."

Nellie's charming contralto murmured in her ear. "Darling, thank you for picking up. You so rarely do. Rude, but then, you were never afraid of showing off your, ah, less appealing qualities."

"What. Is. It."

"Darling, you sound so chilly, even for you." She had the

nerve, the colossal fucking nerve, to sound chiding. Disappointed, even. Leah wondered if she was in danger of biting through her lower lip. *When my teeth meet I will know I chomped too far.* "I wanted to let you know that it looks like *Mother Daughter Hookers Heroes* is going to be picked up! Tom is on his way to Hollywood right now to work out the details; I insisted he get in on this from the very beginning. I simply refuse to get reamed on the gross again."

Leah bit back a hysterical giggle. *So . . . many things . . . to mock . . .* She wondered if it was possible to have a sarcasm stroke. "This has nothing to do with me."

"Darling, of course it does. I cannot star in *Mother Daughter Hookers Heroes* without a daughter."

"So hire one."

"That's part of the hook," she explained patiently, as if Leah didn't know all the steps in the Hollywood dance. As if she hadn't known since first grade, if Nellie would have allowed her to attend first grade instead of hiring tutors to cram her full of multiplication tables and "see spot run" between shoots. "It's *our* comeback, not my comeback and some silly little nobody absolutely no one wants to see."

"You have always overestimated my stardom, because of course it allowed you to overestimate yours. No one knows who I am—or was."

"Is that any way for Little Miss Huggies to talk?"

"Former Little Miss Huggies. No."

"That's just the stage fright talking."

"No."

"So I'm going to messenger the script to you and—"

"No."

"—you'll have to be ready to take a studio meeting first thing Monday."

"No."

"Remember, jewel tones make your skin seem less sallow. And stripes make you seem . . . thick. Absolutely no stripes, darling. And your hair is . . ." A pause while It searched for the right word. ". . . fine. Literally fine; maybe you should try a thickening serum? Something to give you a little body?"

"No! For fuck's sake, no! A thousand times *no*, how are you not getting this? Even for you? No!"

"All right, but at least use some hot rollers to give yourself a little bounce."

Leah pinched the skin above her nose and told herself to stop chewing her lower lip. "No to everything. No to the comeback. No to body. No to stripes. No."

"At last you're speaking sense. You could be pretty, but not with the distraction of horizontal stripes. Remember that dreadful two piece you wore for the Fourth of July special? You looked so very thick."

"I was two."

"Yes, well, you're not getting any younger."

"Pay attention: no to everything. Comebacks, stripes, my matricidal urges, your utter inability to care for anyone but yourself, no."

"Don't be difficult, dear."

"No to the *Mommy and Me Fuck Fest* television show."

"I don't understand." Her contralto, even when she sounded flat and disbelieving, was still lovely. Leah actually shivered at the power of her voice, and was furious all over again that even she, who knew all of her tricks, wasn't immune to her oldest, and best.

The second-to-worst thing: she could make you think she cared.

The worst thing: not only did she not care, she really *didn't* understand.

Leah took a breath, held it for the count of five, then forced it out through her nose. "What? What was it? Exactly what was it about our meeting the other day that left you any doubt as to my feelings about being in your life at all, never mind going back to Hollywood with you? I will not do this, do you understand? I will never, never do this. Not again, not once, not for an HBO special and not for a toilet paper commercial."

Archer, leaning against her desk, was trying to give the impression of a man who isn't hearing every single awful word. If his eyes got any bigger, they would fall right out of his skull and hit the carpet: plop! In her current grim mood, that might make her laugh. Her mother's legacy was clear: Leah was a terrible person.

"I used to love you, but you managed to stomp that flat by the time I had to take you to court. Now I don't even like you, do you hear me? I don't roll my eyes and tell myself that you'll never change but that it doesn't matter. I don't joke about you with my boyfriend—"

"Darling, you don't *have* boyfriends. Which reminds me, the producer is a lovely woman in her thirties who also happens to be gay, so if you could see your way to being extra *extra* friendly to her during the meeting and also after the meeting, we could get a head start on—"

"—or my colleagues or the mayor of Boston!" She had to raise her voice to be heard over her machinations. "I never speak of you. Ever. I never panic when Mother's Day approaches because I don't know what to get you and I never fret about the holidays because I know I won't have to see you. I never feel any of those things daughters feel about difficult mothers. Absent contempt is the kindest emotion I can summon for you. The very kindest."

"But—"

"Lose this number, or I will lose this phone. Do not call me again, ever, under any circumstances. If you want to give me a kidney, I don't want you to call. If you want to apologize for the abortion of my childhood, I don't want you to call. If you're bleeding out, I don't want you to call. Fuck your fashion advice. Fuck your career. Fuck your comeback. Fuck my comeback. Fuck you. Good-bye."

Leah hung up, waiting to feel devastated and bereft. She supposed she'd burst into undignified tears again, as she had in the driveway. Archer seemed to think so, too; he was already moving to her, his arms out in a pre-hug. He had a "there, there" expression on his face; he was fully ready to kick into Comfort Mode.

She held up her hands like a traffic cop and he stopped. "No, I'm fine." She managed a smile. "I'm fine."

"Okay?"

"Yes. Okay. That's . . ." She paused and considered. "That's been stuck in my head for a while. It feels good to get it out."

"The way you'd feel good after a family therapy session!" he insisted.

"Ah . . . no. Not at all like that." Her smile felt a little more real this time. "You charming idiot."

# TWENTY-SIX

Leah drove him home and to his astonished delight, she wouldn't let him out of the car until they were both panting and his erection hurt. A good hurt, though, the best hurt. The *if you don't let me out of these jeans I'm gonna throw up in your underwear* hurt.

He hadn't been expecting snuggling of any sort. Not after the final-final blow-off with her mother. He'd been a little surprised, and impressed, at how Leah held it together that time. Now he realized that she wasn't so much holding it together as she was celebrating her freedom.

Her hands were everywhere and her mouth was full of kisses, and best of all, most wonderful of all, she wasn't at all stingy with them. Where her fingers went her lips followed, and he felt like he was being marked in the loveliest possible way. Her breath kept hitching and would occasionally suspend entirely which made him feel like he was having a heart attack, if heart attacks were intensely erotic. And ah, God, *her mouth.* Lips and tongue busy against his and he was again reminded his earlobe had a nerve connection straight to his cock.

Oh, sure, he'd read things and done some late-night one-handed Internet research, but nowhere in any of that did someone ever come out and say, "In case you missed that day in anatomy, your earlobe connects to your cock when a lovely dark-eyed brunette has her tongue on it."

Even better, she was letting him put his hands in places his hands had only dreamed of

*(hands dream?)*

as he skimmed his fingers beneath her shirt and over the curve of her bra, mindful, always fucking mindful, of the balisong knives. If she had flinched back or even stilled, he would have immediately withdrawn

*(my hands and I are terribly sorry, ma'am; it would be terrific if you didn't stab me again also please don't cut them off thank you and good night)*

but she pressed forward into his fingers and he groaned into her mouth. "Feel like . . . teenager . . ." was all he was able to mumble against her lips, which curved into a smile.

"I wouldn't know." Her fingers had gone to the button on his jeans. *Ohhhh little fly button, how I envy thee.* "I spent most of my teen years in auditions, or studios, or on various hunger strikes to punish Nellie. Once she even noticed."

"Here's a plan: let's not talk about your mom right this minute."

"Agreed." Her fingers had undone the button, he was enchanted to note. "I didn't have a boyfriend until I was twenty." Her fingers had moved to his zipper and he couldn't stand it any longer, he brought his hand up to the nape of her neck and pressed his mouth back to hers, caught her deft fingers with his bigger, clumsier ones

*("what are you DOING?" his libido shrieked, betrayed, "have you gone MAD?")*

and pressed them to his heart.

"Shy," she purred into his mouth.

"Yes, that's exactly what it is. Shush now. More kissing. This is the stuff you missed."

So he showed her and she delighted him with her questions and low giggles, and yeah, it was a little like high school but also a little not, because the girls in school didn't whisper wonderful filthy things in his ear, didn't press and rub through his jeans and ask things like, "There? More? And how about there? Yes?" The girls in school never made the earlobe-to-cock connection. They never made his brain melt.

And incredibly, he could hear "No wire hangers, ever!" somewhere in his head, which was a bit of a mood dampener, but not entirely, since his need for Leah was a great scary throbbing thing. Maybe she heard it, too, because they finally fell apart, *broke* apart, and then he was stumbling out of her car and up the walk to his house, and she was waving at him from the driver's seat. The dome light shone on her dark hair, which was lovely, but the rest of her face was in shadow, and that bothered him, though he was too dazed with lust to put his finger on why.

# TWENTY-SEVEN

She was watching Archer staggering away from her car and realized she was panting, just a little, when her phone twitched again in her pocket, bleating, "No wire hangers, ever!" The noise was muffled due to placement, but no less unpleasant. Her lust instantly damped down and disappeared, ice water tossed on flames.

She fished the phone out and glared at it. Even Nellie couldn't be this dense. Not after the Fuck You medley phone chat. Something wrong? Trouble at the old mill? Something she needed Leah, and just Leah, to handle? Was it possible? Did she have the nerve?

*But I need you to pick me up at the clinic after the procedure. And while you're there . . . I don't mean to be insensitive, darling, but neither of us is getting younger. Now don't worry, I already talked to Dr. Weinman and he'll be happy to discuss a few simple procedures with you. He's got your complete medical history and everything, so don't eat anything the night before you pick me up . . . of course you don't have to have anything done but if you come to your senses, you'll be all set. Okay? Darling?*

and

*But the reporter won't talk to me unless you're there;* People *magazine is doing a "Where Are They Now" feature about celebrity moms. You can take the SATs next year . . . yes, it's wonderful that most fifteen-year-olds don't get invited to take it but that proves my point . . . there's always next year, and also the year after.*

and

*But they loved you, they just loved you, and all you'll need to do is diet down enough so you can play a young girl dying of anorexia and, yes, I know the part calls for a twelve-year-old and you're fourteen, but once you skip enough meals you can pull it off. And darling, really, the dieting alone will bring us—you—more opportunities to work.*

Did she have the nerve? Why was Leah even asking herself such an obvious question? Of *course* It had the nerve! It was made up of fifty percent ambition and fifty percent nerve (and zero percent maternal instinct.) A month ago she never would have asked herself the question. Gah, interaction with Archer was making her soft.

Even as she was wondering why she was doing such a thing, Leah held the phone to her ear. "What." She held her breath, waiting for that lovely shimmering voice, the sound of pain.

And . . . nothing. Nellie was either marshaling new arguments

*It's not that I don't love you, darling, it's that you're not especially lovable.*

or had misdialed

*Sorry, darling, thought you were the colonic clinic. But while I've got you, when was the last time you had a good cleansing? From the look of your complexion, I would guess it has been a while.*

or was sucking in breath for a patented scolding. Most popular: *You Don't Know What I've Sacrificed for You.* Runner-up: *I Can't Believe You Would Deny Your Own Mother Although People Often Mistake Us for Sisters.*

Nothing on the other end but careful, slow breathing. Was she nervous? Working up the nerve to ask for something else Leah could never give her? What could be worse than *Mother Daughter Fuck Fest*? So many, many things. The thought was staggering.

"No," Leah said firmly. "Whatever it is, no."

She shut off her phone for the night, which is why the police couldn't immediately reach her with the news.

# TWENTY-EIGHT

Morning, and for the first time in a long time, Leah could not wait to start the day. Positive note number one: she hadn't been stabbed to death. Positive note number two: it was Saturday, no clients. Positive note number three: Archer had proposed various silly, romantic interludes, all under the guise of researching her eventual murderer. She doubted their ability to get much work done while playing miniature golf

*(I've driven past that place a hundred times and always thought it was a silly activity. But apparently the old saying is, one hundred and first time is the charm. And if you can get your ball to go into the whale's blow hole, you win a free game. Which I may actually play, as long as it's with Archer.)*

or having a picnic at Cat's park

*(that "pond" is nothing more than a glorified mud puddle riddled with duck feces and yet I'm intrigued at the thought of eating near it)*

although she did not doubt that it would be fun—or at least interesting—to try.

Whatever they did, she had promised to call him around lunchtime with a plan. And she had promised under duress, since she would have said almost anything

*("I'm not sure I—"*

*"Oh please please please please please please please please please please please please please please call me or I'll diiiiiiie! I'll just flop over and DIE." Then, in his normal baritone, "What? Too needy?")*

to get him to stop making that horrible noise.

She was in the shower, cursing and trying to get shampoo out of her eye, when she remembered her phone was off. She almost never did that; Insighters got the occasional frantic call in the middle of the night, so she hurried through the rest of her shower, blotted herself dry, then retrieved her phone and turned it back on. While waiting for the thing to burp out various tones alerting her to voicemails and e-mails, she got dressed.

For the first time (in a long time) she dressed for someone else as opposed to clinic wear, or her court suit. Administration preferred Insighters in professional attire—suit jackets, skirts or trousers, like that—while acknowledging that their job was messy, both literally and figuratively. Sometimes clients did not respond well to news that they used to be Mary Mallon, aka Typhoid Mary. Sometimes that meant going home to wash vomit out of her jacket. Many of her colleagues wore a lab coat over their clothing; Leah just tried to stick to wash-and-wear fabrics and a high-quality laundry soap. Insighters weren't doctors, and while many of her colleagues encouraged their clients' dependence, Leah wanted no part of such things, and eschewed lab coats. And also touching.

Today was different;

*(hooray! "different"! what a wonderful word!)*

today she could dress as she liked, so she indulged herself with a pair of rose-colored capris, a cream-colored tank top trimmed at the neck with lace, and a cardigan a few shades darker than her pants. As her phone started chiming, she found her tan oxfords and slipped one on, then glanced down at her phone, which, judging from all the pings and chimes, was about to self-destruct.

*What the hell is this? Four voicemails? Nellie just doesn't know when to quit.*

But none of the voicemails were from her mother.

"Ms. Nazir, this is Detective Preston from the CPD. Please call us back immediately."

Archer.

*Oh, fuck. Archer!*

The other voicemails were from the police as well, though she didn't hear the entirety of the second one, since for some reason the phone was falling away from her, turning over and over before it finally—how was it falling in slow motion?—hit the tile and she heard a faint "crack."

Or would have, if she hadn't clawed for her keys and sprinted out the front door. The phone might be tumbling in slo-mo but she was in overdrive, and it still didn't seem fast enough.

# TWENTY-NINE

She stood on the brakes hard enough to bang her head on the roof, and when the car had more or less stopped, she wrestled free of the seat belt and escaped its confines. She ran up the sidewalk to Archer's front door, barely registering the ting-ting-ting of the car as it chimed its warning that she'd left the keys in the ignition and the door open. And almost on top of a fire hydrant.

She hammered on the front door with her fists and, when that didn't bring an immediate response, started kicking the bottom of the wooden door. It hurt, but she didn't care. She imagined the neighbors would be concerned by the noise, and didn't care. They might call the police; she didn't. The police only called you *after* the unthinkable happened. She had a flash from her past, something about

*("But they cannot! The king is above the law. The king* is *the law.")*

things going bad just when it seemed the good times were back, and shook it off.

"Archer! Open up! Archer, be in there and be unmangled and safe and *open up*!" Part of her brain realized she was sobbing his name and her fists were going numb and her foot hurt but the rest of her brain didn't care, was focused on her worst thoughts being false, being untrue, because Archer was fine, he was fine last night and he would be fine now and all she had to do was keep knocking and he would eventually—

"Jeez, Leah?" The door had opened and he was blinking at her in surprise. "What's wrong?"

She fell into his arms, clutching at him and trying to tell him the CPD had played a terrible prank but she would forgive them because he was fine, he was completely fine and on second thought she would Insight the *shit* out of all of them beginning with Detective Preston, if he so much as jostled a shoplifter during an arrest she would delve into his past lives and tell everyone he used to be Pol Pot.

"Ohhhh you're okay you're okay you're okay oh thank God you're okay." She was telling all that to Archer's neck, as once she'd thrown her arms around him she simply refused to let go. He had staggered, but submitted.

"What's wrong? Ouch, that tickles—what's—yeek!"

"Wait." She stopped talking to his throat and stepped back, looking up at him. His hands went to the small of her back, pressing, and it was absurd, really, how comforting that was. "You're okay."

"Yeah. Well, I went to bed with a chronic case of blue balls, which you've just made worse, but yeah, in general, I'm pretty okay." His blue and green eyes gleamed with good humor. "Where's your other shoe?"

"My what?" She looked down. One tan oxford, neatly tied,

was on her left foot. Her right foot was bare. "I just—I don't recall. I must have . . ." Must have darted, *streaked*, out of her apartment in her rush to get to Archer. "The police." It was hard to think. Relief, she was just now discovering, was as potent a drug as anything illegal. She was alternately giddily light-headed and crushed under the weight of stress. "They called. They said—they said I had to call them back right away and they left lots of messages and they never leave the bad news on a recording I thought something happened so I left and here I am."

"And you thought . . . ah, Leah." He snaked a hand around the back of her neck and pulled her forward for a quick kiss. "You thought I was hurt? Dead?"

She didn't answer, just nodded. Her relief was a palpable force, an enormous thing.

*Oh I am in so much trouble with this boy who I keep forgetting is older than I am. I want to tumble him into bed and divest him of his clothes and find out what he likes, all the things he likes. And then I want to do it again, and again, for fifty years.*

"And you just . . . you quit putting on your shoes and hopped in your car—which you've parked in the middle of the street, by the way, but it's all right, I'm not judging—and came over?"

"Oh my God. I never even—I didn't stop to think. I just assumed . . . you're right, I'm a fool."

"Whoa!" He held his hands up and then—much better—put them back around her and gave her a slight squeeze. "I didn't use that particular F word, so simmer. I'd never use that particular F word in reference to you." He squeezed her again, which was lovely. She was amazed at how quickly he was calming her down. "And now this is the part where I pretend I'm not wildly flattered by your panic. Because I absolutely, totally am. Instead, I'll play it cool. Like the way I'm playing it now: coooooool."

She giggled in spite of herself and had a quick thought

*(you've laughed more in the last week than you have in the last year)*

that was gone before she could grasp it. "But the police did call. And they don't leave voicemails like that unless it's personal."

"They call you a lot?"

"For Insighter business, yes." She nodded and realized they were still standing on Archer's front step. "This was an entirely different voicemail. Personal, you know? I just assumed—but why would they even call me about you? They don't know how—" *Important you are to me.* That was the rest of the sentence, the sentence it was much too early to say. The sentence she might never say. "They don't know we're, ah, dating."

"We're, ah, dating?" He grinned at her, which was a great relief. Yes, let Archer think this was all very cute and very funny, when it was neither. That was fine. It would make things easier, later.

"Yes."

"The cops left you a personal voicemail?"

"Three, actually. At least."

"Okay, let's listen to them."

She stood on the step, perfectly silent, as she realized, and then uttered a sentence she had never before said: "I dropped my phone and ran out of my apartment in my haste to get to you."

"Oh my God." Archer actually staggered, right there on the stoop. "That is so hot. Oh my God."

"And I think it broke. I can't be sure. But I heard something break but was in such a rush I didn't go back to see."

"Oh. My. *God.*" He groaned and clutched at her. "You always have your phone, fucking *always.* You're one of those. I can't believe . . . Jesus, that's hot."

"Shut up," she grumped, feeling horribly exposed, like the entire street could see she cared for this idiot. "Just . . . shut up."

"Ohhhh, you're so cute." He clutched her to him and gave her a hearty smack on the lips. She wriggled, but not very hard. "And so hot." Smack! "And so cute." Smack! "I said that already." Smack! "But it's true." Smack! "I can't believe you rushed out of the house." Smack! "And dropped your phone." Smack! "And left a shoe behind." Smack! "In your rush to get here." Smack! "And show me your cuteness." Smack! "And parked too close to a fire hydrant." Smack!

"Get off." She gave him a light shove (not—she was careful!—on a stab wound) and he backed off, his wide mouth twisting in a good-natured grumble. "I suppose I could call Detective Preston from here, if you'll . . . oh."

Archer, too, had gone quiet. Had obviously realized the only person the police would be calling Leah about.

"Oh." She stood there a moment, thinking. "It's . . . it's her. It's my mother. Isn't it?"

"Well, unless you've got a dad I don't know about . . ."

"She went to a sperm bank," Leah replied absently. She tapped her bare foot as she thought. "The whole thing was for publicity. My birth. My childhood. It was to boost her career. I have no idea who my father is."

"Okay." Archer's fingers, rubbing at the knots in her neck she didn't realize were there. "Okay, so let's call—"

"No." Now that she could think again, she took him in at a glance and was relieved he was fully dressed. He was wearing knee-length navy shorts, a crisp, clean T-shirt with the slogan "Home is where the Wi-Fi connects automatically," and the de rigueur loafers without socks. "Come on."

He held up a finger, ducked back inside for his wallet, then shut and locked the front door and followed her amiably enough. "I assume you have a plan? Which involves fixing your awful middle-of-the-street parking?"

"It's McMansion." No need to even open her door; she'd obligingly left it open for herself. They both climbed in and buckled. "We're going to her McMansion. It's where the police are."

"Oh. You sure?"

"No."

But they went anyway.

# THIRTY

Detective Preston was talking like this was just another day on the job. Which for him, it was.

"The way it looked . . . our crime scene guys say it looks like your mom was trying to stop him, or her, from leaving."

Leah watched his face as he talked at her and knew that in 1941 his name was Aaron DeSalvo and he loved his big brother more than anything. His big brother protected him from their father; his big brother would goad his father into beating *him* instead of Aaron. His father knocked out all of Mama's teeth and his father broke Mama's fingers and was capable of much worse and his wonderful brother would pull that rage toward *himself*, his brother took beatings meant for Aaron and Aaron was so, so grateful.

And when his big brother killed neighborhood pets Aaron covered for him. And when his big brother started stealing and beating people Aaron covered for him, and when his big brother started stealing cars Aaron covered for him, and when his brother started strangling old ladies Aaron covered for him, and when his brother started strangling young ladies Aaron covered for him, and when his brother was charged with rape Aaron defended him, and when his brother confessed Aaron defended him, and when his brother went to prison Aaron defended him, and when he was killed in prison by a person or persons unknown Aaron gave up, he gave up and eventually he died a lonely, dismal death and no one cared, or noticed.

And his beloved big brother was Albert DeSalvo, his beloved big brother was the Boston Strangler.

So here he was, life number two, Detective Preston, who has convinced himself he is an avenger, here he was atoning for a past life by investigating murders in this life and it wasn't just a job, not to Detective Preston, and Leah knew these things about him and didn't care.

Leah watched Detective Preston's lips move and seriously considered hitting him, *bludgeoning* him, with his past life, hitting him over and over again until he would shut up shut up *shut up* about her, about her mother, about the dark moon of Leah's childhood.

But she didn't do that to him. And she wasn't quite sure why. Archer, maybe? But maybe not. Whatever the reason, Detective Preston, né Aaron DeSalvo, was still talking.

*Oh, God, let him soon stop talking.*

"This is total speculation, but she maybe thought you were the next stop," the Boston Strangler's brother continued, "so she threw herself at him or her. The killer must have panicked or maybe she made more noise than he planned . . . he had to leave before he finished her. He probably thought it wouldn't take long, he'd bludgeoned her pretty thorough—ah—" Preston cut himself off, remembering this was a civilian next of kin. He was, of course, used to dealing with Insighters in the course of his work. He had just forgotten, for a moment. Insighters experienced loss, sure. It was hard to think of them as victims, though. "She must have found her cell phone and . . ." He shrugged.

Leah heard a roaring in her ears

*(how odd, the ocean? how odd, what is that?)*

as the implication sank in. "She tried to warn me," she managed in a voice that cracked and shook, a voice that made Archer's eyes go wide with alarm, a voice that made him seize her arm. "While she was dying. She tried to warn me. And I wouldn't take the call."

And then the world went away for a while.

# THIRTY-ONE

"Stop that," she said, batting away the hand tormenting her. "Stop that right now." She was not quite sure what had happened, but whatever *had* happened, she simply refused to stand for it. Whatever it was.

She opened her eyes and saw that for some reason Archer had taken her to the piano room, the last place she had seen Nellie alive. Her mother had been murdered, of course, in the photo room. The room where Nellie had hired Archer to follow Leah. The room Leah hated more than any other room in any other building in the world. Fitting, yes. And horrible. Yes.

"I don't think you should . . . ah, hell," he sighed as she pushed his hand away and sat up. She had been resting on the low bench opposite the piano no one could play. She wondered who would dust it now. And she wondered why she was thinking about such a silly thing, when she had no idea how she had gotten to the piano room. "You were kind of out of it for a minute."

"I did not swoon," she said sharply.

"I'm pretty positive I didn't say swoon," he replied, his expression mild. His eyes, though. His eyes. They were anything but mild. For a cold moment she wondered if he was angry with her, then realized he was angry . . . but not at her.

"I didn't faint, either."

"Didn't say faint, either."

"Because I have never done such a thing in my life unless I was acting and I have no plans to start. Certainly not today of all days."

"You bet. I'm right there with you."

"And frankly, she had a lot of nerve getting murdered last night." Leah shut her mouth so hard her teeth clacked together. Archer would be vanishing from her life soon enough without seeing the truly nasty side of her personality; no need to bludgeon him

*(like how the killer bludgeoned your mother and you stabbed him moments after your first meeting, how much of your nasty side did you think you'd successfully hidden from the poor man?)*

with more of her awfulness.

"She sure did. You thought you were free—"

"Yes."

"—you loved that you were free—"

"Yes!" She nodded so hard her neck hurt. He understood. It was incredible; unbelievable.

"—and she had to go and fuck all that up."

She stared at him, at the blue and the green of his eyes, eyes narrowed in concentration but not—was it true?—judgment. "Yes. It's awful, I know."

"It's also true. Sounds like on top of everything else, your mom's timing was terrible. All the time, not just last night."

A hysterical giggle burst out of her before she could lock it back, and she slapped her hands over her mouth. But then, to her amazement, Archer slipped warm fingers around her wrists and gently brought them down from her face.

"You can laugh," he told her, as if he were the Insighter and she the fretful client, afraid and angry and not knowing why why *why* she was feeling so strange. "You can cry. You're entitled. Who cares? The cops have seen worse. I've seen worse. Remind me to tell you about my dad sometime."

*When would you have seen worse, you gorgeous idiot?*

"No." She cleared her throat and said it again. "No. Later. I'll do that later. Right now I want to speak to Aaron."

"Who?"

"Detective Preston."

"Feeling better?" As if appearing because she called his (other) name, the man was suddenly in the piano room with them. He was dressed in civilian attire, brown pants and matching jacket, cream-colored shirt, brown tie, brown shoes. His hair was so light a blond it was almost white; his eyes were pale blue; his skin was also pale, with very faint color at his cheeks and nowhere else. He almost seemed to glow in his dark, dull clothes. "You seem to be feeling better. We can certainly have this conversation somewhere—"

"Tell me," she said. "Everything. I want it all. I insist." Leah had no idea how much Insighter privilege Preston was going to allow her, but intended to push for every bit of it. Cops, as a rule, tended to accommodate those in her profession. More, perhaps, than most other fields, cops needed them. "Please," she added, because that seemed called for. And it wouldn't kill her to be polite. Being polite when she felt anything but wasn't exactly—ha, ha!—like getting murdered.

He looked at her for a long moment, doubtless assessing if she was as ready for the information as she seemed. He must have seen something that convinced him—or perhaps he simply didn't care if his words would make her crack and break—because he gave her exactly what she said she wanted.

# THIRTY-TWO

"Your mother let the killer in, so we're thinking it was someone she knew."

"That is incorrect thinking," she said at once. Archer heard her Insighter tone and raised his eyebrows, but mercifully said nothing. "My mother was a fame whore, an attention whore, and, for a few years in the early eighties, an actual whore. All anyone needs to do—needed to do—to get into this house is to recognize her. Or pretend to recognize her. Something as meaningless as 'weren't you the lady from *It's All Relative* back in the nineties?' would get anyone, anyone at all, the grand tour. And sometimes dinner. And sometimes dessert. And sometimes breakfast."

"Oh." Preston gave her a long look. Leah stared back. "All right. Well. The killer wasn't here very long before the attack started. He—"

"—bashed her brains in with my Emmy." She turned to

Archer, whose eyes were wide and horrified. "Outstanding Guest Actress in a Comedy," she clarified. "I was ten. And my mother *hated* that I won. Of course." She turned back to Detective Preston. "And you're thinking it's difficult to believe a killer-by-chance just happened along last night and just happened to grope around and just happened to grab my Emmy and then happened to beat my mother to death with it."

"Okay, maybe that's—"

"Except she prominently displays it. Displayed, I mean." God, why was it so hard to remember that Nellie was now strictly past tense? How long had she wanted that to be the case? Now that it *was* the case, you'd think she would catch up. Sure, loved ones often spoke of the murder victim in the present tense, but Leah had never been a loved one. She had never even been a liked one. "It's the first thing you see when you walk into that room. She hated that I won, but later, when I had quit the business (again) it was the best way to prove she had been relevant. So she kept it where a guest couldn't help seeing it. So, in fact, it could be just chance."

"Ms. Nazir, I don't quite get what you're doing here—"

"I am helping you," she said coldly, "do your job. Please continue."

There was a short silence while Preston checked his notes. "Okay. The killer left while she was still alive. And we think he or she knew your mother was alive but wasn't too worried about it."

"Or was in a hurry?" she asked. "Because of the noise?"

"We're still working that. We figure she lived another fifteen minutes or so. We'll know for sure when the labs come back."

Ah. The labs. A medico-legal autopsy was mandated, as in

the case of any death thought to be criminal in nature. Which this certainly was. Even now, Nellie Nazir was cooling at the morgue in her body bag, her beautiful pale hands, with their long tapering nails, bagged to keep any evidence of her killer in place. She was waiting for a clinical pathologist to photograph her—her last photo shoot!—and then they would put her under an ultraviolet light to pick up any evidence not seen by the human eye. Then they would strip her

*("it's just nudity, darling. think of it as a documentary")*

and examine her wounds. They would weigh her

*("a moment on the lips, darling! you know how the rest of that goes")*

and measure her. Then they would prop her up with a body block, making the chest easier to open, and cut her with the standard Y-incision, which starts at the shoulders and plunges down past the belly button to her pubic bone. There won't be much blood, since her blood pressure is now (and forever) zero over zero.

They'll use shears to open her chest to get a good look at her heart and lungs. Which will be pristine—she took fanatical care of herself, as only the very vain can make the time for. When the rare part called for her to smoke, she strictly adhered to herbal cigarettes, and when not working wouldn't touch tobacco, alcohol, or red meat. She will be in perfect health for her autopsy.

They will examine her organs, make note of all wounds, all damage, obtain biological specimens for testing, take samples for toxicology tests, and examine the contents of her stomach. Knowing Nellie, her stomach likely contained a salad and maybe a chicken breast, washed down with glass after glass of milk.

*("Strong bones and teeth, darling, take care of them and they'll take care of you and don't roll your eyes at me, clichés are clichés because they are truth.")*

Finally, they'll examine her mother's brain, peeling her scalp away from her skull, then cutting the skull (likely with a Stryker saw) to expose the brain. After that, they'll put her back together again, exactly like Humpty Dumpty, except in her case . . .

"She'll be a gorgeous corpse."

"Pardon?" Detective Preston asked.

"Are you okay?" Archer asked in a low voice.

"I'm fine." She made a determined effort to stop picturing her mother's autopsy. "What you're telling me, Detective Preston, is what we already know: my mother lived long enough after her attack to call me."

"Yes, that's—"

"Twice." Beside her, Archer winced, no doubt recalling hearing "no wire hangers, ever!" while they were trying to hurt each other in the front seat of her car last night. "But she couldn't speak. And I—" Leah cut herself off and shrugged.

"And we know it wasn't your creepy ex-agent?" Archer asked, still sounding skeptical.

Leah shook her head. Tom Winn of Winner's Talent™ (ugh)? No. "No, remember—Tom was on a plane to Los Angeles when she and I last spoke."

Detective Preston looked up from his notes. "We'll check that, of course. And I thought you said your mother called you more than once."

"One of the times we last spoke," she corrected herself. "You have to understand, we have a difficult relationship. Had."

"Yes, I'm getting that impression." Preston managed that with a straight face.

Leah elaborated. "I did not love her. I did not like her. I did not tolerate her. We were done."

"Done, huh?" Preston took a long look around the richly appointed room, the piano, the art, the glossy, polished floors . . . all the wonders of the McMansion, the first of which could be noticed from the street, as Nellie had planned from the very beginning. Leah wondered if he thought he was being subtle. "So she disowned you?"

"I wish. I disowned *her.* The third to last time she called me last night, I told her we were finished, that I wanted nothing to do with her again. Again," she added. "I wanted nothing to do with her again, again."

"This wasn't the first time you disowned her?"

"Correct."

"And that was the third to last phone conversation."

"Correct."

Preston's demeanor was changing, and Leah wondered if it was another cop trick, designed to trip up a subject, or if she was actually seeing him wonder if she was a murderer. "And you're telling me you fought?"

"*I* fought. She was being her normal passive-aggressive self and pretending everything was super-duper fine. Neither of us touched each other. You will not find my skin cells beneath her fingernails."

"So the anger—it was all on one side."

"The acknowledged anger was all on my side, yes. My mother

would not admit she was angry with me, ever. At most she would voice disappointment." How Leah had lived to disappoint her. Hmm, was that some sorrow, at last? Was she a little sad at the thought that she would never disappoint her again? Was that mourning?

"And then?"

"She called again, and I didn't answer." *As I was far too busy trying to corrupt Archer Drake's morals, which were annoyingly concrete.* "And the third time, it was just . . ." Something in her throat; God, *why* was it so fucking dry in here? Her mother cranked the AC year-round, how was that for foolish and extravagant? Cranked it and so it was like the Sahara in there, if the Sahara was entirely contained in a McMansion. She barked an angry cough into her fist and finished. "Breathing. I could just hear her breathing over the phone."

"So your mother was breathing . . . like gasping? Panting?"

"Like the breathing exercises you do to improve your vocals."

"Your mother, dying from multiple head wounds, called you and did breathing exercises into your phone?"

Leah shrugged. Sure, if you didn't know Nellie, that would likely sound strange.

"And your phone is . . . ?"

"Broken." At his look, she elaborated. "When I got your voicemail I panicked and dropped my phone."

Preston took in her chilly demeanor, her eyes, which weren't welling with tears, her hands, which weren't shaking, and her face, which (most likely . . . she couldn't see herself, after all) wasn't pale. "You panicked? *You* panicked."

"Yes." Leah refused to believe that in the entirety of his career, Preston had never seen a loved one not fall apart at a murder scene. Humanity was an endless variety of good and bad, mostly bad. People reacted to loss in many different ways. On the other hand, if he was letting Aaron's life cloud his thinking . . .

"But even if my phone wasn't broken," she continued, shelving that thought for later, "it would only give you the times of the calls. Which you can get from the phone company or her phone, which I'm betting *isn't* broken."

"So during the last call, when your mom did vocal breathing exercises into your phone, you panicked."

"No, I panicked this morning when I listened to your first voicemail, Detective. As I told you."

"Oh." He consulted his notes again. "But you didn't come here right away. You went to your . . . uh . . ."

"Future boyfriend, eventual husband," Archer said, cheeks flushing just a bit. "We're preparing to fall in love once she tackles a few problems in her life. You know how it is."

"Not at all, actually." Preston turned back to Leah. "So you panicked, but only enough to go see your boyfriend."

"Yes, it was stupid."

"Stupid?"

*Argh. I know this is how they teach you to do it, all the boring repetition and the trick about repeating the last word in the witness's statement, but I honestly would rather be getting one of It's stupid clinic colonics right now.* "Yes, stupid. I thought you were telling me Archer had been hurt. I panicked and broke my phone when I thought Archer was hurt. I put one shoe on and drove to Archer's house and did a terrible parking job and left my keys in the ignition and the door open when I thought Archer. Was. Hurt."

He glanced at her feet. "Yeah, I was going to ask you about

that. But how would I have known to call you if Mr. Drake had been harmed?"

"You wouldn't. Which is why my reaction was . . . wait for it . . . stupid. As I said, I panicked. When people panic, they are not especially bright, do not think clearly, make foolish decisions, and we are all prone to it. Or so I am discovering this week. No need to look so skeptical, Detective."

"Was I?" he asked mildly, scribbling, scribbling.

"You know I'm capable of such behavior. Panicking. Overreacting. I . . ." She paused, gritted her teeth. ". . . blacked out for a bit. Earlier."

"It sure seemed like that's what you did." Unspoken, but she could read him like a chart: *convenient, too. The whole on-site team saw you go down, saw your brand-new lover oh-so-solicitously help you into another room where you could talk about God-knows-what until I followed.*

"All right. I see it now." *That is goddamned enough. Doing your job is one thing. Willfully blinding yourself is quite another.* Leah met his openly skeptical gaze, held his eyes. "It must be awful."

"What?"

"You know, but you don't know. You can't ever escape the feeling that no matter how much good you do, it will never be enough. And what's really maddening is you can't figure it out, and you're too scared to find an Insighter and ask."

He *looked* at her. "What."

"ReallynotthetimeLeah," Archer muttered in one breath.

"Because really, you don't want to know. What you did. Or didn't do. You dream about it, though, don't you?" she asked kindly. "And the dreams are like everything else. You can't ever tell anyone. Of course not. But don't worry, Detective Preston."

She dropped one eyelid in a slow wink. "Your secret is safe with me."

First thought: *That is an alarming shade of red he's turning. I wonder when he last had his blood pressure checked?*

Second thought: *Huh. I've never been arrested before. Is he arresting me because he thinks I killed Nellie, or because I've made him scared and angry? Either way: this will be interesting.* Better yet, it got her out of the room she hated above all others.

# THIRTY-THREE

Clusterfuck!

Total, utter clusterfuck. And all Archer could do was sort of stare, horrified, and be pulled in—sucked in—like Leah's rage and hurt was the damned tide and he was the hapless swimmer. And that made Detective Preston Jaws.

She'd been a block of ice once she recovered from her "it's not a faint, dammit!" It was funny that the one thing in all this awfulness, the one thing about the murder that threw Leah and freaked her out was the realization that her mom, the poster mom for selfish maternity, tried to *warn* her only daughter as she was dying.

Her mother's dying act had been selfless and Archer could see the exact second Leah made the connection; the color just *fell* out of her face and her eyes rolled up and then he was moving and sort of walking her out of the room, into the piano room. She never lost her feet but she wasn't exactly all there, either.

He'd made her sit on the nearest bench and just sort of held her wrist to check her pulse (ninety-plus, yikes) and stroked her hair away from her face until her eyes came back and she was glaring at him and batting his hands away. Relief? Putting it mildly. It had been damn near joyful to have Leah back to her old grumpy chilly self.

And then shit got *really* weird. Even for a murder scene. Even for a murder scene when your *mom* had been murdered with your Emmy from when you were a resentful, talented child actor. That Preston cop was telling her all sorts of awful things, things that would have made anyone else throw up or cry or both, and Leah just got icier and icier. Archer wanted nothing more than to get her the hell out of there, back to his house, where he could comfort her and maybe even get her to laugh and kiss her until they were dizzy, which probably wasn't the best way to deal with grief (if that's what Leah was even feeling) but it wasn't the worst, either.

And then it was like she was going out of her way to make the cop think she had guilty knowledge, when Archer *knew* she didn't. And she kept calling the cop Aaron for some reason, and then made a whole bunch of guesses about him, except they probably weren't guesses because by the time she was done Preston had the cuffs out.

"You can't arrest her for making you mad!" he yelped, torn between taking a swing at a cop and getting his own set of cuffs, or trying to stay calm so he could bail Leah out.

"No, but he can arrest me because I have motive, means, and opportunity," Leah told him, and the horrible hilarity of it was, she was trying to soothe him.

"But you were with me!"

"Yes, but we're each other's alibi." Soothe, soothe. "If one of us is the killer—"

"*What*?"

"—my alibi is worthless. Oh, and so is yours. Plus I was recently here; my prints will be here somewhere."

"You were her daughter! Of course your prints are here!"

He tried to beg her with his eyes. Leah liked his freak mismatched eyes, so he stared at her and thought really really hard: *Do something! Come on, Leah, be your brilliant self and read my mind.*

And she did.

"I do not deny it: I wanted her dead."

Just not the way he expected.

"Wanting her dead is not a motive!" Archer howled.

She blinked. "I'm pretty sure it is. Also, my mother died in the picture of health. If someone hadn't coshed her over the head with my Emmy, she could have lived for decades. Perhaps I was after her money. Which, the police will soon discover, is my money. She spent her life robbing me and my resentment is a matter of public record. I knew I should have told that stupid judge he used to be Lavinia Fisher."

"Leah, stop it!"

"What? I haven't said one thing that isn't the complete truth. The judge was stupid, and he did used to be the first female mass murderer. And of course, all the things I said about Nellie, and my relationship to her, are true."

"*Don't be . . .*" He stopped, tried to calm down, tried again, softer. "Don't be stupid."

"I'll be stupid whenever I like!" she snapped, a crack in her control showing at last. "You don't get to decide when I'm stupid. I decide when I'm stupid. You are not the boss of how and when I am stupid!"

"Do you hear yourself? This is nuts. Tell him you didn't kill her."

*And I thought it was weird when she stabbed me. That was the most normal interaction I've had with this woman. The stabbing!*

"Oh, that reminds me, the murder weapon: my Emmy. Come on." She glanced over her shoulder at Preston, who was cuffing her. "That's pretty indicative, don't you think? Symbolic of my crushing resentment, which I then used to crush her skull? It's pretty perfect."

"You have the right to remain silent," Preston said, but he was talking like he wasn't at all sure what he was saying. In fact, Preston looked like someone had hit *him* over the head with an Emmy. Just not repeatedly. There were three dangerous adults in the room (well, two at least) and none of them seemed to know what they were doing. Leah had that effect on people.

"Don't feel bad, Aaron." Leah actually sounded comforting now, instead of chilly. "It's not your fault that the Boston Strangler was able to kill many more women because you were an ineffectual crybaby."

"*Leah!*" Archer screamed, fingers plunging into his hair and yanking, hard.

"Don't mind him," Leah told the cop as he dragged her away. "He thinks I have it in me to be a good person. Isn't that hilarious?"

"Actually," Preston replied in a low voice, carefully steering her out of the room, "yeah."

# THIRTY-FOUR

"I've never had to do this before."

"What?"

"Bail someone out of jail."

Cat shrugged. "It's easy. It's just paperwork, right down to the money part. How much do you need?"

Appalled, Archer stood—no, practically leaped off the park bench. He'd watched them haul a weirdly cheerful Leah away, asked questions of the cops remaining at the scene, then came to the park to tell Leah's only friend what had happened. "I'm not here for a loan."

"Oh yeah?" She squinted up at him, deep brown eyes narrowed, one side of her mouth tipping up in a smirk. "You've got . . . hmm, let's see . . . fifteen percent of a six-figure bail bond to piss away?"

"Uh . . ." *Oh, shit.* "Six figures?"

"If they arrested her for aggravated homicide, which it sounds like they did, yep."

"Okay, I guess I *am* here for a loan."

"Mmmm. Might not need it. I'm betting that detective's boss is gonna look over the paperwork and have a chat with—what's his name?"

"Preston. Except Leah kept calling him Aaron. I guess he used to be related to the Boston Strangler."

"Trust Leah to *not* keep that to herself," Cat said dryly, and Archer barked laughter. "Okay, well. Here's how it goes: they would've arrested her and hauled her to jail, booked her. They would have taken her before the magistrate, but that's assuming they're really gonna stick with the homicide snatch. I don't think they will."

"Why? You weren't there, Cat. She practically dared them to arrest her."

Cat waved that away, then dug in one of her many sizeable tote bags and extracted a bag of carrots from the depths. She offered them to Archer, who declined with a head shake, then helped herself. Crunching, she continued. "Yeah, but they can't afford to piss off the Insighters. Leah's not popular, but she's generally acknowledged as the best. Her colleagues will get pissy about it, and that's gonna put pressure on the suits. The suits will pressure the cops, and shit flows downhill. The detective might let her go, or he'll knock the homicide charge down to disturbing the peace or some horseshit like that. In which case, bail's gonna be much cheaper. Since she was born here—"

"She was? But she lived in Hollywood all those years."

"Her mom was born here, Leah was born here. It was only after people kept telling Nellie how pretty her baby was that she hauled them to L.A. When Nellie's career went into the shitter, she came back. And that's important, because it might mean no bail is needed. Either way, you go to the jail, find out what the charges are, or if she's even still under arrest—it's too bad her phone's broke, but there's nothin' to be done about that right now—and if you can bail her out, you've just gotta sign a bunch of paperwork. You're legally responsible for getting her home, and for making sure she shows up for her court date. If there is one. Which hopefully not. I mean, she didn't kill her mom, right?"

"Right." At Cat's long, inscrutable look, he repeated himself. "Right! She honestly didn't, Cat. She was with me."

"All night?"

"I wish," he sighed. Then, "Her mom called Leah while she was dying. Leah didn't do it."

"That's interesting."

"Why?"

"Well. Who did? It wasn't you, and it wasn't me. You'll have to take my word on that one," she added dryly. "Or not . . . last night I was at the Four Seasons, and I had dinner in the hotel restaurant. The receipt will be time-stamped. Depending on what the ME decides is the TOD, that might clear me."

"We don't think it was you," Archer said, horrified.

"No? That's not very smart, Arch." Cat's dark gaze was cool, almost clinical. "You liked me right away, but people always do. It's why I went into politics. Some people, they can *make* you like them. It's a knack, like being able to raise one eyebrow. I can do that. But you don't know the real me. You know what you've seen and heard, which isn't much, and you know whatever Leah told you."

"Did you really lose your job because you weren't a bigot?"

"Yeah. Check the headlines from back then if you've got

nothing better to do with your life. Anyway, it's foolish to dismiss suspects because you like them. But you're right, I didn't do it. Although I don't give much of a rat's ass that she's dead. In fact, if she'd been murdered a decade or two earlier, your would-be girlfriend wouldn't be the fucked-up future recluse we know and love."

"Okay." Archer was thinking that he needed to spend a lot more time in the park listening to Cat's Theories of Life and Politics. And yeah—he *did* like her. He just hadn't known Cat had *made* him like her. "What else?"

"It wasn't me, it wasn't you, it wasn't the agent. It wasn't Leah. So who'd kill a has-been B-list actress? And in such a wicked nasty way? Maybe it's the guy who keeps killing Leah. Maybe he's trying something new this life. Or maybe he can't find Leah, so he—no, that doesn't make sense, if he could find It, he could find Leah."

"Yeah." Archer hadn't even had time to consider any of the things Cat had instantly thought of. His respect amped up a few more notches. "Who would? And why kill Nellie at all? She was a threat to exactly nobody. Not even Leah."

"Yeah, well." Cat crunched a final carrot and put the bag away. "If you knew why, you'd know who. Get going," she ordered, "and let me know if you need a wire."

*Ah, yes. I'll let the homeless rich woman in the park know if I need a loan to bail out my future girlfriend for not killing her mother. What has happened to my life?*

He didn't know. And there wasn't time to wonder about it now. He took Cat's advice, and got going.

# THIRTY-FIVE

Archer was more than a little nervous about walking into the CPD to pick up Leah. Or bail her out. Or maybe only visit her. It brought back memories of his childhood. Of course, his bad memories were the equivalent of skinned knees and neighborhood bullies compared to hers of shattered trust and exploitation and tampon commercials.

*Shattered trust and exploitation? You're losing it, pal.*

Well, sure. That seemed about right, after the week they'd had. His inner voice always correctly deduced when he was losing it, or when he was cock-blocking himself, but the rest of the time it was unhelpfully silent.

Speaking of unhelpful: the CPD website. Nothing there about how to bail someone out; nothing about which building to go to or department to call. But if he wanted to take the Police Entry Level Exam, he was all set. And if he wanted to go to a CAPS meeting (whatever that was; the website never really explained), he was good to go. Also, if he wanted to apply for a building permit, he knew exactly how to go about it. The mayor of Boston had been much more helpful.

So here he was, after another Cat consultation, parking his car in the ramp across the street, plunging through the front doors, and nervously following signs directing him to what was euphemistically called the detainee station (which made it sound like they were all waiting together for a bus or something and no laws of any kind had been broken).

Along the way he read posters helpfully explaining that the Chicago Police Department was the second largest (after the NYPD) local law enforcement agency in the country, and also one of the oldest. And also, Sergeant Thomas is starting up another softball league so you should definitely call his cell if you're interested. And it's Patrolman Roger's birthday today and there's cake in the briefing room.

*You'd think they'd make a sign that would handle helping citizens bail out other citizens.*

He realized he had no actual problem with the Chicago Police; his nerves were getting the better of him. Oh, and also the consistently bad memories of his childhood. And then there was the niggling fear that Leah had pissed off one or two or all of her cellmates and been beaten to death, not unlike her mother.

Leah was charming and likeable, but you kinda had to work for it. It was there. Um, under all the layers of blank hostility.

*Oh please please don't let her be dead or battered. Oh, man, they probably took her bra knives. She'd be helpless without her bra knives!*

No checks, the posters told him. No money orders. Bank or cashier's checks only, presented during normal banking hours.

Because apparently there was nothing more annoying than being presented with a cashier's check for low five figures at 2:00 a.m. You could pay cash, by which they meant credit card (not cash) or debit card (also not cash, but no one had told the CPD). He had his debit card, and a balance of $614.23. And Cat, who would wire five figures if he called and asked.

("Of course a homeless rich ex-mayor of Boston has a cell phone," she'd said irritably when he'd expressed surprise. "Third graders have them. What exactly is your day job again?")

It would take up to about two hours to complete . . . whatever it was that needed completing. He still wasn't sure if Leah was under arrest for murder or if Detective Preston had been brow-beaten by a suit into dropping the charges. He figured, if nothing else, he could at least find that much out.

Ah! Here was the large desk, behind which sat a sergeant of some kind. Behind him, he could see rows of desks, and hear ringing phones, and see people going back and forth, some in uniform and some not, and here and there people were in handcuffs, but most of them weren't, so that was encouraging. It didn't look scary. Just busy, like any office on a weekday.

There wasn't a line, so he could go right up to the desk sergeant, whom TV had led him to believe would be a harried, heavyset, sassy African-American woman who was busy but also cared deep down inside. The reality was a heavyset white guy who looked like an accountant who had just heard the IRS had no interest in any of his clients.

"Well, hi there!" Bright hazel eyes blinked up at him; the man's light brown hair was neatly combed. His uniform was crisp and clean; his badge gleamed. The man radiated good fellowship; Archer was dazzled in spite of himself. "Help you?"

"I hope so. I'm here to see Leah Nazir. Or try to bail her out. Or look at her through plate glass while we press our hands together like they do in prison on TV." Given his family history, it was absurd how all his prison knowledge came from *Sons of Anarchy* reruns. Ooh, that Gemma! What a wonderful bitch.

The cop who looked like a cheerful accountant blinked faster. "Leah Nazir?"

"Yes."

"Ah."

"Yes."

He held up a finger. "Just a moment." Then he left his desk, something they weren't allowed to do on TV but was apparently okay in real life.

Archer waited by the abandoned desk and fretted. What did "ah" mean, coming from a cop?

*"Ah, that Leah Nazir. Yep, she's dead."*

*"Ah, Leah? Nazir? I think she escaped, sowing death and destruction on her way out . . . I'll go check."*

*"Ah. Hmm. You're a friend? Of Leah Nazir? Yeah, you're under arrest. Come along quietly or we'll all shoot you."*

*What if she was fated to meet her killer in a holding pen? What if the whole path of this life was to put her in lockup at just the wrong time with just the wrong person? What if she's bleeding out? What if she's dead? All our stupid little meetings, trying to figure out who her murderer is this time around, playing at detective, and she could be dead right now. And in a way, that would be Nellie's fault this life, too.*

He rubbed the heels of his palms over his eyes and shook his head. This was useless and worse than useless. The desk sergeant would know where she was. Leah was alive, somewhere in the building. Right? Right.

*Come on, buddy. How long does it take to get an update? Hurry up or my paranoia will have its way with me again. Where IS he?*

But then! Before the desk sergeant could return! There she was, walking toward him—except she didn't see him. She was walking next to (yikes!) Detective Preston, whose head was bent attentively toward her, clearly soaking in every word.

". . . for God's sake, he was your beloved big brother. He saved you from countless beatings, he protected you in the face of your mother's helplessness and who *wouldn't* worship someone like that? He never showed you the side his victims saw and he never would. Do you think I would be this fucked up if I'd had a protective older sibling? You can't blame the man you were for the dead; that was on Albert. All of it: on Albert. The man doing the actual murdering. If, in your other life, you had gone to the police and said, 'Hey, I'm pretty sure my brother is the Boston Strangler,' you *know* what would have happened. They would have had the cuffs on *you* in about five seconds . . . and that's if they believed you at all."

Detective Preston nodded, but Leah barely noticed.

"You have been carrying all that around, and for what? You're one of the good guys this time. And what if you were a farmer, and not a detective? There still would be nothing to make up for. You could, I don't know, milk your cows in peace. Or whatever you would do if you were a farmer. That old life is done. I insist you stop having nightmares about it immediately."

Not bothering to listen to his response, Leah looked up and her eyes widened when she saw Archer waiting for her. Then they narrowed, and for a heart-stopping moment Archer thought she didn't want him there.

But that wasn't it. Instead, when they walked right up to him,

Leah again turned to Detective Preston and said, "It was unprofessional and cruel to bring this up outside of a session, in your workplace, in front of other people. I have no excuse. It was unacceptable. I . . ." Archer could almost hear her teeth grinding together. ". . . apologize."

Preston barely seemed to notice; his thoughts were miles away, possibly imagining his life as a farmer. He nodded almost absently. "That's fine; it was just as inappropriate for me to arrest you. I didn't really think you killed your mother; I was upset by what you said. My boss and your boss are insisting we play nice, so let's just do that."

"All right."

"Are you okay?" Archer asked in a low voice. Leah seemed unbeaten. Unstabbed. Un-bleeding. And alive! Even better. In fact, if you didn't know, you wouldn't be able to tell she'd been cooling her heels in the hoosegow for the last few hours. He wondered if it was inappropriate to ask her if any *Chained Heat*–type stuff had gone on. He also thought it was adorable that she still had only the one shoe. He thought the cops might have at least offered her a flip-flop. "Leah?"

"Oh, sure." She waved it all away: the arrest, booking, brief imprisonment. "It was interesting. I've never been on that side of the bars before. And some of the other women were interesting. I'll have stories to tell my colleagues. Too bad I loathe my colleagues."

"Mr. Drake." Detective Preston seemed to notice him for the first time. "Ah."

*What is it with cops and "Ah"? Do they mean to make it sound terrifying?* "Hey. Glad you two worked it out."

"Yeah." Preston was staring at him, and given the man was

investigating a horrific murder, Archer found his regard more than a little unnerving. "That's interesting. About your family history."

"Oh, here we go," he sighed. He glanced at Leah. "There's really no way to make this not sound awful. And I promise I was going to tell you. You have to admit it's been a crazy week."

"What?" Leah was looking from him to Preston and back again. "Oh, God. What is it now? What horrific dreadful thing is going to happen now?"

"If this is the Archer Drake, the only son of one William T. Drake—"

"The detective is coyly leading up to the fact that my dad's in federal prison for murder." After a beat, he added helpfully, "He didn't do it. If that helps."

# THIRTY-SIX

"You stabbed me," Archer said for the third time, "which I generously overlooked—"

"Stalker," Leah said as if talking to the air. "Stalker hired by my mortal enemy."

"Okay, that's a fair point, but you're breaking up with me?"

"How can I do that? We were never boyfriend and girlfriend."

"We were negotiating, dammit!"

"A month ago I didn't even know your name. You, of course, knew mine. Because, as earlier: stalker."

"I let you feel me up in your car!"

"Oh, 'let' me?"

"I gave you my innocence! Repeatedly! Which wasn't part of the plan except you've got great hands and oh my God, your mouth . . ."

"That is quite enough about my mouth."

"You used your sexuality as a weapon! And now, after you've callously gotten what you wanted—"

"What did I want, exactly?"

"—you're breaking up with me because my dad *didn't* kill my uncle? Cat will understand where I'm coming from," he added darkly. "She, like me, was vilified for shit she didn't do. Or people related to her didn't do."

"I'm breaking up with you—dammit!" As this was all happening outside a curiously empty desk (on TV the desk sergeants were always at their desks) while Detective Preston looked on with the unapologetic air most cops have ("yeah, sorry, I know this is none of my business, but you'd be surprised how often 'none of my business' turns into 'totally my business,' so I'm just going to linger and shamelessly eavesdrop, and sorry in advance") while witnessing heated exchanges, she plucked Archer by the elbow, nodded a terse good-bye to a bemused Preston (who turned out to be almost okay given his previous life nonsense and propensity to yank the handcuffs off his hip before he had all the facts), and marched Archer out of the police station. As she expected, he bitched incessantly, and loudly, and didn't appear to give a single shit about the stares and interest they were attracting.

Until then, the arrest-jail nonsense had been almost . . . not fun, but . . . interesting? Alarming yet intriguing? She wasn't sure there was a word for it. She had never been frightened. She had never felt threatened. Mostly she watched and listened and, when she thought it was appropriate, commented. As at work, when she felt it was appropriate to comment, and when the person she spoke to felt it was appropriate, were often different. As at work, she didn't especially care.

She had started on Preston in the car on the way to the, as Archer put it, hoosegow.

"All right. Here is my confession." When she caught Preston's startled gaze in the rearview mirror, she continued. "That was inappropriate. I should have prepared you before confronting you with past-life stressors."

He made a strange noise from the driver's seat, an amalgam of a sigh and an annoyed grunt. "That's not even close to the confession I was hoping for."

"Yes, well." She watched the perfectly manicured lawns roll by, somewhat startled to observe that they looked exactly the same to her even though she was under arrest for murdering her mother. Was this her dearest dream or most awful nightmare? She had imagined Nellie dead so many times. She had imagined killing her so many times. Never by Emmy-induced head trauma, though. She had to give the killer points for symbolic originality. "I can't oblige you on that one, sorry to say. But as to the other matter—"

"You're going," he muttered, occasionally glancing at her in the mirror, "to keep talking at me about this. Aren't you?"

"Yes, I am. Because it's important, Detective."

"How is *not* convincing me you didn't kill the mother you admitted wishing dead important? How is anything else we could be discussing more important than you getting clear?"

"Sorry, I misspoke. It's not important to *me*."

"Aw, hell. Look, there's nothing wrong with me."

*Excellent.* He was ignoring Cop 101, to wit, don't engage with the psycho in the backseat. She had worried he would blithely ignore her, or feign interest while toting up an imaginary scoreboard in the middle of his brain (Reasons I Can Justify Arresting That Pain in My Ass Leah Nazir).

"Nothing," he said again, as if saying a word meant anything, or changed anything.

"Of course there is."

He sighed. "The polite thing to do—"

"Don't waste my time with Etiquette 101. You're arresting people for homicide because they scared you and pissed you off—"

"You're half right," he retorted, managing to drive steadily out of pure force of will.

"—which will not be at all good for your career. And honestly, Detective, aren't you tired of being afraid of not knowing? You've been worrying for years that you feel guilty because you were a killer of some kind. Well, you weren't. Don't you want to know who was? There's a reason you're a homicide detective instead of a cable repairman."

"That's not relevant to your mother's murder."

"Of course it isn't." He sighed, possibly in relief. "Except for the whole false arrest debacle." He groaned, probably not in relief.

"I don't want to discuss this."

"But it's a long dull drive." She guessed. She had no idea which precinct/ideal body dump site he was taking her to. "And I *do* want to discuss it."

"Change of subject."

"But it's so foolish, especially when you consider how close you are to putting the nightmares of your childhood behind you."

"Change of subject *right now*."

"You're right. There is one more option." *You realize you're antagonizing a grown man with a gun, yes? Have you considered the fact that he might be your killer?* Leah ignored her inner voice, which often made cowardly suppositions. Here was a man who had a problem she could assist him with. If he was her killer, so be it. At least she wouldn't wonder anymore.

*Oh but Archer . . .*

She shoved that thought away. "You could go the other way, I guess."

"Miss Nazir, I do not fucking want to talk about this!"

Hearing a sworn officer of the law shriek in a closed vehicle as she sulked in the backseat with her hands cuffed behind her was a definite first. Oh, the colleagues she loathed would *adore* this. Perhaps she would embellish the story for them: "And then he perpetrated police brutality all over my head and shoulders which stung horribly." Mmmm . . . better not. In addition to being illegal, false allegations of police brutality were impolite, and sometimes led to murderous misunderstandings.

"All right," she said after a long moment in which a) she was intrigued and b) Detective Preston was grateful. "I only have one thing to add—stop that," she scolded as Preston banged his head on the steering wheel. It was fortunate they were at a red light. And that the horn was located elsewhere in the vehicle. "You'll kill us both, or give yourself a nasty headache, or both, or you'll only kill you, or you'll only kill me. All those results are unacceptable."

"I. Am. Begging. You."

"My last comment on the subject under discussion—"

"It's not! Under discussion, I mean."

"—is that none of it was your fault. I implied as much because I'm a bitch, for which I have apologized."

"You didn't, actually. Oh my Christ, we're still talking about this."

"Hmm." That brought Leah up short. "Well, I meant to apologize. It was on my list of things I meant to discuss. But as I was saying, none of it was your fault; it was all on Albert DeSalvo."

True to her word, she dropped the subject and contented herself with looking out the window and humming "No Light, No Light" under her breath. Florence and the Machine was one of the more vastly underrated musical acts in the history of music. She wondered if Detective Preston took requests.

At the station she had been booked, which was a series of paperwork, followed by her mug shot, and then her fingerprints were taken (no ink required in the twenty-first century and she was a bit let down, having been looking forward to the drama of ink-stained fingertips), scanned, and put into the System, which, as an Insighter, was redundant, as upon licensing all Insighters were routinely printed and photographed, new photos required every five years.

Then she had been escorted to a spotless, well-lit holding cell

*(does television get* everything *wrong?)*

populated by half a dozen other women of various ages, conventional attractiveness, skin color, and clothing choices. Per television, they should all be prostitutes and/or meth addicts.

Only one of them looked like a prostitute (Leah did not approve of tube tops on anyone, never mind an overweight, sallow-skinned woman in her late thirties) and she was the shoplifter. The others were:

1) Karen the Boyfriend Beater. Karen was a gorgeous young lady ("Young lady? Jeez. I'm twenty-nine, okay, and when I was fourteen, I helped my uncle set the Piggly Wiggly on fire, so 'lady' is off, too.") with skin so dark it had mahogany undertones. She tolerated her boyfriend's gambling habit, his inability to keep a steady job (which was hilarious, as he was a temp worker, so his steady job was to not keep a steady job), and his unfortunate propensity for anal sex. ("That doesn't sound so bad," Renee the Shoplifter said. "*Only* anal sex." "Oh.")

Karen worked both her jobs with an often-throbbing backside, but when she objected to his $1,000 wager on the outcome of an upcoming Cubs game, he backhanded her. Karen's response to this was to hoist a knee into his testicles and, while he writhed and sniveled on the kitchen tile, beat him repeatedly in the face with a container of Clorox wipes. In true douchebag fashion, he called the police.

"That makes so much sense," Leah decided after hearing the lurid and hilarious tale.

"Thanks!" Karen smiled, pleased. "My mom, she said the same thing, and all my sisters did, too."

"Yes, well. You, and they, used to be comfort girls in Japan. *Chinese* comfort girls in Japan," she emphasized, assuming they would catch the reference. "Sometimes comfort girls volunteered. You didn't. So in this life, you're not interested in tolerating male bullshit."

"That's creepy," Karen announced, "but you're pretty good. Normally I'd be super pissy about being called a hooker. No offense," she told Celia the Hooker.

"No, no." Celia waved it away. "S'fine."

2) Terry the Sociopathic Cat Cooker. Terry did not like being on the wrong end of unrequited love. Not that what she felt for her boyfriend was love, unrequited or otherwise. "He's the only one that can make me come," she explained.

"Who can make you come."

"He can. Like I said."

"No, you said 'he's the only one *that* can make me come' and it's '*who* can make me come.'" At Terry's long, unsettling stare (unsettling to someone unused to staring down socios once or twice a month), she added, "Never mind. Continue."

"Right. Anyways—"

*Good God. Anyway! Singular! If she says "towards" or "amongst" they'll have to arrest me for homicide. Again.*

"—he can't make me feel that good all the time and then just take it away. He's too big for me to hurt directly, so Muffin had to go."

"He can, though," Celia said. Leah concurred, but did not waste time or breath agreeing. "Just like you've got the right to dump anybody you want."

"Yeah, that's a totally different thing."

"It's not," Celia tried again, to the same effect.

"And then that crybaby hostess calls the cops! Like Muffin muffins would be so much worse than the usual crap coming out of that kitchen." Terry had indulged her anti-cat politics at her (former, Leah assumed) place of employment, Dan's Diner. "Cat's totally fine. Okay, a little singed. But otherwise fine. It's not like I would have really done it."

"Why lie to *us*, Terry?" Celia wondered. Oh, she was

adorable. Leah assumed it was either a) the sociopath's instinctive, perpetual habit of lying even when it was easier to tell the truth, or b) television's portrayal of what happened to those in jail who became, as John Cusack put it, "garrulous in the company of thieves." Hmm. Is that why she was so taken with Archer? He did remind her of Cusack in *Better Off Dead*, a bit, but not, thank heavens, Cusack in *The Raven*.

"So, what is it? Who'd I used to be?"

Leah shrugged. "You were a sociopath then, and you're a sociopath now." Déjà vu. She'd said that earlier to Chart #6116.

"Yeah, I figured." Terry preened a bit, ignoring everyone's tandem eye rolls.

*How I loathe that sociopathy now has cultural cache.*

3) Brienne the Shoplifter. Brienne alternately claimed entrapment, absentmindedness, and drunken intent. "It can happen to anybody!" she protested. "I was thinking about the rest of my errands and took it without thinking."

"Brienne."

"You can't tell me people don't do that every damn week in this country."

"Brienne."

"It was *one* thing."

"It was a ten-speed bicycle from Wal-Mart."

She threw up her hands. "Without thinking! Can happen to anyone!"

"For God's sake."

She dropped her hands back to her lap, a petite blonde who

could not pull off a tube top. "So what's the scoop? What's my backstory?"

"I have no idea." At the other woman's glare, Leah added, "Sorry. Don't believe what you see on TV; Insighting doesn't explain everything. Sometimes people do silly things." And that, too, sparked déjà vu; it reminded her of Archer. Although these last several days, few things did *not* remind her. How irritating, while also comforting. "If you were my patient, I'd have to put you on reindyne and we'd likely have to do a few sessions. And even then I might not be able to help you." *And regardless, you would be responsible for your actions in this life, whoever you were in another life.*

4) Charlie the Scofflaw. Charlie, the oldest in their group, in her early fifties, was a beautifully dressed woman with skin like hot chocolate with lots of milk, a fifty-dollar manicure, a hundred-dollar haircut, and thirty-eight unpaid tickets. She was waiting to be bailed out by her assistant, or for the mayor to hear of her predicament and do some arm-twisting. At Leah's curious glance, she shook her head.

"Sorry, did you want me to do something?"

"That's okay." Charlie tried a smile, but wouldn't meet Leah's gaze. "I'd rather you didn't."

"That works well, since I can't see you."

She shrugged and examined her long, elegant nails. "No, I wouldn't expect you could."

"At all."

"Don't worry." This time the smile was a bit more real. "It's not contagious."

"Actually it's interesting. Maybe only to me," she added, "but you're the second life-blinder I've met this month. My boyfr— my stabbing vic— My future lover . . . well, hopefully; he is proving a tough nut to crack, no pun intended. Stop laughing at me, Celia, and yes, I'm aware there are multiple layers to that comment. You don't—"

"You said the cops think you killed your mom! *And* you stabbed someone?"

"The one has nothing to do with the other, and it's rude to interrupt. Anyway, I can't see *him*, either. I thought it would be creepy and unsettling, but it's . . ." She had to think about it, something she had not allowed herself to do as of yet. She had outstanding excuses to put off examining her feelings, her mother's murder holding pride of place on the list, but she also understood they were only that: excuses.

"It's nice," she finally decided. "He doesn't expect anything from me. No offense," she added as she saw a few of the women frown, "because you didn't, either. I more or less forced myself on you."

"Yeah," Terry said. "We're the victims."

"No one who had to be forcibly prevented from microwaving their boyfriend's cat unto death gets to claim that status."

"You don't know what it's like to be me."

"I know exactly what it's like to be you," Leah replied, bored. She turned back to Charlie. "May I ask a personal question?" Without waiting for an answer, she continued. "You seem like your life is in order, judging superficially by your clothing and accessories and lovely manicure and diction. You're successful on your own? It's not from marrying well?"

"I run a consulting firm." Charlie's voice was as stunning as she was, rich and dark like pricey chocolate. It wasn't unlike verbal velvet.

That gave her pause. "Consulting firm" could be anything from a food truck empire to the mafia, but Leah had no interest in quibbling. "And you never thought that your inability to see what happened in your life before, that never held you back. Right?"

"Of course not. What matters is . . ." She trailed off.

"What you do in this life." That sounded like a sufficient cliché. But the thing about clichés is, as Nellie had pointed out, they are truth. "It works both ways, doesn't it? A lack of previous life knowledge can be considered crippling by some—" *My entire profession, for example. Me, earlier this month.* "—but as freedom for others. There's not one thing to hold you back, yes?"

"Just me," Charlie replied, and they shared a smile like it was a sweet secret. "And I don't think I'm blind. I think I'm *rasa*."

That made Leah's smile drop off. "Oh, I don't—ah—interesting."

The woman gave her a level, unblinking look. "You don't believe it."

"I'm not your Insighter," she hedged like a craven, cringing coward.

"And you're too polite to tell me I'm full of shit." She glanced around the cell, a pointed but silent reminder that Leah was outnumbered. "Or too cautious."

"Is there a way to answer you without upsetting you?"

She smiled. "It *does* happen, you know. You, especially, would know."

Not really. Not for decades upon decades. As with religious miracles, the further past the Age of Enlightenment society crawled, the less often miracles were acknowledged. The chances of a random *rasa* being really, truly *tabula rasa* were the same as the image of the Virgin Mary in a basement water stain being an actual sign from God. It wasn't a miracle, it was simulacra.

"It doesn't matter," Charlie finished. "I know what I know."

"Then let's leave it at that."

"Let's."

5) Celia the Hooker. Leah had met more than one in her professional capacity, but not one so thoroughly undamaged, unashamed, and indifferent to Leah's services. "Don't worry about it," she said after the other girls had begged Leah to, as Terry put it, "Insight the shit out of us!" "I'm fine on my end."

"But don't you want to—"

"Tom Mulligan."

Leah blinked. "Who is Tom Mulligan? Besides you, of course."

"A regular guy. Nice childhood, nice college, got a nice job, married a nice girl, had nice kids." Celia smiled a little. "Died a nice death at home, at age seventy-two, holding his wife's hand. Cancer. He blew off chemo the third time; he felt the radiation was making him feel much worse than no radiation."

"Imagine that."

The other woman's smile widened. "Yeah, crazy talk, right? That radiation can hasten your death? Anyway. I'm not in the second-oldest profession—I'm pretty sure agriculture was the first—because I was raped by an older brother or because I used to be Anne Boleyn. These were my choices." She shrugged. "It's boring."

"You're not boring." Though it sounds as though Tom Mulligan was. Leah respected Celia's wishes and did not express aloud the sentiment that Celia's choices brought her to a Chicago jail cell in the middle of the day, something Tom Mulligan never experienced. "But it's nice to have someone prove what I always say. That we didn't all used to be famous people. Sometimes we were just John Smith. Or Tom Mulligan."

"None of this is helping me with my problem," the sociopath interrupted, and Leah had to laugh, because the thing was, Terry truly felt that sense of being wronged. Her sociopathy provided gargantuan levels of entitlement. It was never, ever her fault, she deserved everything she desired, and she believed that catechism the way the pope believed in tithing. Leah knew people felt sorry for people like Terry ("Oh but their lives are so empty since they can only love themselves and they're forever chasing highs and never holding on to them so they're always unfulfilled poor deluded creatures") but Leah never bothered. People so ruthlessly set on forwarding their own self-interest needed no one's pity.

So jail had been interesting. Just when they decided to play "weirdest place you've ever done it" (Celia was disqualified, and asked to be the judge), along came Detective Preston, wearing an unmistakable "just got chewed out by my boss" expression. He had let her out, then took the time to walk her out. If he could be gracious in defeat, Leah could be gracious in entitled bitchiness, and gave him a proper apology. He seemed to appreciate it, and she was gratified to see he seemed to be paying attention to her words. Time, of course, would tell.

And then Archer.

And then Archer.

*And then Archer.*

# THIRTY-SEVEN

"You're going back to your life, Archer." Leah spoke with a firmness he was sure she didn't feel. "And I'm going back to mine."

He spoke without thinking, and wasn't sorry. "You don't have a life and you *are* my life."

"Stop it," she said absently, looking for a cab.

"*You* stop it, I'll drive you home, obviously."

"No. And where the hell are the cabs? I can't be the only newly released detainee in the history of Chicago to leave a police station and require a ride."

"You're not listening. I'll give you a ride and you're my life." *Nope, still not sorry.*

"You sound like a Hallmark movie. Is it intentional?"

He was now a tiny bit sorry, and pulled up short at that—she'd been tugging him by the elbow out of the police station and onto the sidewalk, and they were both blinking at each other in the sudden sunshine. "You're not breaking up with me—"

She made an impatient gesture, the kind busy restaurant patrons make when they're asked if they want dessert and they don't; they're in a rush for the bill. "We've been over this. Several seconds ago, remember? I cannot break up with someone I'm not dating. Now if you'll excuse me, I have a funeral to plan." She looked like she wasn't at all sure how to feel about that. "Run along."

He scowled at her. "I'm older than you, for Christ's sakes, don't dismiss me like a kid off to naptime." Anger deepened his voice, but his crossed arms probably showed his stress. *Oh God she's doing it she's freaked she can't see me and freaked my dad's in prison and freaked because her mom was murdered and oh God I can't let her do this I won't let her do this.*

"Older. Hmm." Leah's eyes were tipped up in thought. "I always seem to forget. And then I remember, and it goes on the list."

"List?"

"The list I've been compiling of all the reasons you would be an incompatible intercourse partner."

"If you're gonna call me your 'intercourse partner,' we should definitely break up," he said at once, then slapped his forehead. "Argh, see? The worst has happened. I've gone and said something I can't take back."

"Stop hiding behind humor to cover your anxiety."

"I'll hide behind whatever I want to cover my anxiety," he snapped back.

Leah blinked, but went on. He was pretty sure she would go

on if he had a heart attack on the spot. "Speaking of the worst, you need to vanish from my life now."

He nodded like she'd said something he agreed with. She hadn't, but this—this he could work with, at least. "I don't blame you for being upset, but I swear to you, I was going to tell you about my dad. Nellie knew and it didn't bother her, and so much has happened this week I never had a chance to bring it up."

"I made a list in jail, all the excuses not to think about what these last weeks have meant, and realized making a list of reasons why you put off something unpleasant is proof of cowardice. And it's not about your father. Or Nellie wouldn't have given a shit."

"Of course it is!" he snapped. Then, "What?"

"Of course my mother knew your family's history; she would have checked it out. Remember, in her mind she was a huge celebrity and that's what a huge celebrity would do. So she knew, she just did not give a shit, which is what I'm ninety-five percent sure I'll be chiseling onto her tombstone. Ugh."

She slapped a hand over her eyes and wouldn't look at him. "I've been trying to suppress the memory but I just realized I'll eventually have to go to the playing of her will. Her *video* will, because of course she would never refuse the opportunity to perform. If she's wearing the birthday outfit with all the feathers, I will somehow reanimate her corpse and then kill her all over again." She took her hand away and speared him with her shark's eyes. Cold. Nobody home behind them. "You were perfect for her. You aren't perfect for me."

"You're wrong." He stood quietly on the sidewalk, ignoring the stares as people streamed by. "You're not dumping me because of my murdered uncle, are you? And you don't think I killed your mom." No. Stupid to even consider that for a moment. Who would know better than the maddening creature before him that you weren't what your parent was? It hadn't given a shit, and Leah didn't, either.

That was worse. That made it all so much worse.

"We have nothing in common."

"We both think you can be kind of bitchy," he suggested.

"Very well, we have one thing in common. That, and our continual need for oxygen to survive. And you're far too stubborn."

"Oh my God, the pot has spoken! You don't fool me at all, Leah Nazir. It's the life-blind thing, isn't it? You thought you could handle it and you can't, so you're pitching me over the side."

"That's not it," she said at once, so he recognized the lie.

"So you're not just chilly and distanced, you're a bigot, too."

"I am not, in other lives I've been African-American, Korean, Chinese—I can't afford to be a bigot, I'm in glass houses all day long."

"You are, but not for the reason you think." He was starting to get *very* angry and put his hands behind his back so he wouldn't be tempted to choke her. "You hide there. You like it there. You're always a nobody, whether you're slicing off Anne Boleyn's head or watching the revolution burn through a royal family."

"Irrelevant."

"Ha! You're fine watching history instead of making it. You're fine with everything. Look, Leah, there's nothing wrong with keeping your head down, which in your case resulted at least once in keeping your head. If more people followed that example, you'd have less clients."

"Fewer."

"What?"

"I'd have fewer clients."

"Forget it!" He stuck a finger under her nose and shook it. "I refuse to find the Grammar Police thing sexy right this minute but might later! As I was saying! You're so used to being on the sidelines in past lives, you can barely participate in your current one. I might not agree being life-blind is *blind*, but you refuse to see that always being on the outside isn't healthy, either. And the thought of admitting you need someone, it's fucking paralyzing, isn't it?"

"Don't try to make this a commitment phobia," she said sharply. "If anything I'm phobophobic."

"You don't like having your picture taken? I'm not trying to be funny!" he yelped, holding out his hands to placate her. "I have no fucking idea what you're talking about."

"Also part of the problem," she muttered. "It's fear of having a phobia."

"Well, that's just *great*. Of course you do. Or of course you are—do *not* fucking correct my grammar on that one. You're the planet's best Insighter—"

"Actually, Moira McKinnen in Edinburgh is probably the planet's best."

"Please shut up, sweetie. You spend your time helping people see their past fears, screwups, and deaths."

"I'm aware of my own job description, Archer." But he saw it at once; her sharp tone was hiding her unease. He was getting to her and he thought he knew what button he was pushing.

*Are we really thrashing this out on a public sidewalk with dozens of witnesses streaming by on either side of us?*

*Yep.*

"You help clients you view only as medical charts see themselves make the same lethal mistakes over the centuries, and then you help them fix it. Sure, it's a noble calling and all, but sometimes, no question, it gets old. Jaded comes with the territory. As does phobophobia, sometimes. But it doesn't have to define you!"

"Archer," she said, her voice low and sorrowful, "it does define me. It *isn't* just a job. I'm also possibly a thanataphobe." He must have looked helpfully blank, because she elaborated. "Fear of death."

He threw his hands in the air. "Well, yeah! This goes back to what I was talking about! If I'd been murdered a dozen times, I'd be afraid of death, too."

"But I shouldn't be." Her tone—he actually wished she would go back to shouting. She just sounded so young and lost—like a girl who'd lost a mom she *loved*, as opposed to losing It. "I know I'll come back again. Except—" She cut her gaze and looked away from him. "What if I don't? One of these lives might be my last and I'll never know why. I'll never get another chance to fix things. Or worse—what if I come back like—like—"

He took a breath. Let it out slowly. "Like me?"

She said nothing.

"That," he said, "could be a blessing. You guys are so busy feeling sorry for people like me, it hasn't occurred to any of you that a person who has the experience of one measly lifetime can be emotionally and psychologically stronger than someone busily screwing up life number xix. Don't you get it? We can be like that because we *have* to be. We can't hit rewind a hundred times until we figure out our—I dunno"—he groped for something that sounded scientific—"our autophobia is because we've died a dozen times in a dozen car crashes." When she said nothing, he went on. "Fear of cars? Right?"

"Fear of being alone," she said slowly and *why* wouldn't she look at him? He thought he knew.

"That's one thing you *never* have to be afraid of." He reached out, wanting to cup her cheek in his hand, wanting to feel her smooth warm flesh, wanting her to tip her face into his hand and rub like a shark-eyed cat. He wanted to feel the muscles in her cheek flex as she smiled up at him. "Not ever, Leah."

None of those things happened; she took a calculated step backward and he only cupped air. "That is inappropriate, as we are no longer seeing each other."

Each word was like a needle in his chest, long and sharp and hot going in. He dropped his hands, took a calming breath. Tried to take a calming breath. "Leah, I love you, but my God: your knowledge of past lives hasn't made you smarter or braver or stronger. It's paralyzed you. Please, please let me help you."

*Oh, shit. What did I say?*

Her eyes widened.

*Oh, shit! She heard me say the words!*

If they got much wider, if any more color fell out of her face, she'd do a face-plant on the sidewalk.

*Ohshitohshitohshit.*

He braced himself to catch her but wasn't sure he could move fast enough—

"I don't love you and what's more, I never could. I tolerated you because, much like a Vulcan, every now and then I need to mate. You're not worth the time nor the trouble. Get out of my life. The next time I see you, I'll call the police. *After* I plant a balisong in your voice box."

—and it was just as well he couldn't have gotten there in time, because he might have let her smack into the sidewalk, purely for spite.

She turned and walked away.

He let her.

# THIRTY-EIGHT

Had to be done. It absolutely had to be done.

*Oh, God, forgive me, the look. The look in his eyes.*

"I had to do it," Leah tearfully told the cabbie. She was a matronly woman in her forties, blond and brown-eyed and fair-skinned and running to plump, she and a million others like her in the Midwest. She wasn't at all alarmed by the crying once she made sure Leah wasn't physically hurt, or needed a hospital or the police.

"Don't take me back to the police," she begged, "I just got out of there. I had to get him clear of me. Of my life. My mess. Everything. I had to get him away. But oh, you should have seen. How he looked, oh, God. God."

She burst into fresh tears, accepting the box of tissues and instantly going through half of them. "Please put the price for these on the meter," she ordered between sobs.

A snort from the driver. "Not charging you for tissues, honey."

"Thank you, that's very nice. If you had a daughter you wouldn't make her do cattle calls for tampon commercials unless she really wanted to, right?"

"A what for a what?"

"An audition where they call in dozens of actresses and see them all in the same one- or two- or three-day period."

"*Cattle* call?" the cabbie (Brenda Morgan, per the ID helpfully posted on the plastic divider between them) said, lips thinning in distaste. "Is that what they call those? Awful. Well, hon, here it is. I have four daughters, two in med school, one in law school, and one is teaching history to seventh graders. None of them ever wanted to do a cattle call and never have."

"You're a good mom. Your daughters are so fortunate," Leah said, more grateful than she could express. Although why she was grateful to a strange cab driver for not charging her for half a box of tissues she did not know. Was she so starved for positive maternal attention that she would latch onto any older woman who was nice to her?

No, of course not.

No, except for Cat.

Cat!

*Oh holy hell.* Leah clutched damp tissues in her fist and thought hard. Her killer wasn't content to murder Leah and be done with it once the purpose of both their lives was fulfilled. Sometimes he was arrested and sometimes he lived to a ripe old age and sometimes he was killed while killing her, but one way or the other, they both ended up dead.

This time around he went for Leah's mother first, doubtless

assuming that their parent-child dynamic would dictate a bond. Next time, he could beat someone to death she *did* care about: Archer. Or Cat. Archer was safe, she hoped.

"Can you please go faster?" she begged. "Please please go faster. I'll tip you one hundred percent."

"You won't," the cabbie said with an envious air of serenity as she took the second-to-last turn to Leah's apartment. "I'm not letting you do that when you're obviously not yourself."

"You have no way of knowing what 'myself' is; you don't have a baseline," Leah argued, annoyed out of her tears. "This could be daily behavior for me. I might often weep in cabs and tip one hundred percent. Two hundred percent!"

"Somehow I doubt it," came the dry reply. After a pause, the older woman continued. "I'm not charging you for the ride, either."

Leah sat up straight and bit off the words. "That. Is. Just. Ridiculous! How do you expect to make a living if you don't charge?"

"My husband works, too."

"But that doesn't—"

"You helped my niece. Years ago."

Blowing her nose, she looked up in mid-honk and caught the cabbie's gaze in the mirror. "I did?"

"If you're Leah Nazir, yeah. You were on TV a couple years ago, you helped the cops figure out who that Cereal Rapist scumbag was."

She vaguely remembered the Cereal Serial Rapist. A local reporter, one more insensitive than the rest of the herd, hung the nickname on Marcus Farrady, who, after he raped his victims, hung around long enough to have a bowl of cereal (his first preference) or toast. Something breakfast-y, at any rate.

He took the bowl and utensils he used with him. When the cops caught up with him, a full quarter of his unfinished basement was shelf after shelf of mismatched cereal bowls, small plates, bread knives, and spoons.

Leah had been called in to consult, and reasoned that he could have been the reincarnation of three deceased serial rapists (deceased number 1: electric chair, 1990; deceased number two: succumbed to cancer in prison, 1991; deceased number three: shot and killed by last victim, 1992). She backtracked birthdays to their dates of death and was able to come up with a list for the cops. It helped that the Cereal Serial Rapist actually looked and acted like a rapist: shifty eyes, blocky hands like bowling balls, murderous temper, bull-like shoulders, crippling misogyny, juvenile record of peeping, adult record of assault. Leah found it refreshing; bad as their crimes were, it was always much more horrible when the monsters looked like they could be your next-door neighbor.

It also helped that he obsessively ate bowl after bowl of cereal while being interrogated. Obtaining a warrant was not difficult. And though he'd had ample time to ditch the evidence in his basement, Farrady hadn't bothered. That behavior was not at all refreshing. She had ceased wondering why so many serial *anythings* wanted to be caught years ago.

"Yes," she said, remembering, "just a couple of years ago. They stuck a microphone in my face and asked me why I hadn't figured it out sooner, preventing the last two rapes."

"Oh, dear."

"I invited them to fuck the fuck off."

"I sure hope so!"

"Sorry about the language."

"It seems appropriate in that instance."

"That was the part of the interview that didn't make it past their editors." Not to mention one of the last interviews she'd had to endure. She should have tried the "fuck the fuck off" method earlier. She should have tried it on . . .

No. She couldn't think of Archer now.

The cabbie snorted. "No doubt. Anyway, that's how I knew what you looked like. I never met you when you treated my niece for her chronophobia. Five years ago?"

Leah thought about lying, but couldn't stomach the thought. "I . . . I apologize, I don't—"

"It's fine. I wouldn't expect a doctor to remember every single patient she saw."

"But chronophobia isn't that common, you'd think I—"

"Stealing clocks?"

*That* socked the memory home. "My God, yes! I can't believe I forgot." Leah giggled in spite of herself. "Your niece, Maya. She was . . . well, kind of a treasure."

The old-fashioned endearment perfectly fit Maya Ryan, who feared time and the passing of time. She was Leah's second client with chronophobia, and by far the most interesting. Maya believed the best way to prevent time from passing was to break every watch or clock in her home, and steal and hide/bury/destroy every watch or clock outside of her home. The police, of course, eventually got involved.

"My niece couldn't sit in a classroom, she couldn't go to a movie theater or the grocery store or a school play without being obsessed with the clocks, with the watches people around her were wearing . . . she was a wreck. So was my sister. But you were pretty nice about the whole thing."

"I was?" Nice? Really? Was it possible there were two Leah Nazirs living in the Chicago area?

"Yeah, you figured out that she'd died some ten or fifteen times already, always because she'd run out of time."

Leah remembered. In 1881, Maya had ingested poison as a child in Wyoming and hid rather than confess what she'd done; by the time she'd been coaxed from her hiding place and rushed to the hospital, her time had run out. In 1927, she had ignored all the *Danger* signs, found a hole in the fencing, and sneaked into the William A. Clark house, which was (as the signs had warned helpfully) set to explode. Tick-tock boom. As a young mother-to-be in Seattle twenty-three years later, she hadn't realized she'd developed eclampsia; when her labor started, so did her convulsions. By the time the baby had been removed via emergency C-section, Maya had been clinically dead for three minutes.

The cabbie brought Leah back to the present by saying the last thing she expected. "'You were right to be afraid then, and you're right to be afraid now. Your fear is a gift; not a thing to suppress or fight.'"

"How did you know what I—"

"She said it at least once a week, often enough that I memorized it. She was so grateful to you. I am, too."

"Oh. Well, thank you."

"She's dead now. There was an accident by the side of the road and she got out to help. Got clipped by a truck crossing the midline."

Leah groaned. "Of course she did. I'm so sorry."

"Us, too. But you *did* help her when nobody else could." The cabbie adjusted her rearview mirror, the better to gaze straight into Leah's eyes. "I've hopes I'll see her again in her next life.

I've hopes she'll live a lovely long life and die old and loved in her bed. You helped her break the cycle, you know."

"I did? Hmm. *She* did, at any rate," Leah replied, thinking hard. "Or it was broken for her. Something changed and the pattern broke. That's . . . hmm."

She didn't say another word until the cab pulled up to her apartment building, which looked a lot like a long gray Lego upended on its side. The cabbie didn't, either, but got out of her seat and gave Leah a slow, careful hug, which Leah managed to return in kind without bursting into fresh tears.

# THIRTY-NINE

Leah's studio apartment always made her sad, but never more than today. She much preferred Archer's place. He might be only renting the tower, and his landlord might be gone all the time, and the place might be on the market, but it nonetheless felt like a real home.

Or maybe that was just the Archer Effect. Either way, her small studio (or was that redundant?) seemed to scream "this is the home of someone who does not care, does not anticipate marriage and children, and is only waiting to die." Maybe it was the beige wallpaper. If she lived through the end of the month, she promised herself she'd repaint everything in Wild Moss. Or maybe Fennel Seed. Wild Turkey?

Her plan—get to a working phone to warn Cat—worked perfectly until she picked her broken cell phone up off the floor. She couldn't believe she had forgotten such a vital detail. "Son of a *fuck*," she swore, poking ineffectually at the thing. She had no landline as they were almost obsolete in the twenty-first century, and even if she did, Cat's number was stored in the dead phone. She almost never called it, and couldn't begin to recall what it was. Cat was one of those people who just appeared when they were needed, and existed quietly offstage when they weren't. Which was a terrible way to think of her best friend, but if she got mired in her faults, nothing would get done.

Dead phone. Hmm. She had another phone. This one wasn't dead so much as on near-permanent vacation. A homophobic client had not taken well to the news that he used to be Oscar Wilde. He managed to snatch her phone away, then tossed it into the vase of flowers on the small table beside her desk. Unfortunately they weren't silk flowers but real ones that required water. (She'd never made *that* mistake again.)

She'd gone home and plunked her dead phone into a bag of rice, but assumed it wouldn't work, assumed she'd need another, and acquired a new one. But rather than ditch the old one she behaved the way most people did: tossed it into a drawer and forgot about it. Did the rice work? Or not? Cells being so cheap these days, it didn't much matter.

She went to the kitchen junk drawer, pawed through the mess of seed packets (she had never planted a seed in her life), Elmer's glue (she could not remember the last time she used it, literally years and years ago), twine (did people even use that anymore?), expired stamps (or send snail mail?), broken pencils (why in God's name did she save broken pencils?), and a battered cell phone.

She plugged it in to charge, gripping the thing so hard her knuckles ached, waited a couple of minutes, and then gave it a tentative poke.

"Yes!" Cat's number, Cat's number, CatCatCat . . . "There!" She pressed it at once, hoping she was catching her friend on a rich day, not a park day.

"Have you fucked up this thing with Archer yet?"

She was so relieved she could barely summon the energy to bristle. "Excellent, you haven't been stabbed." Then, "How did you know who this was?"

"Who else would be calling the crazy homeless lady who lives in the park? Social services? An Air Force recruitment center? AT&T?"

"Listen, my mother—"

"Should I bother to waste your time with condolences?"

"Probably not. Listen, get the hell off the streets, you understand? Check into the Ritz—"

"No way. They don't have streaming. After a hard day of panhandling and feeding pigeons, I really need classic *Daily Show*."

*Ugh.* "The Peninsula?"

"Pass. No room service after eleven."

"Listen, I don't care where, but do *not* loiter at your usual haunt, which would make it easy for my killer to kill you. Anybody who's been watching me for more than a few weeks will know about you and where to find you . . . in the park. They won't have a clue you're the former mayor of the nation's twenty-first-largest city."

"Yeah, well. If this were a TV show—"

"TV is getting everything wrong this month!"

"—I'd say something tough yet caring, like 'I can take care of myself' and then promptly get my big ass murdered. So to Hotel Felix I shall go."

"Is that really a hotel?"

"Yes, you plebian."

"Sounds like the name of a hotel in a cartoon."

"Wicked plebian."

"Stop that. Maybe you should leave town altogether," she fretted.

"If he knows me, he only knows Cat, not Catherine Carey. It's a good idea, Leah."

"So you're going, right? Right now? You're on your way? Right now?"

"Cripes, you're a bigger nag than my handlers and my private school tutors combined. Yeah, I'm going."

Relief made her knees buckle; she sank into a kitchen chair with more than a little gratitude. If the chair hadn't been there, she'd be on the floor. "Great, Cat. That's wonderful. Okay."

A pause. "You *did* screw up the thing with Archer, didn't you?"

"I had to get him away from me. This wretch went for my mother."

"Yeah, he must have thought you loved her." She could hear Cat's sigh over the phone. "Friggin' moron. So you . . . let's see . . . went into bitch overdrive to drive him away?"

"Bitch four-wheel overdrive." Was that a thing? Possibly not.

"But once you prevent your murder, you'll fix it. Right? Leah? Right?"

"I . . ." She shook her head, viciously swallowed the lump in her throat. She had *zero* time for that nonsense. "I can't imagine, Cat. And it's just as well."

"Friggin' moron."

"I suspect you're not referring to my killer."

"Come to the hotel with me. Stay as long as you want, we'll

get a suite. *My* treat. Because you've got that 'I think I'll do something so fuckin' stupid I'll top every stupid thing I ever did' tone in your voice."

"No more hiding."

"That's *also* something they say on TV, and it's usually followed by the hero having to duck a hail of bullets."

"Bullets, ha. If only. Go. *Now.*"

"Fer Christ's sake think it o—"

Leah hung up. Archer was safe. Cat was safe. She, of course, was not. But she never was, not in any life. She had never, ever felt safe and for a moment she couldn't help thinking of Maya the Clock Snatcher, who always felt terrified at how time slipped by no matter how much she tried to slow it down. Who died an untimely death, but not the one she'd been doomed to relive dozens of times.

Leah had no plans to be hit by a car while helping someone else who had been hit by a car, but she did know the variable in this life: Archer. He was the thing that never happened before. He was the key to tricking fate into cutting the shit already.

But the cost was too high. His life for hers? Never.

Oh, never.

She stepped to the kitchen window and looked down at the streets. Archer was out there somewhere, which was fine. Her killer was, too. Which was not.

"Come on, come on," she breathed, fogging the glass. "You know you want me. Come and get me."

# FORTY

"You're horrible and I could almost regret meeting you and I'm probably not the only guy out there who wants to strangle you—I'm literally not the only guy out there who wants to strangle you—but I'm not gonna just slink off into the sunset and let you get fatally stabbed a lot."

"Huh."

"That's it." Archer nodded so hard he almost gave himself a headache. "That's what I'll say to her when I see her again."

"Might work," Cat conceded. She and Archer were walking toward the downtown area. Archer had called Cat with updates, she gave him an earful, then orders, and he'd met her to walk her to the hotel. The day was too gorgeous, and they were both too keyed up, for a taxi. "Or you could just kiss her a whole bunch."

"Plan B. Also Plan C through ZZZ."

"Good to know. So you figured out her incredibly transparent ploy, eh?"

"Please, God, let it be a ploy." He shoved his hands in his jeans and hunched while they trudged, Cat because she was loaded down with Target bags of just-purchased travel toiletries, he because he was dead like a dodo inside. Thanks to Leah, his heart was extinct. *I need to remember to never say that out loud because, even to me, it sounds lame.* "Pretty please? God probably owes me a favor, right? I do all sorts of stuff for Him." Part-time job number five: bookstore clerk at St. Peter's.

"Trust me, she was as awful as she could be, but not to be awful. Not to just be awful," Cat amended. "You always, always have to remember what you're dealing with."

"Who."

She narrowed her eyes at him. "Are you correcting my grammar, boy?"

"Yeah, it helps me feel closer to the Leah who corrected my grammar and forget the Leah who talked to me like she hates me."

"First off, it's 'whom,' you doorknob, so you gotta turn in your Grammar Police badge."

"It is not! It's 'who,' and I don't have a Gra—"

"Second, she doesn't hate you. Opposite, in fact. This is a woman who operates almost entirely out of fear while refusing to acknowledge she's scared shitless pretty much all the time." Anticipating his question, Cat elaborated. "Scared of putting herself out there, scared of opening up to you, scared of making a friend who doesn't put 'feed pigeons chunks of Big Macs' on her weekly to-do list, scared the world's gonna drown in aluminum cans because not enough assholes recycle." She paused. "No. That last one's something I'm scared of. Leah doesn't worry much about the planet, just the people who live on it. Scratch the last."

He shrugged, feeling bitchy. "I dunno. She had a couple of good points."

"Shut up, don't buy into that shit," the mayor ordered. "Depending on my schedule that day I'll either cut you or smack you upside the head with my platinum Amex."

*She must have been terrifying in office.* "So, what? She drove me off like a dog at a picnic for what? Leah's just gonna just put herself out there? Make herself bait? Write 'please come stab me, big boy' on her forehead?"

"Dog at a picnic, heh." Catching his scowl, Cat shrugged. "Sorry, hilarious mental image. But listen, I think that might be pretty close to the plan. It might even work. Her whole deal is that she's always passive, always on the sidelines, right? She's never tried getting in the killer's face before."

"She's never lost her goddamned mind before, either," he muttered. "I'm pretty sure."

"I don't think the killer's gonna hang around long after doing her mom. He's gonna have to make his move real soon."

"Guessing." He slashed his hand through the air, dismissing the argument. "It's all just guessing."

"Yep. But I think Leah's an accurate judge of his methods. She might not always know who he is, but she remembers enough things to be careful."

"Except she's not being careful. Is she?"

"No."

*It's unreal that we're even discussing this. Only three weirdos: a shark-eyed Insighter, the rich homeless former mayor of Boston, and . . . well . . . me . . . could have problems like this. Does that make us lucky, or fucked?*

They walked in silence for a few moments. "You know what

I can't figure out? Besides almost everything? How someone who thinks she's a terrible person would go out of her way to protect you and me."

"She's her own worst critic," Cat agreed, "and she's still terrible. Just not as terrible as she thinks."

"This whole thing is making me ill. I don't know dick about serial killers—any kind of killer, since my dad didn't *really* kill my uncle—"

"What the frig, Archer! Minor detail I'm only just hearing about!"

"It's not relevant to this month," he argued, "so I want to stay on topic. And the topic, horribly, is the guy who wants to kill my shark-eyed sweetie."

"It's maybe not relevant, but it adds to the Mystery of Archer. You're older than her but look younger—"

"I have a really good moisturizer."

"—you're a private eye with only one client, now deceased—"

"I needed a vacation anyway."

"—who lives in a tower with a landlord who's never there—"

"The economy's tough and she's job hunting in California."

Cat snorted and swung her Target bags. Archer jerked back, saving his nose from getting clipped. "What the hell do you do all day, Archer?"

"Asked the bag lady."

"Please," Cat huffed, annoyed, "we prefer the term 'home-impaired.'"

"I do lots of things," he replied cheerfully. "After my dad went to prison I helped out my mom by taking on some part-time jobs, blew off college, and decided I liked being a permanent self-appointed temp worker. So I do some Pee Eye stuff and sometimes I dog-sit and sometimes I pick up a few shifts at the diner around the corner from the tower—"

"Waiter?"

"Cook. I dunno how to explain it; those little tiny jobs are all nice but they don't move me."

"Be thankful it's not a career that doesn't move you. You know how many lawyers I know who hate their jobs? College *and* law school and they just about cry every morning when their alarm goes off."

*Was there a lawyer anywhere who doesn't hate being a lawyer? Someone should do a study.* "Yeah, and the little jobs are fun until they're not and then I quit and do something else. I think I'm sort of testing everything out. I'm like a compass with the needle spinning all the time."

"So you're a professional bum. Bum as in goof-off, not a politically incorrect term for the home-impaired."

"Pretty much. Good thing Leah can't see all the jobs from my past lives, since I've had a million just in this life. Her brain would implode."

Cat was giving him the oddest look, which was unsettling to say the least. (Okay, technically saying nothing was saying the least, but he was a slave to cliché.) "Have you thought maybe you're not life-blind at all?"

"Huh?" He nearly tripped over a parking meter, and a bike messenger nearly clipped him, and they resumed walking. "Where'd that come from?"

"Something Leah said a few months ago. A theory about the life-blind. I thought she was bullshitting out of boredom, but now I wonder."

"It's a myth, Cat. It's the fairy tale nobody actually buys.

Believe me, I used to play that card when people were feeding me overdoses of patented 'you poor blind idiot, you'll never get it' crap. It's like the things orphans tell themselves: my *real* parents are rich but I was stolen from them. I'm not supposed to be here."

"Whereas the *tabula rasa* have never been here at all."

"No." He shook his head. "I'm not that. I was disabused of it pretty early on. And for the zillionth time, being life-blind is no handicap."

"Can we even say 'handicap' these days?" Cat fretted. "I'm a little behind on my PC jargon."

"Focus! Listen, I *like* not having the weight of a dozen lives smashing me down with everything I do. Most people don't get that. And besides, Leah's my proof."

"Proof of what?"

"That I'm not a true *rasa*. If she doesn't know, then I'm not."

Cat laughed. "Your faith in her is adorable. And not misplaced," she added as Archer frowned. "She's among the best in the world at what she does, no question. But you're acting like Insighters are infallible, and you gotta know they aren't. Just because Insighters all over the world want to refer patients to her doesn't mean she doesn't ever get it wrong. Besides, what's it all for?"

"What?"

"This. Us. Life." Cat gestured vaguely at the air, the people around them, the traffic. "Everything we go through, all our past mistakes. Our attempts to fix things in *this* life . . . what's it all for, if there's never a chance to be born with a clean slate? Well, a clean slate until you fuck something up severely. Then it's back to the end of the line, pal."

"Kid stuff," he replied, feeling uncomfortable. He didn't like thinking about this, and not just because their focus should be on Leah. It brought back painful memories. Because there *had* been a time he thought he was different because he was a clean slate. Not a cripple, not someone so stupid in all their lives they could never see them. "Like I said. Fairy tales for grown-ups."

"I don't think so," was Cat's only response, and to his relief she appeared to get back on track when she added, "And I don't think you're a bum. And d'you know how often Leah takes to a guy under the best of circumstances?"

"I have no—"

"Years. Okay? As in, she *never* takes to a guy right away. Never mind one working for her mom. Never mind one who's been stalking her while he works for her mom. But she didn't chuck you out the back door, which I think is interesting. Just stabbed you."

"'Just,' huh?"

"And then forgave you. My point, get it?"

"Yeah, she took to me right away but chucked me out the back door in under a month, so it's *not* interesting. And speaking of her mom, getting back to what I said earlier, why'd the killer decide to kill her mom first? He would have known he was killing the wrong woman, right? All he or she did was bring attention to himself or herself. The cops know something's up, Leah knows he's close now. Pretty dumb. Pretty obvious and dumb." It was strange to be discussing such things while walking down a beautiful street in sunny Chicago, where almost everyone was smiling and enjoying the day.

*Sad and scary how much bad shit went on when everything else looked great.*

"What happened? What'd Ms. Nazir do to make him lose

his shit and kill her? Not just kill her. He didn't shoot her, didn't stab her, choke her . . . he or she picked up Leah's Emmy and whack-whack-whack."

"I get it, I get it, stop drawing that mental picture." Cat paused and swallowed. "If you knew that, you'd probably know who did it. And maybe it wasn't anything. Because, you know. Psycho killer. That's for the cops to figure out. They're checking alibis, all that behind-the-scenes stuff, right? Canvassing the neighborhood, and even B-list celeb deaths make the news, so people are talking about it, thinking about it . . . Again, he's exposed. He's gotta kill Leah quick and get out."

"Yeah. Not that there are many alibis to check. Leah and I are each other's alibis, so I'm not sure how that works. And Leah's old agent, what's-his-face. You should have seen this guy, Cat. He looks like he's always on the verge of hay fever, or sobbing uncontrollably. Big watery eyes, runny nose."

"Yeah? Why's he even a suspect?"

"He was there when Leah blew off her mom for the tenth time. At the McMansion."

"Huh. Doesn't make sense for an agent to kill his client, though. Much easier to just drop 'em. Like there's a shortage of B-list actresses in Hollywood?"

"Right. Anyway, he was on a plane to L.A. when Ms. Nazir got iced with Leah's Emmy."

"Oh." A short pause, then: "How d'you know?"

"Leah figured it out, and the cops were gonna follow up. They've probably verified by now." Archer shuddered, recalling the crime scene (the McMansion had never seemed more bleak, or more sinister) and Leah's white face and tight, clipped voice as she explained how she could have killed It while knowing damned well she didn't kill It. "Beaten to death with Leah's Emmy. I didn't know Leah even had an Emmy. But then, you know. Known her less than a month."

"Yeah, Outstanding Guest Actress in a Comedy." At Archer's stare, Cat shrugged. "Okay, I was a fan. I loved the stuff she did in the nineties. Recognized her straight off when one of her clients chased her through my park." He was still staring, so she elaborated. "Her eyes are the same. It's why they always cast her as the smart-ass kid who acts tough but is a big sweetie inside. And don't worry. Leah knows I was a fan. She decided we'd be pals anyway."

"Okay, well, when this blows over and Leah's pregnant with my twins—"

"Whoa!"

"—I'll need to borrow some of your DVDs."

"Okay, I can't think about your weird twins right now, or the fact that you think I have a DVD collection stashed somewhere. So how did you know her agent was in L.A.?"

"Leah's mom told Leah."

"Leah's mom."

"Uh. Yeah. Problem?"

Cat was walking faster, a frown spreading across her broad face. Archer knew there were two kinds of people in the world: the ones who slow down when they're thinking hard, and the ones who speed up. Almost jogging, he tried to match her pace. "Told Leah when? Over the phone?"

"Yeah. I was right there; I heard Leah's whole side of it. Did you know her mom's ringtone is 'no wire hangers'? Creepy as shit."

"So you weren't at the house. Neither of you. You didn't actually see the agent *not* be there."

Archer was having trouble figuring out the source of her growing alarm. "No, but Cat, it's like I said, Nellie cleared him, even if she didn't know she did at the time."

The mayor shook her head so hard, Archer got sympathy dizziness. "And you believed her? Jesus!"

"Sure I did. Why wouldn't—hey. Hey!" He grabbed her elbow and planted his feet, though the mayor could move him if she was inclined. The mayor could toss him into a pile of garbage if she was inclined. "Please, stop sprinting and explain this to me. What's the big deal? Why wouldn't I believe Nellie? Leah did."

"Yeah, well, the *problem* with that is that Leah's a little too close to the *problem*."

"Okay, I appreciate the emphasis on *problem*, but I'm new to the story, here. You've got to give me more," he begged, "and standing still, please. Me, I go slow when I think, that's the kind I am."

"Okay." She shot him an annoyed look, doubtless wondering at the relevancy of going slow. "The *problem* is that Nellie Nazir set the standard for unreliable narrator."

He blinked and absorbed that. "She lied?"

"Unreliable narrator doesn't necessarily mean lying. She could have believed it herself. Or convinced herself that if it wasn't true right that minute, it *would* be true."

"Okay . . . I have faith you're gonna get there eventually, so I'm hanging in."

People streamed around them as they again stood in the middle of a public sidewalk discussing lies and murder. "I think she lied about the agent being out of the house. I think he was right there with her. And I think Leah didn't catch on at the time because she had plenty of other shit to worry about. Which brings me to the 'baaaad shit' part of our program."

"No, it's good shit!"

She peered up at him. "I think you're getting too much sun. It's bad shit."

"Cat, don't you get it?" Archer was so excited he danced the mayor in a little circle, right there outside Burger King. "The cops will check his alibi and know it's bullshit. They'll have him!"

"I know. Stop spinning me." The mayor was growing pale, which was alarming as she normally had a healthy tan from all her time in the park. "They'll have him. And the thing about that, Archer, is that he *knows* they'll have him."

"Oh."

"So he knows he's almost out of time."

"Oh!"

Without another word, Archer whirled, stepped off the curb, ignored the bus about to kill him, flagged a taxi, then leaped out of the way of the bus about to kill him.

"Cops!" Cat yelled after him, but he didn't see, didn't hear, didn't turn. He was climbing inside the cab, totally focused on getting to Leah. "Cops would be a good thing now!"

The taxi never slowed.

# FORTY-ONE

Leah turned impatiently toward her front door when the doorbell chimed. Finally! She felt as if she had been waiting forever for her killer to show up and murder her. And so she had, for over two decades. An entire life wasted waiting. If Archer was here, he'd laugh and—

*Do not think about Archer.*

"About time, thank you!" She stomped to her door, observed all the secured locks, and peeped through the aptly named peephole to observe Tom Winn of Winner's Talent™ (ugh) blinking at her from the other side of the door.

"Go away, Tom, I'm waiting for my—never mind."

"Gotta talk to you, Leah. About your mom."

She hissed out breath. Tom had the tenacity of a bred-in-the-bone Hollywood agent; he would never quit until he'd talked to her about Nellie. This was no doubt the "but Hollywood loves when famous relatives of famous murder victims do reality TV" pitch. Or the offer to play herself in the Lifetime movie inevitably written about her mom, *New Life, Old Murder.* Or perhaps *Hushed Killing.* She could send him away and have him come back and back and back, or she could deal with it now, be rid of him forever, and hope he didn't scare the killer off.

*Of course, he might be the killer. On TV it always seems to be the one you never suspect. However, TV has gotten nothing right this month.*

*But still.*

"Make it quick," she warned, unlocking the three security locks and swinging the door wide. "I'm a little pressed for time."

"Yeah, me, too." He shuffled inside, past her, and she closed the door.

"You missed the reading of her will," he told her with gentle disappointment.

"Her last performance? Yes. Well. I was, at that time, in jail for her murder, talking Celia into judging our Oddest Place You've Ever Done It contest. But it's not like it's a lot of trouble to hit rewind on the disc."

Tom's wispy blond hair always looked like he was in a gale, even inside, and his big wet eyes got bigger and wetter. "Yes, I—yes. I knew that. That's what the police—yeah. They said. Um, I know you didn't do it, Leah."

"How very kind. You did not swing by to reprimand me about missing the will."

"No."

She ground her teeth. "What. Is it. Tom?"

"The cops. I had to talk to them while you were in jail. They'll check my alibi."

"Yes, and?" He couldn't be worried about negative press. The only press that could hurt an agent was embezzlement coverage.

"I'm almost done here."

*Hopefully that includes this tedious meeting.* "That's fine."

"She lied," he whined. He hadn't taken off his trench coat (trench coat? in summer? really?) and sweat was beading his forehead and running down his face like tears. Wait. Those might *be* tears. Well, he had just left his biggest client's last performance. He had been a part of Nellie's life for so long, perhaps he could not imagine his without her. Certainly he had also been a part of hers; some of her earliest memories were of Tom coming over to their overpriced Beverly Hills condo with contracts for Nellie to sign. Distracted pity rose in her and she stomped on it. Absolutely no time, not for any of that nonsense. She had her murder to get on with, dammit. "She lied about you."

"Who? It?"

"You shouldn't call her that," he said in mild rebuke. At five, she had bent an attentive ear to such rebukes, since he gave her far more attention than Nellie and she wished to please him. By the time she was in her teens, her contempt for the man and her mother had long smothered her need for his approval, or hers. "It's very disrespectful and the press wouldn't like it."

"Yes, it's almost as bad as stealing your only daughter's childhood and then all the money you forced her to make. And trust me: the press did not give a shit."

"She was disrespectful, too. About you."

"That. Is. So. Fascinating!" She smothered a groan. Ninety seconds, that's what he could have. A minute and a half and then out he would go.

"But the lie, that was the worst. I couldn't forgive that."

Leah softened at once. Holy God, she had never considered this. That Nellie's death would force him to reexamine her life,

Leah's life, and his complicity in the ruin of her childhood. That he might feel regret. Perhaps he always felt regret. Perhaps he could never admit it while It breathed and dominated and terrorized as she walked the earth in her pink satin kitten heels.

"I . . ." She could not believe the words about to leave her mouth. "I appreciate that, Tom. Which lie? When she told the casting director for *A Thousand Rapes* that I was eighteen when I was fifteen? When she told the casting director for *The Huggies Musical* that I could play two when I was eighteen months? The lie to the judge, so she could keep my money?" He opened his mouth and she held up a hand. "Whichever lie you regret, I'm grateful. Well, not grateful, but I despise you somewhat less now."

"I'm tired. I'm tired all the time."

"Well, it has been a stressful week for us all, Tom, and you really must be going." She started toward the door. "But thank you for stopping by and being sorrowful and vague, I guess."

He stepped in front of her, blocking her path to the door.

"Tom."

"She said she had changed your mind about *Mother Daughter Hookers Heroes.* She said you were on board and we'd all go back to Hollywood and it'd be the way it was when you were—when you didn't hate us. She said that. To me."

"Tom."

"But you made it clear, that last call. I figured it out, then. How she tricked me; I forgot how good she is at tricking people. Me, an agent, and her, an actress! The worst kind, the desperate kind. That goes for both of us," he added.

"Tom!"

"You said you were done with her at the house but I thought

maybe . . . maybe you weren't—well, all right, I knew you were serious but I hoped you'd change your mind. We knew how much you hated Insighting. Knew you'd turn your back on it if you could. But you didn't."

"Didn't hate Insighting? Or didn't turn my back?" She was having trouble following him. Tom seemed weepy and distracted, even more so than usual.

"You didn't change your mind," he elaborated. "And I knew. I remembered what she always made herself forget, how stubborn you are, how unmoving. So there was no point, you get it? When you wouldn't just do the show, you wouldn't be with her anymore for *any* reason. No point to stay in her life. I wasn't ever supposed to be in her life anyway."

"No?"

"I did it wrong this time; I got in her life when you were young. I had to. You see it, right?"

"Maybe talk me through it." She realized she was using her clinical voice, and no wonder. This could be a session like any other session, with one crucial difference: she wasn't bored. She sent a silent apology to all her patients. *Should have been nicer, should have seen you weren't pieces of paper in a chart. I'm paying for it now, if that makes it better.*

"The only way I could be in your life is if I was in hers. I wanted to be near you for a long time, I didn't want to make you go away, because then I don't have you until the next time." This in a tone people used for "two plus two equals four; it's so easy, isn't it?"

"A dilemma," she agreed, sounding like she was speaking through a mouthful of sawdust. *My kingdom for a glass of water. And a shotgun.*

"But I didn't count on the stubbornness. Yours *or* hers. By the time I realized I was hiding too well you'd left and built your own life somewhere else. But she was always sure she could talk you into coming back. And I—I let myself believe it, because it was what I wanted, too. I believed it because she believed it."

"Yes, my mother could take a polygraph and the needles would never twitch," Leah managed, her thoughts whirling. "It's why she was such a good actress. She was *always* acting. Even Nellie Nazir was a role."

He took a step forward. He was three feet away, between her and the door. No other exit. Phone still charging in the other room. She could stand there and shriek, but the door had locked when it closed. No one would get there in time. And she was a fool. It seemed she was always a fool.

Tom's tears weren't for Nellie. They weren't even for her. They were for himself, only for himself. *Never thought I'd say this, Mother: you deserved better.*

"Is that why you beat her to death?" She couldn't believe how detached she sounded, attentive yet slightly bored. Ho-hum, just another day in the salt mines. "Because I refused to do the show?"

"No. Because she told me she knew how to get you to Hollywood. To get you back. She was so proud for thinking of it. So she made me wait there in the photo room, the shrine to your careers—"

"I honestly would rather hear about my mother's murder instead of the photo room, and I don't want to hear about my mother's murder," she admitted.

"I heard her lie. She said you had a deal and I was on my way to L.A."

"She gave you an alibi." Christ. How awful and disturbing and wrong. She pictured Nellie on the phone, winking at Tom while purring in her lovely voice at Leah, unwittingly giving her killer an alibi. Not a great alibi, but one that would buy him enough time. Time to do . . . this. Which was all he was living for anyway.

*She would have known. At the end. Realized what he would do in a day or two or a week or two. Remembered how I predicted my murder when I was five. Remembered dismissing it, ignoring it, all those years. Put herself in his way. She was ready for him to ruin her face, destroy her beauty. He never touched her face but she couldn't have known. She put what she loved the most on the line to save what she loved the least and oh Mother I am SO SORRY.*

"You pathetic piece of shit." Her voice sounded so distant to her ears, distant and distasteful. Like hearing about a nasty story in the news but not feeling how awful it was. "You ridiculous awful man." She was once again surprised yet not surprised at how evil could look like a frail sniffling man huddled in a cheap coat.

"She lied," he whined. He was still closing the distance, inching toward her. She was still letting him. "The lies kept us apart all those years. It's her fault, all that wasted time. And his fault."

"His?"

"Your idiot boy, the one you've taken up with."

"First, *he* took up with *me*. Second he's not *my* anything, third he's not an idiot, and fourth, I've had boyfriends before now, what's so special about Archer?" Dumbest question ever. Everything about him was special. His smile, his eyes, his laugh, his toenails, his morning breath.

*Hmm, I get quite sentimental when I'm about to be murdered. Who knew?*

"He's a young fool, not worthy of—"

"He's not young," she corrected, "he's *rasa*." Somehow saying it—defining it—out loud to someone else made it even more real than it had seemed in her head. Which made sense, because it *was* true. She'd seen glimpses over the past couple of weeks, but now she saw the entire portrait of Archer: a clean slate, a new beginning. All past-due accounts squared up, firmly in the black. A fresh start . . . for both of them.

Tom, meanwhile, had let out a disbelieving snort, for which she could not blame him. "I know. Absurd to contemplate, much less pronounce. Which makes it no less true. Archer is the man you'll never be: someone who could face what he'd done, and become a better person for it."

"Shut up!"

"It's all right. I had no expectation you would understand."

"You're mine, you're for me, and Nellie lied and now I have to—don't you understand?"

"I do understand. Understanding is irrelevant. Shall I compile a list of all the fucks I don't give about *your* pain?"

"I'm tired," he said. "I'm tired all the time."

"Well, so am I!" she snapped back. "What, you think waiting around for you to kill me in every life isn't exhausting?"

"I'm tired of thinking about you and needing you to bleed on me. I feel like I've been tired for a thousand years."

"Oh my God, enough sniveling! And yes, that's about right, that's how long it's been, give or take a century. Is that my cue to feel pity for you? 'Poor killer, ultimately he was a victim, too'?

Tom, you've known me most of this life and in an awful lot of others. When, in any of them, did I ever feel sorry for you?"

Except she did, a little. A *very* little. He was as locked into his pattern of murder as she was in hers to be murdered. She knew he was in his forties, but he could have passed for sixty. She wondered what it was like, stumbling through life after life with the same maddening itch, never being able to rest until it's scratched, even knowing the scratch will destroy you. And then returning again and again, waiting for Leah each time, and then being alone again and again, until the next time.

She would have let him kill her a thousand more times before admitting such a thing aloud.

His hand was glittering. The knife, of course. In his hand, of course, he had pulled it from somewhere in one smooth motion she hadn't noticed. That was bad, because she was paying attention to the proceedings but still hadn't seen it. He would be good with the knife, quick with it. Of course. He never minded getting his hands dirty, which made him perfect for Hollywood.

"You are tainting everything the industry stands for, you're betraying your own kind. Nellie Nazir made a lot of money for you and you do *this*. No Agent of the Year wall plaque for you."

*Hmm. Did I just defend Mother?*

"I loved you so much."

"I don't care," she replied evenly, "so much." She remembered thinking how tedious meeting with him was. How she would give him ninety seconds. His time was up. Hers, too, maybe.

She began to move to his left, opposite his knife hand. She knew she would get cut; several clients had told her that anytime the other person has a knife and was within five feet, *you will get cut*. She didn't mind that; she minded bleeding out.

"So is that it? You come here, babble your insipid woes, and then on with the stabbing—ah!" She jerked back in time, felt the air displaced as the blade hissed past her cheek. "I guess so. What a surprise, you're not original in this life, either." Hysterical laughter bubbled out of her nose as she dodged another swipe. *He's here to kill me and I still find this meeting tedious! And why, exactly, am I goading him? Oh. Yes. So I can do this.*

She was too jittery to try a martial arts move, and to be honest, she liked the symbolism of the blade. So she popped the balisong knife free from her bra and the handle was snug in her palm one second later. "You aren't the only one who practiced, Tom. And unlike all the times before, I will fight. Do you know why?"

They were circling each other like alley cats. "Because you love me," he said with a shining smile.

*Ugh.* "I love the idea of *killing* you," she corrected. "I'll be honest, Tom, the idea of slicing you into cat food makes me salivate. But if I can't, I'll be a pragmatist and at least take you with me."

"Together," he breathed. "We'll go together."

"Ugh. Just . . . ugh."

He swiped and she lunged, and felt a line of fire streak along her temple. *Going for the face this time, no head or belly wounds for you. Did not ruining Nellie's looks make you want to ruin mine, stupid man? My mother was a thousand times more beautiful. I don't CARE if you ruin my looks. Archer loves my looks; Archer thinks I am a sexy shark, which should be off-putting but is endearing.*

*Don't think about Archer now.*

"You do not get this, any of this, and you never did and you never will. It's 2017; do you think I mind a few scars? With all the surgical advances? Idiot."

Despite her words, perhaps he thought she did. He remained stagnant, always seeing her as a past victim instead of the person she was now. She had been able to force change within herself this time; he could not. Or would not.

Perhaps he recalled how Nellie fought him. He had expected Leah to pull back, to flee from him. Instead she jerked her head out of the way and as his knife zinged down the side of her face, she planted hers in his breastbone.

"If this were TV," she shouted, her spittle speckling his reddening face, "I would say something clichéd like 'this is for my mother,' but this is for *me*, you festering poisonous penis!"

Triumph filled her like a drug, but then she looked down and saw what she had done, and cursed her rookie mistake.

*So comforting to know about the error that kills me. After all that time, wondering . . . at last I know.*

# FORTY-TWO

Archer was out of the cab before it stopped moving, sprinting into Leah's apartment building. He'd shouted—babbled—at the driver to call the police, but the poor guy was just relieved to get the hysterical nutjob out of his cab. And Archer wouldn't wait for the cops. In TV, as in real life, they often arrived too late.

He would have needed a key to get through the outer door and into the lobby, but all he had to do was bull past the young mother with her arms full of kids and groceries. Any other day he would have helped. Any other day he could have repacked her groceries for her (part-time job number nineteen, bagger at Dominick's).

Any other day but not today and, thank God, she couldn't fumble the toddlers and the food and her key fast enough. He had plenty of time to race past and ignore her startled, "Hey!", glance at the elevator and see it was on sixteen (Leah was on four), and plunge into the stairwell.

There was an old horror movie that scared the crap out of him when he was a kid, *A Nightmare on Elm Street*. A babysitter let him watch it and he never forgot it.

Most of it was cheesy and silly (he still didn't understand why Nancy got so freaked when she unplugged her phone from the wall and it still rang (good Lord, was this movie made in the 1800s?) but there was a part at the end that terrified him. Nancy, the last (wo)man standing, was running down the stairs to flee the bad guy when the stairs became all gooey. They were carpeted on top but like giant marshmallows inside and the faster she tried to go and the harder she struggled to wrench her feet free of the mess, the more her feet got stuck in the goo.

He'd slept with the lights on for a week and refused to use the stairs for a month. This proved problematic as the only bathroom was upstairs, but that was why, eight-year-old Archer reasoned, God made backyards. During the course of that month, he spent so much time in the yard it eventually led to part-time job number three, lawn boy.

This was just like that. He knew the stairs were concrete but he also felt like his feet were sticking to them, preventing him from making any headway. He knew he was taking the stairs as fast as he could, but it felt like he was stuck in goo. Like he wasn't moving at all and somewhere Leah needed him and he knew no matter what he did or how he did it, he wouldn't be there in time.

He made it to four after a thousand years and barreled through the door and into the hallway right outside Leah's apartment, slumping against the door

*(breathe you've got to breathe you're no good to Leah if you pass out in the hall so for Christ's sake breathe and then get in there and take that fucker apart starting with his eyes if he can't see her he can't knife her come on come on COME ON)*

for half a second.

And in that half second, the door to Leah's apartment opened and Tom Winn stumbled out. Archer had never been more horrified in his life, and that included part-time job number nine, the month he spent working on a Wisconsin dairy farm (some of the things livestock did, like give birth, were so *gross*). Awful enough that Tom was here. So much worse that he was leaving. Because if Tom was leaving, that meant Leah was dead.

There was also something wrong with him, besides the psycho killer thing. It was so obvious, but so startling, Archer's eyes had a tough time processing the image and reporting it to his brain: Tom had a knife in one hand (to be expected) and a knife sticking out of his chest (unexpected). Quivering out of his chest, to be specific; it looked like it was only in partway, half an inch or so, and it wiggled back and forth when he moved.

He realized at once what had happened, and as if Leah were standing beside him, he remembered what she said when she'd stabbed *him*.

*It's just as well I could not ram it home in your heart. All those ribs to get through—ugh. Most of the time the blade just glances off them. In the end it's often too much trouble.*

She'd gone for a kill shot and the knife had gotten stuck in the guy's breastbone. It must have hurt like a bitch, but wasn't fatal. It was barely slowing him down. But it had served to scare him off—for the first time in all her lives, Leah had finally fought back.

"I loved her," Tom the Psycho was saying, sounding amazed and hurt, like he couldn't believe Leah had the gall to actually resist being murdered. His trembling fingers kept coming up and trying to pluck at the knife, but would skitter away at the last second and he'd let out another whimper.

*Awwww, poor baby. Don't like the pain of getting knifed? Buck up, little camper, just make sure you take your antibiotics! Take it from one who knows.*

"Do not touch him!" Leah, screaming from very far away. The most beautiful sound in the world, the universe, the most beautiful sound in the history of sounds. No one screaming like that was dying, not if they were getting *that* much oxygen. (Part-time job number eleven: EMT.) Her shrieks sounded like a seagull set on fire, which, for some reason, he found sexy.

*I'd like to love you in your tower, so bring me there.* The thing she said to him he'd loved the most (so far). The thing he replayed in his brain before going to sleep. Or getting out of bed. Or fixing breakfast. Or mowing the lawn (part-time job number seventeen). Or in the shower. Especially in the shower. Several times in the shower.

*Hold that thought*, Archer promised himself.

"I loved her," Tom said again, irritatingly lively for a stabbing victim. He said it like he assumed Archer gave a shit. He said it like Tom was the victim.

"You don't know one goddamned thing about love." Archer kicked the other man's legs out from under him. He didn't have much of a plan, he just wanted the man on the ground. What happened was kind of spectacular: Tom fell over Archer and plunged face-first into the stairwell. He and Leah heard the "crack" as the weight of Tom's falling body punched her knife through the bone. He lay crumpled at the bottom of the stairs and didn't get back up.

Too bad. Archer would have liked to pull the knife free and reinsert it somewhere else twenty or thirty times.

Maybe in the next life.

# FORTY-THREE

Leah was on Archer like a hurricane with shark eyes. "Are you all right?" she cried, stumbling, falling to her knees and then wrenching herself back up. Blood was trickling down the side of her face, which for some reason she hadn't noticed. "Did he hurt you? There's blood, Archer. Are you bleeding? Are you? Ohpleaseareyouallright? Where's your phone? The police. Where is—"

"It's your blood, Leah, I'm fine. You're the one bleeding; c'mere and sit down with me," was all he managed before she reached out.

She groped for him, clutched at him, then ran her hands over him to assure herself he was unharmed. She rained small kisses on his face, the backs of his hands, his palms, his neck. "I did not you must know I did not mean what I said I did not I said those hateful things to drive you away and I am so sorry so sorry so sorry it always worked before so I thought I would do it to you and I didn't mean a single world of it, I swear, I swear, not one word, not ever any of those words oh please I am *so sorry*."

He was trying to blot the blood off her face with the tail of his shirt and saying, "Of course not I know that Jesus are you okay I can't believe that fucker are you okay did he hurt you are you okay?" Stupid questions, stupid comments, she was *bleeding*, of *course* Tom had hurt her, it's what he does/did. Archer wished the pathetic fuck was still alive so he could trip him down the stairs all over again. "C'mon, let's go call an ambulance, the dispatcher will put out a Code 3 and we'll get cops, too."

She nodded tearfully, still clutching him. "All right, that sounds—what? Code 3?"

"It doesn't look deep," he said, still wiping her face. "Good job dodging." He kissed her on the cheek. "And also stabbing."

"A shit job stabbing. I couldn't get through the breastbone and I know better, so frankly I deserve to be dead." She batted his hand away. "I'm fine, are you all right?"

"You're the one bleeding, I'm just out of breath. Ran all the way up the stairs."

They both heard approaching sirens.

"Hey, the cab driver called the cops! Or Cat did," he added, remembering. "She was yelling at me about that when I left to get here."

"You galloped to my rescue in a cab?"

"The bus I needed wasn't due for another fifteen minutes."

Leah let out a hysterical giggle, then clapped a hand over her mouth. Archer reached for her wrist and gently pulled her hand down. "That's an okay sound. Any sound you're making right now is gorgeous. I'm pretty sure you're in shock, though."

"I am *not*." All hysteria had fled; she was again Leah the Insighter, firmly in control. "He's dead. We killed him. *We* did." She looked at Archer as though she couldn't believe he was there, right there, within touching distance. Hugging and kissing distance. "He's dead and we're still here."

"You're still here," he corrected. "That's the most important thing."

"It is *not*." He could see the cuts were already clotting; she likely wouldn't need stitches. "I can't believe you came for me. After those things I said. I can't believe you're here. And my mother. She tried to help me."

He was rubbing small circles beneath her shoulders. "Yeah, hon, I know that, remember? I was there when she called—"

"No. She knew what Tom was going to do. She put herself in his way. She put her face and her body in the way of his blade. To help me. And when he left, she found the strength to call me, knowing I wouldn't talk to her. She used up the last of her life trying to warn me, and died knowing I wouldn't care."

"Is that so incredible, so hard to understand?" Frankly, it was the first time Ms. Nazir probably acted like a real mom.

"Yes," she said bluntly.

"All right. That's fair, but maybe she was ready to change her next life, too. Maybe the weight of always hurting you was too much this time around."

Leah leaned against him, looking down at Tom's sprawled, broken body. "Maybe so." She took a long, shuddery breath. "For someone who's lived over a dozen lifetimes, I'm still learning."

"Oh, Leah. That's . . . so TV."

"I can't help it, I spent my formative years mouthing clichés and fake-crying. Or fake-laughing." She shoved his shoulder, gently. "Less criticism, more hugging."

"Oh, absolutely. For the next several decades. Yes?" He leaned in and kissed her carefully on the mouth.

"Yes." She could not seem to stop looking at the body. She remembered Tom's clumsy kindness as a child. She remembered him pleading with Nellie when Leah brought them to court. She remembered him crying as he tried to kill her. Whatever she was feeling, it wasn't shock.

"He tried to break his pattern, too. He didn't want to kill me right away. He wanted to be around me for a while; years and years. He told me. And I—" Leah pulled away from Archer, bent at the waist, and barfed in the stairwell. Coughing, she stood, wiped her mouth, and glared. "Not in shock."

"Fine, you're not in shock. But the CSI guys aren't gonna like that. Your neighbors won't, either." He took her back into his arms and resumed rubbing slow, soothing circles on her back.

"Please tell me you don't find that attractive, too," she groaned.

"Congratulations. You've found my one turnoff. I temped as a janitor at the high school last year, part-time job number twelve, and you wouldn't believe how often teenagers throw up."

"Change of subject." Then, "Part-time job number twelve?"

"It's a long story. Which, thank God, I now have all the time in the world to tell you."

*Thank God, yes. That's exactly right. Thank you, God.*

Leah leaned forward while remaining in the comforting circle of Archer's arms. "Good-bye, Jack. Good-bye, Buck. Good-bye, Fritz. Good-bye, Béla. Good-bye, Elias. Good-bye, George. Good-bye, Peter. Good-bye, Gilles. Good-bye, Delphine. Good-bye, Tom. Good-bye."

# FORTY-FOUR

"And they lived happily ever after. Except I don't think so."

They were on Archer's porch, swaying back and forth on the porch swing. Leah had been unaware such things existed in the twenty-first century. It was nightfall of a long day.

"You promised to forgive me for being horrible to you in order to save you," she scolded. "You can't tell me you knew I didn't mean it and then decide perhaps I did mean it."

He had been bringing her hand to his mouth to nibble on her knuckles, but snorted against them instead. "That's not what I'm talking about, okay? I was talking to Cat about what you said—"

Leah groaned. The mayor had had choice words for them both. Some of the words had been "idiots" and "dumbasses" and "thank God, you're all right" and "cripes, the shit I put up with" and "you swear you're both okay" and then a lot more in the "idiots" vein followed by "they don't have any carrots here!".

Cat had, in fact, called the police, careful to have them take her statement at the hotel as Catherine Carey. The three agreed that the cops taking her statement in the park might cause unnecessary complications. ("Wait, ma'am, *what* did you say your old job was?")

The police had plenty of questions for Archer and Leah, mostly because the two of them were involved, once again, in a violent death. The second that week, in fact. So . . . yeah.

Fortunately, the police seemed satisfied with the answers. It helped that they had Nellie Nazir's killer, complete with the de rigueur creepy killer motive. And Tom's shrine to Leah had been found almost immediately, which made sense because it was basically his entire house.

When asked how she'd known him most of her life but never saw his house, Leah's reply was particularly Leah-ish: "I made it clear to the late Tom Winn of Winner's Talent™ (ugh) that I would rather be hooked up to an IV of my own vomit than ever set foot in his home. And my mother would never deign to visit; she made him come to her. Always. So, yes: I knew that man my entire life and never saw his home."

Archer's cab driver was found and questioned, and confirmed Archer was the hysterical young man who kept begging him to call the cops "before he kills her again oh my *God* when will this horrible wonderful month be over?" Leah's cab driver also came forward, but more to explain to the police (who already knew) what a help she had been to those in need and if she killed anyone she had a damned good reason and why don't the cops leave Leah alone and go after actual criminals. Huh? Huh?

"Anyway, Cat knew what you'd done—that you'd pulled a *Harry and the Hendersons*—"

Leah groaned again.

"—but you have to admit, you made a couple of good points. We might be too different. I'm not sure I'm the right guy for you."

"Don't break up with me for my own good, Archer," she warned. "It's annoying and condescending."

"Can't break up with you," he said, not looking at her. He was still nibbling on her knuckles, so she stayed where she was, content to have any part of him touch any part of her. "We haven't been going out."

"Well, we are now. We are now officially going out. This is our official first date."

"On the porch? We didn't have dinner. We didn't even have ice cream. And we both smell like a police station."

"Official first date. And come out and say it, for heaven's sake. You think being life-blind will be a problem for me."

"Won't it?"

She yowled in frustration, then had to smile when he jumped. She leaned forward, her arm across the back of the swing, and thumped him on the chest with her other hand, well away from his stab wounds. "I don't have a problem with your life-blind status. I decided it makes you far more attractive to me than the alternative, and I told that to all the girls in my cell."

"Uh. What? Is this gonna be a *Chained Heat* thing? Please let it be a *Chained Heat* thing."

"I refuse to be distracted by yet another silly movie reference. Look at me. Listen to me. Of course you fear going forward from here; anyone who isn't severely mentally damaged would be. And that is *my fault*, for saying those dreadful awful things. I swear to you, I swear it, the only one of the two of us who has a problem with being life-blind is you. And also, you're not."

"Sure, now. Today." She could see Archer, her proud, vibrant, endlessly amusing and charming Archer, was having trouble keeping his head up, having trouble looking her in the eyes. *My fault. This is my fault and I'd better fix it or I'll wish Tom had killed me.* "But eventually you'll get tired of living with someone who's missing a bunch of their parts."

"You're not missing anything!" she almost howled. "Except knowing when to quit being an idiot!" She took a steadying breath. "Sorry. And did you not hear what I said? You aren't life-blind."

"I love your love talk. Um. What?"

"You're not life-blind. You're *rasa*. You've done all this before. Just like the rest of us, you've had baggage to clear in order to move on. The difference is, *you* eventually got it right."

He shook his head. "Leah, you don't have to make up some fairy tale about *rasa* to make me feel—"

"It's not a fairy tale. It's just, we're all so jaded, so far from ourselves, we told ourselves it was. It's not. You did it. Other people did it. Other people *can* do it. I was top in my field when I was jaded and passively waiting to be murdered. Think how many people I can help, not that I'm not either of those things. Because of you, Archer."

"And you."

"Yes. And me. And I don't know how I couldn't see it before. I don't know how other people in your life couldn't see it. Idiots. And me, too. I'm an idiot. I'm a fool—"

"This is getting me so hot."

"Stop that. I'm not such a fool I cannot learn from mistakes. I will be glad to put that in writing and have it notarized if you so require. Besides, you aren't even considering the alternative."

"Alternative?"

"Maybe it isn't just you. Maybe what we've callously dismissed as life-blind aren't blind. Maybe they're new."

"Leah, we've been over this—I'm older than you are, and—"

"I don't think you are," she said softly, reaching out a small, pale hand and clutching his wrist. "I have this theory. I've been thinking about it a lot. You're *rasa*, I'm sure of it now, but I don't think the life-blind are blind at all. I think Insighters can't see them because there is nothing to see. It's not a failing in them; it's a failing in us."

Now he was paying attention. Now he could meet her gaze.

"There have to be *some* new souls, don't you think?"

"You're saying we can't all be reruns."

She groaned yet again. "If it helps you to put it in the context of television, fine, we can't all be reruns. And . . . I think that's what I needed to break the cycles of my murders. All my other sad short lives—you weren't in them. But you were here for this one. I think that's why I'm still here."

He was staring at her like she was a dangerous woman who routinely kept knives near her breasts as well as a careful clinical distance from almost everyone on the planet. And he was staring at her like he found it almost unbearably sexy.

"You might be wrong."

"I am not."

When he continued, he had the look of a man with his mind made up. "And if you are, I don't care. That's . . . yeah. It's fine if your theory goes the way of . . . of other theories that weren't true. I'm kind of drawing a blank on examples, but you get where I'm going. A *lot* of the blood has left my brain," he admitted. "I can't even hold your hand without wanting to do things to you that will make you want to put your nails in my back."

She leaned forward, put her hands on his shoulders, sucked his lower lip into her mouth, nibbled gently, then slowly released it.

"Show me."

# FORTY-FIVE

They made it, somehow, to his tower, and Archer thanked whatever deity watching over them that his landlady was still out of town. They stumbled through the nearly empty living room, past the gourmet kitchen (which boasted a coffee-maker and a microwave to supplement the stove, and that was all), up the suspended staircase, down the hall past the bathroom and two other bedrooms, and up the tower staircase to his little corner of the house. A third of the room was all reading nook, one big enough to sleep in, and another time he hoped to coax Leah into making love in it. People likely wouldn't see them, especially with the lights out, but it would be hot to do it next to a bunch of huge windows and graphic novels and pretend they *could* be seen. But that was for another time; Leah had had a tough week and he had no interest in pushing anything for their first time. He would wait as long as she—

"Oh. Here. Over here." She hauled him to the nook,

rearranging several of the thick pillows and putting his Avengers graphic novels on the floor. Then she was wriggling on her back, her fingers in his, as she pulled him down on top of her, with six-foot-high windows right beside them.

He was worried he'd crush her but her lips broke his fall.

*(Wait, that's not right. Who cares, we're kissing. Who cares, I'm on top of Leah oh my God this is the greatest day of my life back off, long weekend at Disney World, we have a new winner!)*

Her mouth was sweet and warm, and often curled into that smile he was finding easier and easier to coax out of her. Her fingers slipped beneath his shirt and she stroked his chest, her touch skimming over his wounds, his belly, his nipples. He shivered in her embrace and she helped him pull the shirt off. She examined his wounds, which were carefully taped and healing well. "Are you sure it will be okay if—"

"S'fine."

"I don't want to hurt you." Her smile turned sad. "More, I mean."

He couldn't stand it. "Leah. It's so completely totally fine I can't even." And it was, but he would have lied. He could have been bleeding out and would have said it was fine. And it *would* have been fine. "Please touch me more or I'll curl up and die, no pressure."

She laughed and pulled off her own shirt, then sat up to wriggle out of her tan shorts. Archer may have helped—his hands were shaking too much for him to be sure—and then she helped with his jeans and, with a devilish grin and a whispered "Do you mind?"—his black boxer briefs.

"You didn't wait for an answer," he said, thinking he should mind that he was naked and she still in her bra and panties

*(pale green satin,* his dazzled, fevered brain reported, *like early*

*spring, her underwear is like early spring I didn't even know sharks could pull off pale green)*

and deciding he didn't mind. At all.

*Oh my God this woman is perfection and I don't even know what color her nipples are.*

"It was a rhetorical question," she admitted, reaching behind her and unhooking her bra. The straps fell down her shoulders and he leaned forward and gently pulled them down her arms. She raised her hips and he slid her panties off as well.

"Pink!"

"Excuse me?"

"Your nipples. Now I know what color they are."

"I'm so glad to please you," she said primly, then ruined it with another of those grins. He felt dazzled and, more than that, *lucky*. He was getting to see a side of Leah that he doubted anyone else knew existed. *Nobody knows how playful and adorable she can be. Nobody but me, how did I get so lucky?*

And that was all he could stand to consciously think about; she was pale and perfect and studded with pink and her mound was dark silky hair and he pounced on her, and the nice thing about being stabbed by the future mother of his children was, if she had a problem with anything he was doing, she would have no problem stabbing him. Or letting him know some other way.

"God, you're—"

"Yes," she murmured, her hand on the back of his neck. "Oh. There. Right there."

He was kissing her with zero finesse, more intent on pressing his mouth everywhere on her tender flesh than seducing, he was clutching her and groaning into her mouth and she *wasn't minding*, she was getting pretty enthusiastically vocal herself.

He left her mouth only to kiss her nipples, his tongue curling around the hardened buds, and she shivered beneath him. He closed his eyes and reminded himself it was not cool to leave off the foreplay to get on with the pounding already but, ah God, it was hard—well, it was *hard*, of course, but—

"Stop thinking," she whispered, her hands in his hair. She arched her back, pressing her breasts into his mouth. "It's very distracting."

"Sorry," he managed, his hands slipping down her waist to clutch her hips and then sink lower, fingers skimming across the damp dark hair between her legs. "Oh, God. You're so beautiful."

He anticipated denial, and was happily startled when she murmured, "I know you see me that way. Thank you."

"You like a tender boyfriend, right? Because I'm probably going to burst into tears in another few seconds. It doesn't mean I'm not all man, baby. It probably doesn't mean that. All right, there's a chance I'm not all man."

She giggled and her rosy flesh, flushed with arousal, trembled against him. "I've cried more than you have this month. *Have* you even cried this month?"

He let it go, since it was old business and settled, but she must have seen something in his face, because she was sitting up and gently pushing until he was sliding off her to sit back on his heels.

"Oh my God. You cried after I drove you away. You came up here to your tower and wept when you thought I—I did not want you—"

"Leah."

"I should have thought of something else, I'm so sorry, I—"

"Leah! C'mon. It's fine. I promise I'll cry plenty of other times when you don't do a damn thing to set me off. AT&T

commercials make me cry, okay? iPhone commercials. When you want me to mow and it's really hot out, I'm gonna cry like a little girl whose pet bunny got hit with a lawn mower."

"Promise?"

He held his hand up in the Boy Scouts salute. "I swear."

Then she was drawing him back to her, taking his hands, guiding him, touching him, stroking him, and she was whispering the same thing over and over and he groaned and shuddered and when she helped him inside her he made out the words she was saying—"I'm so sorry, I love you"—over and over, and when she arched beneath him and shivered all over, his own orgasm swamped his brain and he was slurring, "I love you, I love you, Leah" all the way down into exhausted, sated sleep.

# FORTY-SIX

He itched, a constant burning itch, and hated himself and hated the people around him. They had everything and he had next to nothing; they thought he was scum, and he hated that sometimes he thought they might be right.

He knew how to get rid of the itch and the maddening thoughts and feelings that came with the itch and she was coming toward him, some bitch in nice clothes with mousy brown hair and shiny black eyes, kind of a dumb bitch, too, walking like her shit didn't stink, walking down *his* alley like her shit didn't stink.

Easiest thing in the world to step up to her. He liked this part, though the first time he did it he threw up afterward. He liked when their eyes changed and they realized their safe comfortable boring lives weren't safe or, as long as they were in *his* alley, comfortable. He liked how at first they pretended they didn't notice he was in their way, and he liked how they looked when they couldn't pretend anymore.

He stepped out, blocked her. The alley was wide, but she couldn't slip past him without getting stuck. He waited for her steps to falter, her expression to go from determinedly not seeing him on purpose to not being able to look away from him.

"Give it up."

She stopped. Put her hands on her hips. Shook her head like she was amused but disappointed at the same time, and what the fuck was *that* about? "I honestly don't know how I should react to this."

He blinked and scratched. "Just gimme." Best to keep the transaction short and simple. No one was gonna fall in love here. Her face wasn't changing but that didn't mean he couldn't take what she had.

"Normally I'd impugn your manhood and dare you to shiv me—that's the term, yes? shiv?—and then we'd grapple and I wouldn't especially care if you killed me."

"I'm not gonna kill you!" Shocked in spite of himself. He did *not* need that kind of heat, ever. Mugged at knifepoint was as far as he was willing to go, and it took years to work up to that. "Just give me your fucking purse, okay?"

She ignored him and kept talking like he hadn't interrupted. "But I have something of a new lease on life this week. God, I hear myself saying it and ugh. New lease. Ugh."

"Gimme!"

"It's not like I would miss the forty bucks," his victim was speculating. "But it's the principle of the thing, do you understand? Nobody ever calls you on your shit. So life after life you just take-take-take and then die alone."

"What?"

"I know! Awful. But you can break the cycle, you know." She

sighed. "Aaaaand I just heard myself again. It seems I am unable to stop spouting clichés. I really hope that particular Archer effect wears off."

"You just—"

"You think I hear it? Of course I hear it. I recognize it and the worst part is, I am unwilling to stop the romance clichés. And perhaps unable."

Okay, fuck this shit, and fuck this crazypants bitch. He swiped the knife at her and she sidestepped. "No-no-no. Not like that." She mimed his action. "I had all the time in the world to move, you silly man. Like *this*." He jerked back and avoided her hand, but not the invisible knife she was swinging at him. If it had been a real knife, his guts would be hanging around his ankles. *Why isn't she crying or screaming? Why am I standing here letting her teach me Mugging at Knifepoint?*

"You're fuckin' weird."

"Yes, I am! Good of you to notice and comment. And in these few seconds you have stupidly given me, I have decided. So we can get on with it now." She gestured at him, bending at the waist in what his amazed eyes reported to his brain was a short, polite bow. "Whenever you're ready."

"Last chance."

"It's not, though." She smiled, big and wide like a kid eyeballing a hot-fudge sundae. She was kind of almost pretty when she did that, which made him want to stick her more. "It's not my last chance at all. Which I find singularly wonderful."

Enough was fuckin' enough. He swiped again, copying the motion she showed him. But it went wrong, like this whole encounter had gone wrong from the second he blocked her path.

She somehow stepped inside his swing and then his wrist

hurt and then his balls exploded into two white-hot suns of agony and the sidewalk jumped up and hit him on the back of the head and when he woke up in police custody he counted himself lucky to be alive.

Fuckin' weirdos! The city wasn't safe anymore.

# FORTY-SEVEN

"What . . . is this?"

"C'mon, baby! Let's ride."

Leah blinked and took in Archer and, odder, the gigantic silver car he was leaning against. "What is this? You promised me a date the likes of which I had never seen. I was skeptical."

"You were," he agreed, smirking.

"You said you'd show me more things I missed by not going to high school. But . . . ?" She gestured. "I have seen you. I have seen cars."

He slapped the side of the car, then winced. "Wow, they really don't make 'em like they used to. It's a rental, and I got it for a great rate for the day, part-time job number fifteen." He went to her, dropped a quick kiss to her smile, then escorted her to the vehicle. "It's a Crown Vic."

*As if that would have any meaning for me.* "All right." Bemused, she slid into the passenger seat as he held the door for her. "So we are in a Crown Vic." It was nice, if you liked gas-guzzling monsters. She herself was indifferent, but with much of the country in an uproar about going green, she suspected people would start throwing gasoline on guzzlers the way fur activists used to throw red paint on women wearing mink. "Where you shall show me what I missed."

"Yep. Buckle up, baby."

"I insist you stop calling me that," she said without heat, and got another kiss for her trouble.

He drove with easy confidence, one hand on the steering wheel and (often) one resting lightly on her leg. She pondered part-time job number fifteen and his many other jobs (her current favorite, part-time job number four: lemonade stand franchise owner) and thought his exhaustive need to try *everything* might help prove her theory that life-blind weren't blind, just new.

They drove out of the city and eventually parked at the end of a scenic lookout, where they could see hills peppered with fields for what seemed like miles, even as the sun set and swept the land with shadows.

Then he pulled her to him and she could feel herself opening for him, wanting him, not just her mouth but her entire body seemed to want him, and his tongue stroked into her mouth, slid along her tongue, nibbled her lower lip, and her hands were under his shirt, clutching the long muscles in his back, and things got rather more delightful every minute, every *second*, and then they were tumbling into the backseat and he was showing her what she missed in high school.

# FORTY-EIGHT

"We've done it!"

"Eh?" Leah was struggling back into her bra. "Have you seen my balisong—ah! There it is." She had explained to Archer that although Tom was moldering in his grave, and good riddance, she felt naked unless she had at least one knife concealed on her person. Far from being put off, he'd nearly tackled her on the spot and they spent a delightful hour experimenting with cowgirl and reverse-cowgirl. "Yes, we have definitely done it; it seems obvious."

Archer was back in the driver's seat, shirtless. "We are the first couple in the history of backseat banging to have terrific sex in the back of a car! You have no idea how unprecedented this is."

"The word 'first' tipped me off." She couldn't help the grin, an expression she suspected would eventually become more or less permanent with Archer in her life. "It's good that it's unprecedented, though. That makes me glad. Until you pointed that out, I was sad about missing high school sex."

"Yeah, that? About that. Typical high school sex: picture what we just did, but suck ninety-five percent of the pleasure out of it and factor in muscle cramps and a paralyzing fear that you may have knocked up the girl in question, and also that your folks will find out what you've been up to, calculate all that, and it's actually much, much worse."

She sniffed. "Then why indulge?"

"Um . . . sex? Even bad sex is still pretty great. Because: sex."

She tossed his shirt at his head. "Spoken by every man ever, and no woman ever," she muttered, but it was impossible to maintain her pique. "So I should not actually miss this, because backseat sex tends to be unsatisfying?"

"Not the way we do it," he replied with deep, masculine satisfaction. She rolled her eyes, but nothing would bring him down. "You know that feeling you get when you're positive you haven't done this before? Déjà new? That's what Leah and Archer backseat sex is. Déjà new."

For some reason, that made her laugh so hard she dropped her knife. And then there was nothing for it but to slip into the back again and go for Round Two.

# EPILOGUE

**NELLIE NAZIR**

*1985–2017*

*The World Remembers Her*

*Always*

Archer took a long look. "Wow. It's beautiful." And it was. The headstone was purple marble and when the sun hit it, it kicked up a glitter effect that made the stone seemed to glow. Even on a cloudy day, the effect was striking. The letters and numbers were deeply, crisply chiseled and unlikely to rub off for at least a couple of centuries. There were trees nearby, and the grave was nearest the pond full of koi, which Nellie had always thought were the epitome of class, though she went to her grave having no clue how to tend to them.

"It's a lie, of course," Leah said, smiling at him. She had dressed in a sober black business suit, black stockings, and black high heels, attire she loathed and would never wear in the course of an ordinary day. Which this was not.

Archer knew she was trying to show respect to It—um, to Nellie—the only way she could, and made a mental note not to tell her how sexy she looked in mourning. God, the high heels alone . . . ! "It's really beautiful." This in an attempt to keep his Leah-obsessed mind out of the gutter for five entire minutes.

"It's a lie," she said again. "I've paid for a lie, and that's not the only one. My mother did not die at thirty."

He smothered a laugh against his fist. "Ah . . . no. Probably not."

Leah shrugged. "But she deserves the lies. In a way, they're perfect for her, entirely suited to her personality. If my mother was here, she could believe those lies; she would make herself believe them. So it's okay. Besides." Leah took a deep breath and smiled at him, though her eyes were bright with tears she refused to let fall. "*I'll* remember her."

Photo courtesy of the author

**MaryJanice Davidson** is the *New York Times* bestselling author of several books, most recently *Undead and Unforgiven*, *Undead and Unwary*, *Undead and Unsure*, and *Undead and Unstable*. With her husband, Anthony Alongi, she also writes a series featuring a teen weredragon named Jennifer Scales. MaryJanice lives in Minneapolis with her husband and two children and is currently working on her next book. Visit her website at maryjanicedavidson.net or find her on Facebook at facebook.com/maryjanicedavidson.